SEED

Published by 47North
P.O. Box 400818
Las Vegas, NV 89140

ISBN-13: 9781612183664
ISBN-10: 1612183662

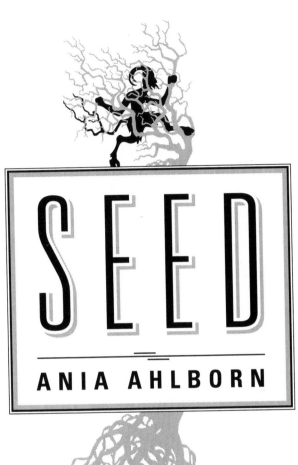

SEED

ANIA AHLBORN

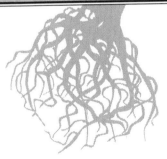

47NORTH

To my little brother, who battled his demons and lost.

CHAPTER ONE

THE SATURN'S ENGINE RATTLED LIKE A PENNY IN AN old tin can. The car was a junker—its headlights pale and off-kilter. It was a temporary fix that had become a permanent mode of transportation. Jack had insisted that when they had the cash they'd buy themselves a pair of fancy wheels—a ride that had that new-car scent. And then Abby broke her arm. Charlie got bronchitis. Aimee needed a tooth filled. Years passed; that secondhand Saturn became their lifeline, but Jack refused to lose hope. He collected loose change in one of Aimee's old Mason jars, squirreled away an extra dollar here and there. He worked extra hours at the boat shop, sweating through Southern summers that buzzed with the soothing hum of locusts. Now, after all that effort, they were only a month away from finally reaching that distant goal, and the idea of that shitcan Saturn rusting in the Louisiana bayou was enough to make Jack smirk as the engine rattled and coughed. The humor of it trumped the migraine that was blooming behind his eyes, creeping along the inside of his skull, growing with each reflective flash of broken yellow line.

It would take them an hour to get back home. Live Oak was a blip on the map—a place you drove past and thought, *Oh, how quaint*, before blowing through without a second thought. It was the kind of place people ran from, the kind of place that was heavy with dark secrets and strange people—strange because they stayed there, somehow having found a way to survive in a nowhere town. But Jack loved Louisiana, from the bridges that stretched over swampland, to the long gray moss that hung from ancient trees like a tangle of witch's hair. Most averted their eyes, avoiding the dilapidated houses that skirted the everglades and sank into the marshland—swallowed by a quagmire that could only exist in the South. Jack never looked away. Those skeleton-houses drew him in.

Aimee dozed in the passenger seat as they sped down a rural road. She and ten-year-old Abby had the infant gene—they fell asleep as soon as the car was in motion, lulled into dreaming as if by magic. His gaze jumped to the rearview mirror. Charlie sat next to her sister, tucked into her car seat, humming a tune the Pizza-Rama rock band had played on a loop—a torturous two hours for any adult, no matter how much that adult loved his kids. She was inspecting the high-bounce ball she'd won with a stack of game tickets. That little ball proved she wasn't a baby anymore. She was six, and she could hold her own in a game of skeeball. Nobody would catch *her* on the baby rides.

Charlie never slept in the car, not even when she was a newborn. With Abby, all it took was a quick drive around the block, but driving only made Charlie restless. Jack often wondered whether there was something spiritual that tied Charlie to their house, something that called her back if she strayed too far after dark.

Reaching the turnoff, he steered the car onto the road that would take them home. They passed Live Oak's single grocery store—conveniently closed at eight on the dot, seven days a week. They sped by an old gas station—the kind that required cash and had a tired attendant working the register—and a blinking stoplight, hanging heavy on its overhead power line, swaying in the breeze. The highlight was Bijou, a little diner that served the best red beans and rice in all of Louisiana. That place, in Jack's opinion, was a national treasure. It survived off passersby and a handful of unfortunate truckers—the ones who were forced off the freeway and into the sticks for a random delivery. Jack was determined to single-handedly keep it in business until the day he died.

Live Oak was so small that the roads in and out were darker than pitch, and the Saturn's yellowed headlights didn't offer much in the way of illumination. It was a murky drive, one that Jack took two or three times a month, most times in the dead of night, sometimes in the pouring rain—trips that were made with the band, miles ticked away on the odometer in the name of a youthful dream: play music, make money, be happy, do what you love. Tonight the sky was clear, the stars were out and burning bright for the birthday girl. And yet, despite the stars, it seemed darker than ever, like someone had reached into the sky and turned off the moon.

Jack furrowed his eyebrows against the throb at his temples and backed off the gas. He couldn't see more than twenty feet ahead of him, and the blind spot in his right eye was blooming like a supernova. He flipped on the high beams, and for a moment he could see the road as clear as day.

The headlights flickered once.

Flickered twice.

The last thing he saw was a pair of animal eyes, reflecting bright silver and wide in the darkness. The headlights went out.

Jerking the wheel was an instinct. Jack's mind wasn't focused on whether the car would fly off the road, but whether those eyes belonged to a human rather than an animal. The trees along the side of the road housed occasional stragglers, and the idea of killing a man outweighed the impulse to keep the wheel pointed straight ahead.

One of the tires caught the embankment. The car was thrown off balance. It jerked sideways, rubber screaming across pavement. And then inertia swallowed them whole, lifting the car off the ground and spinning it into a graceful pirouette.

There was nothing but silence.

Nobody cried out. For that brief moment, the world had gone soundless.

Then: the sickening crunch of metal against asphalt.

The creak and pop of safety glass.

The explosion and powdery stench of airbags.

The grinding of the roof against the road as they slid to a stop.

The first sound that breached the silence was Aimee's hyperventilating. She tore at her seatbelt despite being upside down, determined to get out of the car if it was the last thing she did. Jack dangled from the driver's seat, suspended in the air like an astronaut awaiting ignition. He imagined being paralyzed, wondered if it hurt to sever your spinal cord. Or to die in a car accident like this one. But he could hear Aimee thrashing. He could hear her crying. He couldn't possibly be dead.

And then, a final assurance that he was still alive: Abigail began to scream.

That scream motivated Jack to tear himself free, to fumble with his seatbelt and shove open his door, tumbling onto the glass-speckled street like a clown rolling out of a circus car. Aimee kicked at her door as she screamed. If he had time to close his eyes, her cries would have convinced him that both Abby and Charlie were dead, smeared across the tarmac—roadkill left for the cleanup crew.

Jack got to Abby before Aimee crawled out of the car. He pulled open the back door and caught his eldest daughter around her waist, unbuckling her from the backseat and heaving her from the mangled wreck. Abby stopped screaming the moment she saw her mother. She started to bawl instead.

"What happened?" Aimee yelled. Her face twisted with panic. "Jack? What the hell happened?" She was trying to keep calm, but every word that clawed its way up her throat was a shriek.

Jack didn't reply. He was busy dashing around the other side of the car, his heart stuck in his throat, threatening to choke him. Like a newborn baby fresh to the world, Abby had screamed and assured her parents that she was alive, but Charlie hadn't made a sound. Not a whine, not a whimper.

His every nerve stood on end, buzzing with dread as he wrenched open the back door and stuck his head inside. To his relief, hovering over him like an overturned angel, Charlie dangled from her car seat, her hair hanging in her face.

"Hi, Daddy," she said softly.

Jack's heart swelled in his chest.

"Hi, baby," he whispered back, fumbling with the seat's latch, careful not to let her tumble out of his arms and onto the roof.

"Did we flip?" she asked, her arms around his neck. "Like in the movies?"

"Yeah," he replied, only now remembering that reflective pair of eyes, the ones that had made him jerk the wheel in the first place. He hadn't bothered to look and see if anything was lying dead in the road. Part of him hoped that whatever had caused this had been flattened by the Saturn's front bumper. If the road was clear, he had half a mind to storm into the woods and find something to kill, if only to satiate his sudden compulsion for retribution.

Jack pulled Charlie from the car and set her down on her sneakered feet. Abby and Aimee wept into each other's arms while Jack and Charlie stood silent, both of them transfixed by the smashed Saturn.

"Cool," Charlie whispered under her breath, her eyes sparkling in the moonlight—eerily reminiscent of the eyes that had caused this chaos in the first place. That single word of childlike wonder thrust him out of his thoughts and back into reality, and for the briefest of moments, despite the circumstances, he tried not to laugh. The moment was cut short by Aimee's shouting.

"Call the police," she yelled. "What are you waiting for? Call the police!"

Jack patted down his pockets. Empty. His cell was missing. He ducked back inside the wreck, searched the bent roof of the car for his phone, and found it close to the backseat. Half expecting there to be no service, he imagined a psychopath bursting from the trees with an ax held over his head—that hitcher he'd saved by swerving was, coincidentally, a crazed killer looking for a nice family to julienne.

Reality was never as exciting as Hollywood. There was no killer, and Jack's phone boasted four bars. He had an e-mail waiting. A missed called from Reagan no doubt, thanks to the Pizza-Rama band and their ear-shattering jam.

He dialed 911, reported the accident and their approximate location. Crouching beside a shaken Abigail, Jack wiped her tears from her cheeks while giving the dispatcher details of the incident. Nobody was hurt, but they'd send an ambulance anyway. A fire engine would arrive, accompanying a handful of police cruisers and eventually a tow truck that would drag the Saturn to its final resting place.

The thing was totaled, twisted like a tin can. Under different circumstances, Jack would have set its smashed frame on fire and danced around it like a devil around a bonfire. But instead of whooping with joy, he stared at it, waiting for it to come alive, waiting for the engine to rumble to life and mow them down like King's Christine.

"What happened?" Aimee asked again, trying to compose herself before the cops arrived.

Jack shook his head, bewildered. "I thought I saw something. An animal."

He looked back the way they came, squinted in the darkness, tried to spot a carcass in the road.

"It's like the headlights just went out," he said.

"They went out?"

"I think so..."

"You *think*? Jack, we could have been killed." Aimee shoved the back of her hand against her damp cheek, swatting at her tears. "What were you thinking?"

"It was a reflex."

"What, jerking the wheel instead of slamming on the brakes? Have you lost your goddamn mind?"

He saw something shift out of the corner of his eye, shot a look down the road again.

"Where's Charlotte?" Aimee's voice took on a sudden urgency. "Jack?"

Looking back to the car, Jack saw that Charlie wasn't where he had left her. His eyes fluttered around the wreckage. He charged into motion, frantically scanning the perimeter of the accident.

"Charlotte?" Aimee called out, her voice shrill with panic. "Oh my God, where is she?"

Jack bolted down the road, his pulse hammering against his ears. Aimee's whimpers grew fainter until she sounded like she was underwater, muffled and indiscernible. The air had grown thick and heavy, impenetrable by sound.

Jack finally spotted her. Charlie stood on the soft shoulder a few yards from the car, facing the trees.

"Thank Christ," Jack murmured. "Charlie, what are you doing? Your mother is losing her mind."

Charlotte looked at her father, then looked back to the trees with a furrowed brow.

"Something ran into the woods. Over there." She lifted a hand and pointed a small finger at a tangle of trees.

He looked to where she pointed, his own eyebrows knitting together as he tried to spot movement in the darkness.

"Probably just an animal," he assured her, taking Charlie's hand into his own. "Come on, let's get you back to your mom."

Charlie reluctantly gave up her position, craning her neck while her dad led her back to the overturned car.

"It wasn't an animal," she murmured. "It walked on two legs, like us."

Jack slowed his steps at Charlie's description. His breath hitched in his throat. *No,* he thought. *It was a hitcher. A goddamn hitcher who's lucky to be walking at all.* But his logic wasn't very persuasive.

"I saw it, Daddy," she told him, lowering her voice so her mom wouldn't hear. "I saw it before the lights went out. I saw it just like you."

It was well after midnight by the time the Winters arrived home. To Charlie's delight, the officer who gave them a ride after reports were filed ran his lights all the way home, turning the darkness around them into an electric wonderland of red and blue. Aimee put the girls to bed while Jack sat at the kitchen table, staring at Charlie's high-bounce ball next to his coffee cup. Somehow, she had managed to hang on to it through the accident, having let it go only when her mother insisted it was time for bed. Uncurling her fingers from around the cheap rubber toy, Charlie had carefully placed it next to her father's mug in a silent gesture of alliance. She had seen it too—the pair of eyes that had forced Jack to swerve and nearly kill his entire family.

Jack had seen those eyes before.

Aimee eventually stepped out of the girls' room and quietly shut the door behind her. She took a seat across from Jack, holding her silence for a long while, but Jack knew what was coming. She wanted to know what happened. She wanted an answer that would satisfy her anger. Rather than ask the same question again, she caught Jack off guard with a statement instead.

"You could have killed them. Imagine it, Jack…Charlie dying on her sixth birthday."

Jack blinked at her, stunned.

"Thanks," he muttered. "I wasn't feeling quite guilty enough."

"You were falling asleep."

"I was not."

"I know you were. You're just afraid to admit it."

"What?"

"What do you expect, staying out all the time?"

"All the time?" Jack frowned. "Like what, once every two weeks?"

He shook his head, then lifted his cup and took a swig of cold coffee.

Aimee sat in silence, then got up and walked out of the kitchen without another word.

Jack decided to sleep on the couch.

It wasn't the first time, and he doubted it would be the last.

The next morning Charlie refused to get out of bed.

"I'm sick," she complained, tugging the covers up to her nose while Aimee pulled school clothes out of a dresser, tossing them onto Charlie's bed, confirming that Charlie *would* be going to school today, no matter what had happened the night before.

"On your feet," she said, yanking the covers off her daughter, who, at the shock of cold morning air, flailed atop her mattress like a waterlogged fish.

"But I don't feel good," Charlie whimpered. She sat up anyway, knowing her efforts were futile. Aimee was the last to budge when it came to school.

"Blame it on the piles of candy you ate yesterday. I told you it would make you sick, didn't I?"

Charlie jutted out her bottom lip.

"Maybe someday you'll learn to listen to your momma."

"Maybe someday I'll really be sick," she muttered. "I mean *really* sick. Like green and dying and puking like…" She stuck her tongue out, twisting her face up in disgust. "Like *that*. And then you'll be sorry."

"Oh I will, will I?" Aimee tried not to grin.

"You might be dying," Abigail chimed in from across the room. "But she'll still send you to school."

"Then I'll die at school," Charlie said matter-of-factly. "And all the kids will come to my funeral because the teachers will make them, like they make us go outside when the fire drill goes."

"You can't *make* people go to your funeral," Abby said. "They only go if they feel like it."

"They'll feel like it." Charlie pulled on a multicolored sock. "I'm gonna be buried in the sandbox next to the monkey bars. They'll have to go because it'll be during recess."

Abigail rolled her eyes at her sister as Aimee pretended to busy herself in the girls' closet, eavesdropping on their conversation.

"And if they don't want to go they'll have to stay inside," Charlie continued, "even though it's recess." She paused, narrowed her eyes. "Because they're jerks."

"Charlotte." Aimee shot her youngest a stern look. "Watch your mouth."

"That isn't even a bad word," Charlie mulled. She yanked on her other sock and slid off her bed. "And I can't watch my mouth because my eyes are stuck on my head, and my mouth is stuck on my head, and how do you watch your mouth if they're both stuck on your head, huh?"

Aimee exhaled a steady breath and held Charlotte's pants out, patiently waiting for her to stick her scrawny legs through the holes.

"Hurry up or you won't have time for Lucky Charms," she warned. "You too, Abby. Both of you are running late."

The girls went silent while they dressed, zipping up zippers and pulling on T-shirts. Charlie fumbled with her shoelaces before throwing them down in frustration. After a minute of letting her struggle, Aimee plopped Charlie back onto the bed and tied her shoes for her.

"Momma?"

"Yeah, baby?"

Charlie frowned before raising her shoulders up to her ears. "Is Daddy OK?"

"What makes you ask that?" Aimee asked.

"The accident," Charlie shrugged. "He looked really worried."

"He was just worried that you and your sister might be hurt," Aimee said with a smile. "You aren't hurt, are you?"

Charlotte shook her head no.

"Good. Now hurry up and eat your breakfast. Grandma is giving you a ride to school today."

Jack *was* worried. There was the accident and the mangled car—it was enough to worry anyone, especially since it was their only mode of transportation. But the twisted frame of that Saturn was the least of Jack's concerns. What was really eating at him was that pair of eyes.

The first time Jack had seen those eyes had been along the outskirts of his parents' Georgia property. The house was a run-down double-wide trailer, and its paint was peeling from decades of humid Southern heat. The siding was rusted over and popping its bolts, hanging from the bottom of the trailer like a silver-lined candy wrapper.

The property didn't match the house. It was a great stretch of land: a good two acres, narrower than it was long. Those two acres of grassland stretched back for what seemed like an eternity, ending at a wall of trees.

Beyond those trees and a few hundred paces north, an old cemetery sat surrounded by a rusted iron fence. There were too many headstones for it to have belonged to a single family, yet not enough to have belonged to the small town of Rosewood, Georgia. The day Jack discovered that cemetery, he ran from it in search of his parents, but something kept him from revealing his discovery. As soon as he burst into the house, the urgency to tell them about what he'd found was replaced by a distinct need to keep it a secret—something only *he* knew about. He couldn't explain his sudden change of heart. All he knew was that if he told, the cemetery would no longer be his. If he told his parents, it would be theirs too, and he wanted those headstones. Wanted every single one to himself.

Gilda and Stephen Winter weren't prizewinning parents. That double-wide was an accurate representation of the way their household was run: sparingly and with little attention. They had been blessed with those two acres after one of Gilda's family members had bitten the big one, but the shitty trailer was all Gilda and Stephen's. They'd bought it off an old guy with one foot in the coffin a few months after she got pregnant, and even then that trailer was itching for the perfect moment to fall apart.

Moving to Rosewood wasn't much of a change. They traded one nowhere Georgia town for another, hauled the already dilapidated trailer halfway across the state, and parked it on that inherited land; that was all it took for the Winters to officially become homeowners. A few months later they were homeowners with a kid.

Growing up, Jack didn't have much guidance. He ran around in bare feet throughout most of the year, took a bath every few days—Gilda would throw him in the tub when she was no longer able to take the stink—and brushed his teeth only after seeing other kids do it on TV. He grew up wild, a modern-day Huck Finn. He'd run along the length of the property to the tree line, duck beneath a tangle of branches, and spend afternoons among his secret friends: the dead.

Despite his youth, Jack knew that spending time alone in a cemetery was weird, but something kept drawing him back. Staying away for too long made him feel anxious, as though the wellspring of comfort was nestled among those graves. At first he only visited once or twice a month, but time turned him into a junkie. Eventually, he was there every day—sitting, talking to no one, throwing rocks and tearing wild grass from the earth.

It was there, among the moss-covered headstones and rusted wrought-iron fencing, that he first saw those eyes. After a day of kicking headstones out of boyhood boredom, Jack had picked himself up to leave for the night when he saw a pair of reflective black eyes staring at him from behind the trees—animal eyes, the kind that shone like silver dollars in the dead of night. Like two onyx marbles, they could have easily belonged to a wolf or a raccoon. But there was something off about them. They were soulless, empty, as if pulled from the pit of something twisted and unclean.

He wanted to run just like the day he'd discovered the cemetery in the first place. But like the time before, his initial reaction was overridden by the allure of secrecy. The fear that bubbled at the pit of his stomach went calm, and before he knew what he was doing he was walking away from home rather than toward it. He paused only when he came to realize what stood between him and the trees, between him and those eyes: a single grave marker—one that had taken the bulk of Jack's abuse. He'd gone so far as to etch his name onto the weatherworn stone, nothing more than a thoughtless act of childhood vandalism. Jack stood paralyzed in front of his own grave.

Those eyes were the same eyes he'd seen just before the Saturn lifted off the road and flew through the sky. They were the eyes that changed his life forever. Jack knew those eyes, and it terrified him that they had found him again.

CHAPTER TWO

PATRICIA HAD EVENTUALLY FORCED HERSELF TO ACCEPT Jack as her son-in-law, but this accident was too much. Putting her daughter and grandchildren in danger? If Jack Winter thought Patricia Riley was going to turn a blind eye to his blatant recklessness, he had another thing coming.

"Charlotte is running a fever."

Pat made the announcement the moment she stepped into the cramped little house. That house was another thorn in Patricia's side. She'd raised her daughter in a proper Southern home, and here she was, living in a two-bedroom lean-to stuffed floor to ceiling with what could only be described as "the bizarre." Aimee was a fan of antiques, collecting everything from tarnished mirrors to oversized furniture, and that was fine and good; it was an aesthetic Aimee had picked up from her mother who, naturally, had impeccable taste. But Jack was partial to strange artifacts—ancient books and weird family portraits. He liked taxidermy, which struck Patricia as perverse and disgusting, gravitating to the likes of dancing squirrels and grinning cats. He owned a ferret mounted in a tiny pine coffin, a miniature bouquet of dried flowers clutched in its pint-sized paws. To Patricia's horror, Charlie found the dead ferret—which she named Dead Frank—completely hilarious. It all made for a gruesome collection of home décor.

Patricia diverted her gaze from the stuffed fawn curled atop Jack's crumbling piano to Nubs, the Winters' shaggy black and white border collie. She wrinkled her nose in distaste as the dog approached her, taking a cautionary step backward in case the fleabag decided to jump all over her new skirt. But Charlotte distracted him when she slunk into the house, her eyes rimmed in a sickly red, dragging a bright yellow *SpongeBob SquarePants* backpack behind her. Nubs's interest in Patricia was instantly withdrawn, and he trotted behind his usually exuberant owner like the loyal dog he was.

"She was complaining about feeling sick earlier," Aimee said from the kitchen, wiping her hands on a gingham-checked dishtowel. "I figured she was just making it up." She lifted her shoulders in a shrug. "Guess not."

"You should get her to bed," Patricia advised, approaching the kitchen counter to inspect her daughter's in-process cooking.

Patricia Riley was practically a gourmet chef, an expert at the culinary arts. She'd once overheard Jack say that she fancied herself an expert at absolutely everything, especially the art of rearing other people's children—an easy comment to ignore coming from a guy who collected voodoo dolls and skipped out on his family every other weekend.

"Give her some Tylenol and run a cool bath if her fever doesn't break by tonight."

"Will do," Aimee said.

"And I'd consider keeping Abigail on the couch for the night if I were you," Patricia continued. "Or you'll have two sick kids instead of one."

"Thanks for driving her," Aimee said. "I don't know what we're going to do about a car."

"Well, I have my bridge club every Wednesday and the garden club on Fridays," Pat said. "Your father and I have committed to those dance lessons, and those start next week. I can drive the girls every now and again, but I'm no chauffeur. A family can't survive without a car."

"We'll figure something out," Aimee said. "We're only a few weeks from a down payment on a new car anyway. We'll just settle on a cheaper model, get it sooner."

"A *new* car?" Patricia raised an eyebrow. "You could probably buy two used ones for the same amount of money."

"Jack has his heart set on a new one. He's been talking about it for years now."

"What for?" Patricia asked with a smirk. "So he can flip it down a few more roads?"

"It was an accident," Aimee murmured. She had been hard on Jack herself and the guilt was creeping in. "We were planning on a new car and we're going to get a new car. There's no reason for us to change our plans."

"Suit yourself," Patricia said with a shrug. She knew the more she protested, the more satisfaction Jack would get from making such a ridiculous purchase. "But you'll be wishing you listened to me," she warned. "I'd have expected that by your age you'd have learned that your mother is always right."

Aimee busied herself by chopping a stalk of celery a little too forcefully.

"Either way, I'll check with Daddy to see if he'll let you borrow the Oldsmobile for a few days. That is, if it's OK with Jack."

"If it's OK with Daddy," Aimee said. "We'd appreciate it."

"I hope so," Patricia said. "Because you know how much your father loves that car."

Aimee nodded.

"Thanks, Momma," she said. "And thanks again for taking Charlie today."

Patricia forced a curt smile and pivoted on the balls of her feet, moving toward the front door.

"Don't forget the Tylenol," she warned. "If you don't remedy the problem now, you'll be sorry later. And don't sauté that celery to death. It'll lose its crunch."

As soon as Patricia stepped outside she took a deep breath of fresh air. That house was utterly stifling. She had no idea how Aimee did it, and she hoped that sooner rather than later, she'd come to her senses and make a major change.

Jack's job was far from ideal. He spent his days patching up flat-bottomed swamp boats and resoldering metal joints to keep his customers afloat. These customers came to the shop because they got hammered with the shop owner every other night, and they ranged from crawfish fishermen to bona fide gator hunters. Jack spent half his day listening to stories about "the big one that got away," about the monster that nearly chomped a finger or two.

By the time he came home that night, the familiar itch of a headache was tickling his brain, and the tension that had settled over the house didn't do much in the way of letting him unwind.

Abby sat on the couch, watching television while doing her homework—something she hardly ever got away with. When Jack peeked his head into the girls' room he found Aimee perched at the foot of Charlie's bed looking pensive.

"One-oh-three," she said as soon as she saw him in the doorway. "She came home with a fever and she's up to one hundred and three. I think we need to go to the hospital."

"Did you give her a bath?" Jack asked, approaching his shivering daughter. Charlie was bundled beneath a pile of blankets, her teeth chattering in her sleep.

"Every time I try to move her she starts to cry."

Jack took a seat next to Charlie, pressing his palm to her forehead. Aimee was right; if they couldn't get her fever down they'd have to go to the ER—something they sure as hell couldn't afford.

Peeling the blankets away from her coiled-up body, Jack stuck an arm under the girl and hefted her up into his arms. Charlie whined, squirmed, tried to get away, but Jack didn't give in. He held her tight and walked to the bathroom, Aimee at his heels. Taking a seat on the toilet lid, he ran the bath while Aimee stripped off Charlie's sweat-soaked clothes.

A worried Abigail appeared in the doorway with Nubs at her heels.

"Is she gonna be OK?" she asked.

When Aimee failed to answer, Jack looked at his eldest and offered her a reassuring smile.

"Everything's going to be fine, sweetheart. Charlie just needs to cool down."

As if on cue, Jack lowered Charlie into the tub. As soon as the frigid water bit her skin, the shock of cold made her buck and thrash. She exhaled a high-pitched scream, clawing at the sides of the tub, desperately trying to escape. Abby slapped her hands over her ears. Nubs let out a frightened yelp and cowered in the hall. Jack held Charlie down while Aimee clasped her hands over her mouth. She looked away, unable to watch her baby flail and writhe like a frightened animal.

"Abby!" Aimee twisted toward the bathroom door. "Get out. Go to your room!"

Abby blinked at her mom's unexpected bout of anger and bolted out of the doorway.

"Let her go," Aimee demanded, turning her attention back to Jack. "Let her out; you're scaring her."

But Jack didn't give. Each passing second rendered Charlie calmer. She eventually exhaled a pitiful wail and gave up, going limp with a sob.

"I don't know what's wrong with her," Aimee whispered later, after Charlie was back in bed, having drifted back into a fitful sleep, a damp towel pressed to her forehead.

"Nothing's wrong with her," Jack assured. "She's got the flu or something. She'll be fine."

Aimee nodded and left the room to heat up the dinner Jack had missed yet again. It had been another long night of overtime.

Only after she left him alone did Jack look to his daughter with genuine concern. There was something off about the way she had fought him, something that made him uncomfortable. Had it been Aimee who had held her down, he was sure Charlie would have leaped from that tub and rushed past her like a feral, wild-eyed child. It had been too much fight for a six-year-old.

"I gave her Tylenol, but it isn't doing a damn thing," Aimee complained, watching Jack eat his jambalaya. She'd sautéed the hell out of that celery. "If I hadn't sent her to school this morning she wouldn't have gotten so sick. She told me she felt bad."

Jack gave Aimee a look.

"What?"

"She's a kid. She'd have gotten sick whether she was here or at school, or anywhere else."

"Well I'd rather it have been here," Aimee said. "At least that way I could have had my eye on her."

"You'll have your eye on her tomorrow. And most likely a day or two after that."

"It was probably one of those kids at the pizza place," Aimee mused. "It's just like back-road Louisiana hicks to take their sick kid to a place crammed with other kids. I swear to God…"

Jack grinned. It was one of the things he loved about her; Aimee was sweet and put-together on the outside, but once you cracked that outer shell she was a pillar of brimstone. She'd been raised a strict Catholic, and it seemed that the constant Sunday sermons had infused hellfire into Aimee's blood.

"What?" Aimee gave Jack's smile a suspicious look. "I swear, sometimes I wonder why we even bother living here."

"Where else would we live?" he asked. "New York? You want to move to California and get ourselves a condo out on the beach somewhere? Think we'd fit in?"

"What do you mean 'fit in'?" Aimee looked genuinely offended. "Is there something wrong with us?"

"Sure," Jack said. "We're Southerners."

"And what's *that* supposed to mean?"

"It means we were born here, we live here, and we die here."

Aimee smirked with a shake of her head. "You weren't born here." Of the intricate web of mistruths Jack had told about his past, he was honest about not being a Louisiana native. It was easier to keep the lies in line if they closely resembled the truth.

"The South is the South."

"I don't mind the South," she said. "It's the *dirty* South I can't stand."

It was the dirty South that made Jack who he was and Aimee knew it, but it was something she liked to think he'd grown out of—like growing out of an old pair of jeans. She knew that he'd grown up in Georgia and made his way to Louisiana after he left home. She knew he had been young—seventeen, as the story had been told, not fourteen—when he'd left. She knew that Jack's mother was unstable, that his father had been more interested in protecting her rather than his own son, that the situation eventually "got bad," which was when Jack decided to fly the coop. She was left to assume that there was abuse, which was why Jack had never expressed any interest in seeing them again, not for their wedding or the birth of their kids, and she was fine with that. If there was any reason to suspect they might hurt Abigail or Charlie, she didn't want anything to do with them. Other than that, his childhood was a cipher, and she loved him too much to press the issue. It made him uncomfortable, and at the end of the day it didn't matter. The past was the past. It was behind him.

That didn't mean that Jack didn't wonder how Aimee would react to knowing just how much of the dirty South he had in him. The Rileys were shocked when their daughter announced she was engaged to a roughneck—a nobody who had come from nowhere, like a ghost that had gotten stuck in the bayou. But the thought that got to him most was how shocked, and perhaps disgusted, his own parents would have been to discover he was marrying into gentility. It was hard to forget just how rough Gilda and Stephen had been when it came to "the riches." Everywhere they went, whether it was the market or the movie theater, his parents would scope out the place, pinpointing the people who looked the most refined, tallying up the most expensive cars in poorly lit parking lots. Jack was too young to know for sure, but he had a suspicion his folks lived off more than government checks. Every now and then his dad would show up with a new leather jacket or a necklace for Gilda, but there was never a mention of how he afforded such things.

The Rileys were the type to swear by genetics—after all, the apple doesn't fall far from the tree. If Patricia and Arnold knew the truth about the family Jack had left behind, the fact that he had run away, run for his life…it wouldn't have made a damn bit of difference.

Exhaling a breath, Aimee slumped in her seat and sighed.

"I forgot to tell you, Daddy's going to let us borrow the Olds until we get another car."

Jack grimaced. He hated borrowing anything from the Rileys. The last thing he needed was old Arnold's pristinely waxed Oldsmobile parked in their unpaved driveway.

"They're doing us a favor," Aimee reminded him.

"Sure," Jack muttered. "I'm sure they are."

That evening Jack woke to a tug on his T-shirt sleeve. Charlie stood beside the bed, her hair plastered across a sweat-beaded forehead.

"Daddy," she whispered hoarsely. "I think there's someone in my room."

After pulling himself out of bed, he got her a drink of water and walked her back to her room. Charlie pointed at the closet from her bed, clutching the glass of water in her free hand.

"Here?" Jack asked, approaching the door that was open a crack. He swung it wide to reveal nothing but a bundle of clothes—two girls' worth; one girl too many for the size of that closet. "There's nothing here, honey," Jack told her. "I don't think anyone could fit in here even if they wanted to."

"I saw it," Charlie whispered, unsatisfied with her dad's diagnosis.

Jack closed the door and approached her bed, tucking her in after placing the glass of water on her bedside table.

"Well, there's nobody there now," he told her. "Besides," he leaned in, whispering a secret into her ear, "Abby's bigger. It'll eat your sister first."

Charlie's face blossomed into an uncontrollable grin. She covered her mouth against her laugh, trying not to wake her sister.

The closet door swung open an hour later.

Both girls were fast asleep.

The next morning, Abby came dragging into the kitchen for breakfast. Aimee turned away from the stove, balancing a pancake on top of a spatula, and inspected the girl from across the room.

"Please tell me you aren't getting sick like your sister."

Abby shook her head no, then slouched in her chair like a rag doll.

"What's wrong then?"

"Tired," Abby murmured.

"Did Charlie keep you up?"

Abby shook her head again.

"I think it was an animal," she said. "There was this scratching on the wall outside. All night."

Reagan took a seat next to Jack at the picnic table that served as their lunch area outside the boat shop. Jack met Reagan the day he found himself in Louisiana. Dropped off outside a five-and-dime by an unknown driver in a beat-up pickup, Jack caught Reagan trying to sneak a smoke around the side of the building while his mother did the shopping inside. Reagan didn't have a much better upbringing than Jack had; his mom supported her fractured family by dancing, and he'd never even met his dad. But what Reagan's mom lacked in companionship she made up for in brains. It took her a single night of Jack sleeping over to put it all together: he was a runaway, and because she had been a runaway herself, she took him in despite her meager income. Jack half expected the cops to show up and haul him away, but they never came.

Reagan had always been tall: gangly with long limbs that reminded Jack of a spider if a spider lifted weights. He was the type of guy who liked to buck the norm by fitting his Charger with an exhaust that woke all of Live Oak during his late-night drives. He wore eyeliner and gauged his ears and bought intentionally offensive T-shirts off the Internet, which he would then wear to the shop, betting Jack that today was the day he'd get punched in the mouth by a swamper.

"This Saturday is booked," Reagan said, drawing a cigarette from its pack. "Should be a good night."

Music was another reason the Rileys never took to Jack. Reagan and Jack were the backbone of Lamb. The band had been Reagan's dream before Jack ever picked up a guitar. When they discovered that Jack could write music as well as lyrics, Jack was thrown into the limelight—at least what little of the limelight they had. Reagan's act of selflessness paid off in spades. Lamb became a hit at a few local bars and clubs before they could legally drink, and the boys eventually took to Bourbon Street, where, miraculously, they gained a following that filled the Red Door to capacity every time they played their brooding, bluesy rock-n-roll.

Jack stared down at his bologna and cheese sandwich. It sat there, boring and humorless on a square of wax paper.

"Man, I don't know," Jack said. "This weekend is really bad timing."

"It's already a done deal. I e-mailed you. I called you to make sure it was cool, but you didn't answer. I left a voice mail, which was pointless, I know. You never check it anyway."

"This is going to get me into some serious shit."

"What's the problem?" Reagan asked. "You guys having a fight?"

Jack shoved the bologna sandwich back into the paper bag it came from. Having two kids, Jack got sack lunches along with the girls. Aimee hated wasting money; Jack adored her for it but felt partly responsible. Aimee had been expected to go to college and work on a degree while waiting for an appropriate suitor, preferably a handsome young man working toward a PhD. Someone by the name of Ashley or Leslie or Rhett would have been preferable. When Aimee agreed to marry Jack, the Rileys decided it would be best for their daughter to get a taste of "real life." Tossed from the nest and into Jack's arms, she quickly realized just how little money they had.

Aimee had learned to embrace her bare-bones lifestyle as a direct affront to her parents. It was a giant *fuck you* to the both of them: she hadn't starved to death like they had expected her to, and she hadn't crawled back to them for help either. He knew it gave her satisfaction that her parents were irked. They had expected her to fail, to run back home and beg them to take her back.

In fact, Patricia Riley still hoped for this to happen. Jack suspected she was patiently waiting for Aimee to announce the dissolution of their marriage. Patricia Riley was a gambling woman. He'd bet a hundred bucks she had a ladies' wager on it.

"It's just the whole thing with the accident," Jack said. "And now Charlotte is sick. And we're being forced to use Aimee's old man's car until we come up with the money to buy a new one. Aimee's on edge."

"So what do you want me to do? Cancel?" Reagan shook his head. "You know that's going to make us look like shit."

"I know," Jack murmured. "We can't cancel."

"Then what?" Reagan asked. He paused a moment, then continued: "I mean, if we have to cancel, we'll cancel. I'm just saying it's going to look bad. It's going to piss Sam off. And I'm not really sure if it's a good idea to piss off the owner of the main club we play, you know? I mean, you get what I'm saying here, right? I'm not trying to be a dick or anything. I'm being realistic. Realism, man."

"I get what you're saying."

"I don't want to be the bad guy," Reagan insisted.

"I know."

"Seriously, it's like not my intention to make waves between you and Aimee. I'll even tell her myself. I love her like a sister," he continued.

"Reagan…"

"Like an incredibly hot half sister."

Jack pressed his elbows against the weather-warped wood of the picnic table and put his head in his hands.

"Jesus Christ," he muttered into his palms. "You're so fucking weird, you know that?"

"I know," Reagan agreed.

"Like just…*off.*"

"Oh, I know, dude. Seriously, I'm a psychopath."

"I'll just deal with it," Jack said. "She'll just have to understand. It's already scheduled."

"Sure, she'll understand. And then she'll rip your balls off."

Jack smirked and patted Reagan on the shoulder. "That's all a part of marriage, my friend."

"And you enjoy this?" Reagan asked, truly curious. "You like this better than hanging out, watching movies, playing video games, making late-night Doritos runs…?"

"Love is pain."

"Write a song about it."

"Good idea," Jack said. "I'll do that. I'll have plenty of time while sleeping on the couch."

CHAPTER THREE

When Abby came home from school there was a lump on Charlie's bed. Buried beneath a set of *SpongeBob* sheets and a matching comforter, Charlie had taken up her favorite position of sleeping with her butt in the air. She'd done it since she was a baby—elbows pulled into her chest, her knees pressed into the mattress, her rear end flying high and her thumb stuck in her mouth. Abby didn't have to see her to know that was her sister's exact position.

She dropped her backpack next to the leg of the desk they shared. Most days, if Charlie had homework, she'd do it at the kitchen table with their mom, and Abby would have the room all to herself. Then there were days like these, when Charlie refused to leave the bedroom and Abby would have to do her best to ignore the six-year-old monster on the opposite side of the room.

Squatting next to her bag, she began to rifle through Lisa Frank folders—they were hard to find but Abby's favorite—searching for her homework.

The lump on Charlie's bed shifted.

Abby waited for her sister to pop her head out from beneath the sheets. When it didn't happen, she continued to search for the right notebook—the one with Hello Kitty stickers all over it. She was sure she brought it home.

The lump shifted again.

Abby blinked. "Char?"

Getting no response, Abby rolled her eyes and looked back to her bag, ignoring the next fumbling shift across the room. She had learned from her mother: if Charlie didn't get a reaction, she'd get bored and stop. But when the lump began to convulse as though the person beneath the sheets were suddenly unable to breathe, Abby stared at it with a startled expression. It was moving in a nearly mechanical way—oddly jerky, like an old wind-up toy.

Less than a year before, Charlie had been diagnosed with asthma after an attack at a local park. She remembered how her sister's face had turned blue, how she had clawed at her neck with wide, desperate eyes. As she squatted on the bedroom floor, the memory conjured in Abby's mind and anchored there, forcing her heart to flutter as she pictured her sister beneath those sheets, suffocating while Abby ignored her.

"Charlie?" She got to her feet and swallowed against the lump in her throat, taking a few hesitant steps toward the bed. She was afraid to pull those sheets back, afraid of what she'd see. What if she was too late? What if she yanked the blanket away and Charlie was dead and blue and it was all her fault?

"Charlie, are you OK?" Her question was strained with worry. The closer she stepped toward the bed, the faster the lump panted, as if sensing Abby's approach. She stopped short, her eyes wide, not wanting to see what was beneath those sheets even if it *was* her sister. All at once she realized that her mother was home, that all she had to do was yell and Mom would come running.

She opened her mouth to call for help.

And Charlie appeared in the doorway.

Abby's heart shot into her throat. Suddenly she was the one who couldn't catch her breath. Charlie, on the other hand, peered sleepily at her sister while clutching a juice box to her chest.

"I'm not OK," Charlie said. Abby had posed the question seconds before; Charlie had certainly been out of earshot. Yet there she was, answering the question as though she'd been standing next to Abigail the entire time. "Didn't Momma tell you I'm dying?"

Stepping around Abby, Charlie crawled onto her bed, that lump of sheets now nothing more than exactly that.

Abby shook her head, backing away from SpongeBob's smiling face and crazy eyes. What had always been a pleasant character now looked positively evil.

Charlie shot her sister a skeptical look. "Are *you* OK?" she asked.

"I'm fine," Abby said quietly. "I just…have a lot of homework." She turned away, sank to her knees, and pulled her backpack to her chest, desperate not to cry.

Dinner was tense that evening. Jack picked at his pasta while trying to figure out how to break the weekend news, Aimee watched Charlie from across the table with a look of concern, Abigail sat on only half of her chair—the half farthest away from her sister, and Charlie appeared more serious than usual.

"There's someone living in the closet," she announced matter-of-factly. "I'm pretty sure because today I saw him, and when I went to check, the door closed by itself."

Jack and Aimee looked at each other, then looked to their daughter.

Abigail's breaths were shallow as she sat as still as she could. Jack saw her perk up, alert for noises—for the subtle creak of the closet door to see whether Charlie was telling the truth.

"I think he's the guy who's making all those scratchy noises," Charlie continued. "You know the noises?"

"What noises?" he asked.

"Scratchy ones," Charlie repeated. "Like *scrrrr…*" She lifted both hands to make tiny claws, scratching at the air to show her dad what she meant.

"Probably just an animal," Jack told her. "A raccoon or something." He pursed his lips, then looked down to his plate and poked at his pasta, suddenly uncomfortable with the conversation.

Aimee exhaled an annoyed sigh.

"All right, what's wrong? Is it no good? Why isn't anyone eating?"

"I'm not hungry," Abby said softly.

"I'm sick," Charlie whined.

"Reagan scheduled a gig," Jack mumbled.

The room went silent.

Of the fights he and Aimee had, the biggest ones always started with that very phrase. Their arguments were always about the band, about how much time Jack spent away from the girls on weekends, which, beyond the occasional night Jack didn't offer to work late at the shop, was the only time they really got to see their dad at all. The gigs were erratic, and Aimee had expressed her displeasure with Lamb's mysterious schedule a dozen times before. But now, with the accident, the strain on their marriage was undeniable.

Abby chewed on her bottom lip and rolled a piece of penne back and forth with the prongs of her fork. Charlie put her fork down and put her hands in her lap, which she stared at silently.

"I didn't know," Jack said quietly. "He only told me today." It was a half-truth. There was the e-mail. The voice mail. But Reagan *knew* Jack never checked that stuff. If it had been so damn important, he should have called again, should have called until Jack had answered.

Aimee said nothing.

"I told him it was bad timing. I told him Charlie is sick."

"Dying," Charlie whispered.

"And?" Aimee raised an eyebrow.

"And if we cancel on Sam it'll look bad, Aimes. He already put us on the schedule for this Saturday. The lineup is posted all over the Quarter by now."

"Oh." Aimee calmly pushed her chair away from the table and gathered up her plate.

"I didn't know. If he had said something sooner…"

"Then what?" Aimee asked, snatching Jack's plate off the table.

"Then I could have kept it from ending up on the schedule."

"Really? Because you've kept *so* many gigs off the schedule."

Lamb never missed a gig. Rain or shine, if they were booked, they played. They had even made the journey out just before Katrina. Jack had made it out of town a mere four hours before the first levee broke. That one nearly made Aimee go ballistic— but gigs were becoming few and far between. Letting them slip through their fingers was as good as disbanding altogether.

"What do you want me to say?" Jack asked, desperate for a little leeway. He hated fighting with her, hated that it was happening more often now than ever. "I didn't know this week was going to end up like this. I didn't know we were going to have an accident or that Charlie was going to end up sick. How was I supposed to know?"

"You just *know*," Aimee snapped, dropping the plates into the sink with a clang. "That stupid band shouldn't be your priority. Your family should be."

"Reagan *is* my family."

"You know what I mean."

"Can I be excused?" Abby asked. Her request went unheard.

"It brings in money," Jack reminded Aimee.

"Well, we both know we wouldn't need it if—" She stopped herself.

"Right." Jack sighed. "We wouldn't need it if I'd just grow up, right? We wouldn't need it if I'd screw the whole thing and get a *real* job."

"You have a real job, Daddy," Charlie piped in. "You fix boats!"

"Can I be excused?" Abby repeated. Again, she received no reply.

"Fixing boats isn't going to get us out of this house," Aimee said. "Fixing boats isn't going to fill up our savings account. It isn't going to get us anything but this life, over and over again, forever."

Jack's tone became bitter. "You chose this life."

Stepping back to the table, Aimee grabbed the girls' plates and marched them to the sink.

"Once upon a time, you *liked* this life," Jack told her.

"Once upon a time," Aimee agreed. "And maybe once upon a time I should have listened to my mother."

Jack went silent. He bit his tongue and stared down at the grain of the table.

There was a tense pause. Aimee finally broke it: "Whatever," she said, turning on the faucet. "You just do whatever you want to do, Jack. I'll hold the family together while you're out playing your little songs."

Jack's nostrils flared. His jaw went rigid.

"Daddy?" Charlie stretched a scrawny arm across the table.

"What is it?" Jack asked almost inaudibly.

"Will you play us a song tonight, for bedtime?"

He gave Charlie a weak smile and nodded once in agreement.

"That sounds like a great idea," he said. "Abby?"

Abby looked up from her empty place setting and, after a moment, nodded as well.

"As long as it's one of yours," Abby said.

"Maybe 'Don't Stop Believin'" just once," Charlie added. It was her favorite song.

With her back turned, Jack heard Aimee inhale a shaky breath. She used to ask him to play her lullabies when they had first met. Now she resented him for picking up the guitar—something she'd loved about him a dozen years before. Jack was the same Jack he'd always been.

It was Aimee who had changed.

Charlie knew all the words to Journey's biggest hit, and she sang it at the top of her lungs while using her bed as a stage. Despite Abby's slow-growing apprehension, she laughed as her little sister bounced around like a monkey, using a toilet tube for a microphone. After Charlie's performance, Jack tucked them in, strummed a lullaby on his guitar, and left the door open a crack. The light from the hall slashed through the darkness of the girls' room like a beam of hope.

As soon as her dad left, Abby shifted her attention to Charlie's bed, remembering what she had seen when she had come home from school. She wondered how she'd ever sleep again.

Aimee was already in bed when Jack returned from entertaining the girls, reading *Les Misérables* for what seemed like the eighteenth time since they had met. It was her favorite book—a poverty-stricken romance; a story she could see herself in if Louisiana were somehow magically transformed into France. She'd always wanted to see Paris but doubted she would. Maybe when the girls grew up, when they went off to college or got married and had kids of their own; maybe then she and Jack could take the honeymoon they never had. She wanted to walk the Champs-Élysées arm in arm with Jack, a beret atop her head—tipped just so. She wanted to sip café au lait and eat chocolate-filled croissants and ride a bicycle with a wicker basket, brimming with fresh-cut flowers. Maybe if they had enough money to visit they'd have enough money to stay, move to a tiny countryside town. A girl could dream.

Aimee didn't look up when he entered the room, still determined to be angry. But after a few minutes of Jack rummaging around in the bathroom—brushing his teeth, getting ready to turn in for the night—she lowered her book and allowed her head to fall against her pillow.

"You know," she said after a moment, "if I wasn't big on the idea of a husband running around with his band for the rest of my life, I probably shouldn't have married a musician."

Standing at the closet door, Jack paused when she spoke, then peeled off his shirt and tossed it into the hamper in the corner of the room. Jack's tattoos were all in places that could easily be hidden; she found them sexier that way. She was the only girl in the whole world who knew them all in intricate detail—at least, she hoped that was true. The most pronounced one was emblazoned across his back—a tattoo he had gotten long before they had met. That one had scared her the first time she saw it. It crawled across his shoulder blades and down his spine: a wicked-looking beast with black, leathery skin and glowing eyes. A razor-sharp grin was spread across its horrible face, as if laughing at a joke that only it and Jack knew. The first time she saw it, he had played it off as nothing but rock and roll—a stupid decision made under the influence; booze and tattoos didn't mix, especially when there were rowdy bandmates egging you on. But Aimee knew better. That tattoo must have taken months of repeat visits to a parlor to complete. She was sure Jack had spent hundreds of dollars and dozens of hours beneath the needle, etching the nightmarish image into his skin.

"You probably should have listened to your mother," he said.

Aimee stuck her bookmark between Victor Hugo's pages and sighed.

"I probably should have," she agreed. "But it was either endure the pain of being your wife, or run the risk of my darling mother arranging a marriage for me."

"Well, there *is* one good thing about your darling mother," Jack said.

"Oh yeah? What's that?" Aimee tried to bite back a smile, but the corners of her mouth betrayed her.

"She married an Oldsmobile man."

Aimee exhaled a laugh.

"The guy has excellent taste," Jack insisted.

"Mm, he does, doesn't he?"

"Velveteen upholstery. A tan paint job…"

"Beige," she corrected. Her father hated the word "tan"; "beige" was somehow better. Arnold Riley was particular about vocabulary. "Tan" was boring. "Beige" was more sophisticated. Vanilla wasn't acceptable, but French vanilla was just fine. He watched motion pictures, not movies. He ate rocket, not arugula. Jack had once joked that Arnold wasn't anal; his father-in-law just had a constipated disposition.

"Potato, potahto. It's tan." Jack moved to the bed. "And you know, I'm not knocking tan." He crawled onto the mattress, slinking toward his grinning wife.

"You're not?"

"Why should I?" he asked, his palms pressing into the mattress on either side of her sun-kissed shoulders. "Tan is my favorite color."

"It's a sexy color," she whispered, her fingers walking up his chest.

"My sentiments exactly," Jack murmured against her neck.

Aimee's eyes fluttered closed as his hands moved down to her waist, catching the hem of her sleep shirt between his fingers. The fabric dragged against her skin as he pulled it upward. The room grew hot. The sheets were kicked to the side.

And then there was a scream.

It was amazing how quickly they could go from foreplay to bolting down the hall. The screaming continued as they raced toward the girls' room, as if desperate to outrun each other.

Jack was the winner. He skidded to a stop in front of the door and stared into the darkness. Aimee wasn't much farther behind, covering her mouth as soon as she saw it.

Abby was the one screaming. Still in her bed, she sat stick-straight and terrified, surrounded by a veritable lake of vomit. It was everywhere—Abby's bed, the floor, the desk, dripping off her stack of precious Lisa Frank folders: glossy unicorns and colorful bears swimming in sickness.

Charlie stood in the corner of the room, her chin against her chest, her hands at her sides. Unmoving. Staring through a blank set of eyes at what she'd done.

In spite of its cheerful wallpaper, the doctor's office felt nothing but cold. Aimee sat beside Jack in the waiting room, flipping through an old copy of *Good Housekeeping*, while Charlie sat on the floor, sliding beads up and down brightly colored metal rods. The beads hissed as they slid up and tumbled down with each hill and valley, eventually smacking the wooden baseboard. Jack hadn't been able to sleep after he and Aimee had cleaned up Charlie's mess the night before. Every time he closed his eyes he saw her standing in the corner of her room, shaded by the dark; he saw himself approach, ready to pull her from the shadows, only to catch sight of those eyes—soulless. Abysmally empty.

He shuddered.

Aimee raised an eyebrow, flipped a page of the magazine.

"Chill out," she whispered. "You look more uncomfortable than all of these rug rats combined."

Across the room, a little boy sat next to his mother, flipping thick cardboard pages of a *Thomas the Tank Engine* storybook; another kid pushed a bright red Tonka truck across the carpet, repeatedly smacking it into the leg of an old guy's chair—hopefully a grandfather rather than an unfortunate stranger. A girl on the other side of the waiting room pressed her mouth against the glass of a fish tank, leaving streaks of spit across an ocean scene while the fish cowered behind a plastic deep-sea diver. Her mother hardly noticed, busy conducting business via cell phone.

They all seemed so calm compared to Jack, who was hunched over in his chair, his knees bouncing nervously. He told himself Charlie was just sick, that she had the flu and that was it—but he couldn't unknow what he knew, and he couldn't unfeel the certainty that coursed through him like a quick-spreading disease.

Jack's stomach twisted uncomfortably. His face turned down in a grimace.

Charlie always said she wanted to be just like her dad.

Jack feared that his little girl was getting her wish.

"Charlotte Winter?"

A nurse clutched a clipboard against her chest, her free hand holding ajar the heavy door that led to their assigned examining room. Aimee tossed the magazine onto an empty chair, gathered her purse, and motioned for Charlie to get up.

Charlie strode to her mother, took Aimee's hand, and looked back to her dad with a blink. Jack hadn't moved. He hated doctors, hated this whole thing.

"Come on, Daddy," she said. "You can't stay here by yourself."

The nurse smiled as Jack reluctantly pushed himself out of his seat.

"You must be Charlotte," she said, too friendly to be genuine. "You're just down the hall."

Aimee flashed the nurse a terse smile and stepped through the door. Charlie let go of her mother's hand when Aimee tried to drag her behind, extending her arms out to her dad, waiting to be picked up like the baby she would soon no longer be. Jack didn't argue. He hefted her up into his arms and stepped past the nurse without a word.

"Room C," the nurse instructed.

"C for Charlie," Charlie whispered into Jack's ear.

C for curse, he thought. *C for catastrophe. Calamity. Chaos.*

The examination room felt even colder than the waiting area. Aimee took a seat while Jack plopped Charlie on a padded examination table, her attention immediately drawn to the counter space next to a small steel sink.

"Can I have one of those?" she asked, pointing to a jar full of tongue depressors.

"No, you can't," Aimee said, but Jack was already making a move for them.

"Jack." Aimee gave him a stern look.

"You think they'll be mad?" he asked, fishing a depressor out of the jar. "You think that maybe they can't afford to buy any more of these after they send us our bill?"

"That isn't the point," she muttered. But she averted her eyes nonetheless, checking her nails.

Jack handed Charlie the depressor, which she immediately stuck into her mouth.

He took a seat next to Aimee while Charlie traced the shape of a smiling bear against the wallpaper, ignoring her parents as she sucked on the wooden stick in her mouth. Eventually, a soft knock sounded at the door.

Charlie's doctor looked quite professional with his white coat and horn-rimmed glasses.

"Hi, folks. I'm Dr. Hogan." He extended a hand to both Jack and Aimee before turning his attention to the little girl sitting on his table. "Hi, Charlotte," he said.

"Charlie, please," Charlie requested, her words jumbled around the tongue depressor.

"Charlie, then. How are we feeling, kiddo?"

"I'm fine," she said. "I told that to my mom but she's still mad."

Aimee shifted uncomfortably, clearing her throat.

"Mad about what?" Dr. Hogan asked.

"She was very sick last night," Aimee cut in, but it didn't stop Charlie from telling her version of the story.

"I puked all over the floor. And then Nubs got in the room and started eating it..."

"Charlie," Aimee warned, her voice edged.

"...so that was gross."

Jack held back a laugh.

"Nubs?" the doctor asked.

"Our dog," Aimee clarified.

"Sometimes he eats his own poop," Charlie explained.

"*Charlie!*" The name cracked like a whip. Aimee had the uncanny ability to shut anyone up by hissing their name.

Dr. Hogan cleared his throat, attempting to regain his professional composure before turning to Aimee and Jack, but there was still a hint of amusement dancing in the corners of his mouth.

"So," he said. "Let's see what we can do."

"Completely ridiculous," Aimee snorted, stomping across the parking lot. She reached the passenger door and crossed her arms over her chest, fuming. "Nothing wrong with her," she sneered. "Where did that man get his medical license anyway? Off the Internet?"

Jack put Charlie down next to the car and fished the car keys out of his pocket.

"You don't just vomit buckets the night before to be fine the next day, Jack. That doesn't happen."

He held his tongue, unlocked the doors, and helped Charlie into her car seat—it was the only thing they had salvaged from the wreck. When he finally slid behind the wheel, he sat quietly for a moment, transfixed by the Georgia plates on the back of a rusty red pickup. It was like déjà vu, except this time he was the father and Charlie was the kid.

"Isn't it better that she isn't sick?" he finally asked, trying to calm Aimee down despite the slow roll of nausea within his gut.

"She *is* sick," Aimee snapped. "She's been sick for the last few days. She had a fever of one hundred and three. Or do you not remember her clawing at your arm when you put her in the tub?"

Jack remembered it.

"It was cold!" Charlie yelled from the back.

"It was probably just a bug," he denied, not sure who he was trying to convince. "She caught something at school. It was a two-day thing and everything is fine."

Aimee shook her head and stared out the window, refusing to look at him. Unable to reassure Aimee or himself, he exhaled a shaky breath and started the car, slowly rolling it out of the parking lot and onto the street.

A few minutes later, while idling at a red light, Aimee spoke up again, her voice low.

"There's something wrong with her, Jack. I can feel it."

And at that very moment, Aimee's voice wasn't hers. It was his mother's.

CHAPTER FOUR

THE DAY JACK'S PARENTS FIRST SUSPECTED THERE WAS something wrong with him was the day they found a stray cat hanging from a tree.

The cat had been a nuisance from the moment Gilda and Stephen had parked their trailer on that land. It yowled like a banshee long after they'd turn in and would perch on their deck railing during the day, peering through the front window like a voyeur. Stephen hated cats and had been trying to scare the thing off their property longer than Jack had been alive. Jack had learned from his father that whenever that cat showed its furry face around the Winter estate, all was fair in hunting felines. Stephen made it clear: he didn't care how Jack got the damn thing off their property just as long as it was gone.

Before Jack started school, he spent scorching afternoons chasing it across their two acres, wielding a stick as big as he was in case he managed to catch up with it. When he hit first grade, Stephen bought him a slingshot for his birthday and he spent an entire month nursing his new obsession. He taught himself to shoot rocks as well as Robin Hood, preparing for the next time that roving stray crossed his path.

But after years of poaching, he'd secretly grown fond of the trespasser that drove his father crazy. By the time Jack entered the fourth grade, he was leaving milk in a shallow dish behind the lot's farthest tree. He didn't dare risk placing it any closer: he knew that if he was caught fraternizing with the enemy, he'd get the beating of his life.

The year he went soft on that stray was the year he started visiting the graveyard more and more often. The cat, which had grown fond of Jack as well, crept after him through the tall grass, watching the boy through slitted yellow eyes while he sat among the headstones. It kept its distance at first, but ventured closer as the days wore on until, one afternoon, that feline found itself sitting next to Jack as compliantly as a lifelong pet.

Jack patted the animal on top of its head, his eyes fixed on a point beyond the trees. For a brief moment, two sworn enemies found solace in each other, enjoying the spring breeze that rustled the leaves and bent the grass to the earth in gentle arcs. And then, with his hand stroking the cat's back, Jack saw those black bottomless eyes in the shadow of an oak. He'd seen them a handful of times—a wave of calm washing over him each time they had appeared. He had dared venture among the trees one afternoon, seeking them out, but found nothing at all.

But the day he and the cat sat together in the grass, something was different.

His fingers tensed, biting into the animal's fur like a pair of jaws. The stray shrieked and bounded away, then stopped to glare at its old enemy. It didn't like what it saw. Reflexively, it arched its back, fur bristling with agitation. Opening its mouth as wide as it could, it exposed its fangs with a hiss, then turned and dashed out of view.

Its reaction made Jack's heart bound into his throat. He didn't know why he had grabbed its fur the way he had. Had he hurt it, or just scared it? Whatever he had done, it had scared him back. But his fear was short-lived. Within a second, it gave way to anger.

On any other day Jack would have shrugged it off and forgotten the whole thing, but that particular day he couldn't seem to let bygones be bygones. The way the animal's back bent into an S-curve, the way it had bared its teeth—something about it made his blood boil. Rage curdled his blood. His fingers dug into the soil. All at once he was on his feet, running after it, determined to catch it once and for all, to string it up like he should have long ago. Years of effort burned in his lungs like oil, all the hours he had spent hunting.

The cat was mocking him. It had tricked him into bringing it milk, scratching behind its ears when nobody was looking.

Jack's nostrils flared. He ran harder. He could see it ahead of him, dashing toward the trailer like a fur-covered missile. Jack slowed when Stephen stepped onto the sagging porch, aimed his BB gun, and fired as the stray bolted by him. He missed.

"Son of a bitch!" Stephen barked. He turned to his ten-year-old son; Jack was winded and gulping for air, and could feel his dark hair plastered to his sweat-covered forehead. "You think you're gonna catch 'im with your bare hands?" he asked.

Maybe not with my bare hands, Jack thought to himself. *But I'll sure as hell catch him.*

Jack spent the rest of the day plotting his revenge.

That night, long after Stephen and Gilda had gone to bed, Jack snuck out the front door with a saucer of milk. He crossed the front yard with careful steps and placed the bowl at the base of his momma's oak—a huge old tree that shaded their trailer from the burning Georgia sun. Armed with a spool of his father's fishing line, he tied a slipknot onto the end and looped the line along the ground, leaving that saucer in the middle as bait. Then he climbed up into the branches of that tree and waited, the end of the line held tight in his hands.

Gilda was the first to see it. She had stepped outside to beat the kitchen rug with a broomstick when her eyes snagged on something swaying in the shade. Squinting against the sun, she couldn't make out what it was, so she stepped off the porch and walked a few dozen feet to get a better look.

She wasn't squeamish, but she couldn't help the scream that punched its way out of her lungs. Stephen stumbled out of the trailer to see what his wife was screaming about, spotting his arch nemesis strung up like a hate crime. Rather than exhaling a satisfied laugh, he gave his son, who was sitting beneath that tree like a sentry, a startled look.

"Holy Mary, Mother of God," he said. "Boy, what the hell have you done?"

Sitting in darkness so black he was sure it wasn't real, Jack had stared at the slit of light that shone from beneath his bedroom door—light that leaked into the pitch blackness of his bedroom, too weak to penetrate the lingering shadows.

His mom sounded wounded; that was what Jack remembered most. He could see their shadows dancing outside his bedroom door. Gilda was choking on her own air, and though he couldn't make out her words he knew she was crying. The longer it went on, the more Stephen raised his voice despite trying to stay calm. But after a while he started to yell, his own panic taking control.

"Stop it," was the first thing Jack could make out. "Stop it, Gilda, stop it." He imagined Stephen grabbing her by the shoulders and shaking her like they did in the movies—shaking some sense into her while shaking the chaos out.

"There's…something…wrong." Her words came in gasps, caught between sobs and desperate gulps for breath.

"Something wrong," Stephen echoed. "Something wrong with what?"

She wailed again—a sound that Jack had never heard come out of his mother in his ten short years.

"Something wrong with what?" Stephen repeated, more urgently this time. "Gilda, I can fix it. Just tell me what," he said. "Just tell me what it is and I—"

"With *Jack*," she shrieked. The way his name slithered through the walls and under the door made Jack's skin crawl. There was terror in it, a distinct pitch of absolute dismay.

"What's wrong with Jack?" Stephen asked.

"This is too much," she confessed. "He killed it, Steve. He killed it and then he…"

But wasn't that what his dad had wanted? He had said it himself—he didn't care *how* Jack got rid of that cat as long as it was gone. And here they were, freaking out about it like it was some big deal. His mom hadn't given two shits about what Jack did or didn't do up until now, and suddenly she was losing her mind over something Stephen had told him to do in the first place.

"…he was clawing at the wall," she told him. "Like he was trying to crawl up to the ceiling."

"What?"

"I was bringing in his clothes and he was scratching at it like a cat. And his eyes, Steve. And when he saw me come in…" Her words hitched in her throat. "His eyes…they were all wrong."

"This is ridiculous," Stephen muttered.

Jack's door suddenly swung open and hit the wall, bouncing off the cheap paneling that made up the walls of the trailer. Stephen stood in the doorway, then took a step forward, pushing his hand into the shadows. His palm slid across the wall in search of the light switch.

The light snapped on and the room went bright.

Jack sat silently upon his bed.

When Gilda saw her boy sitting there so calmly, her eyes went wide. Her hands pressed themselves against her chest and she stared at him as though not seeing him at all—looking through him, beyond him, at something behind their son that Stephen failed to see.

"I know what I saw," she choked. "Oh God, I've lost him…"

Stephen looked back to Jack, his expression riddled with such intense confusion it verged on rage. Jack shook his head, confirming that he was just as clueless as his dad. And that was mostly the truth.

But in the back of his mind there was a slight glimmer of understanding, a tiny shard of remembrance. After Stephen had sent Jack to his room, wandering off to bury the cat, Gilda had opened the door to bring in Jack's laundry. He remembered seeing her not right-side up, but upside down. What he couldn't recall was whether his mom had been walking on the ceiling, or whether he'd been standing on his head.

CHAPTER FIVE

DESPITE CHARLIE'S IMPROVEMENT IN HEALTH, AIMEE wouldn't let it go. Jack caught her at his old piano, fishing a phone book out of its bench seat.

He eyed her as he made his way to the front door, holding the screen open for Nubs, who was making a mad dash for the front yard.

"What're you doing?" he asked.

Nubs lost his footing on the wooden floor and nearly crashed into the wall, but righted himself just in time to leap onto the front doorstep.

"Looking for a second opinion," Aimee said flatly. She dropped the phone book onto the piano's bench with a crack. A cloud of dust exploded from between the pages, catching the sunlight that filtered through the curtains, setting the dust particles afire with a supernatural gleam.

"Still?" Jack asked. They had survived the night before without incident. Charlie had slept without getting up for a glass of water, let alone pulling an *Exorcist* in the dead of night. He hoped that would have been enough for Aimee to let it go. But luck, it seemed, was not on his side.

"She doesn't look right," Aimee told him. "She looks...yellow."

"Yellow?"

"Just..." She shook her head. "Never mind. I can't explain it."

"Aimes..."

Aimee straightened where she stood, held up a hand to silence him.

"Just don't. You're busy getting ready to live it up in New Orleans. Your head's never right before a gig, and I'm sorry if you consider at least one parent being concerned as unusual."

"I'm concerned," Jack confessed, glancing to his guitar nestled snug in its case, crammed between a wall and a bookcase. It would be easy not to go. Reagan would be pissed, but he knew all the songs as well as Jack did.

Aimee flipped to the *P*s for a pediatrician; at least it wasn't *P* for psychologist. Or *E* for exorcism.

"At least let me pick up a new directory," he said. "We've had that one since we moved in. It's completely useless." Not that they needed one. She could have confiscated his phone, pulled up a number on the web, but he was trying to stall her—throw her off her groove.

Aimee stared down at the phone book, fighting an internal debate. Eventually, she looked at Jack, rolled her eyes, and relented.

"Fine."

She turned to leave the living room when Jack stopped her with a question.

"Hey, Aimes?"

Exhaling a sigh, she turned to face him. Her arms hung at her sides in defeat. For a moment, she looked like the girl Jack had fallen in love with a decade before—beautiful despite her irritation. Aimee was always beautiful, no matter how annoyed she was.

"Watch a movie tonight," he said. "Pop some popcorn. You deserve it. Just like old times." It had been one of their rituals before the girls had been born—bad B-movies and cheap microwave popcorn. They always finished the popcorn but hardly ever finished the films, too smitten with each other to keep their hands to themselves.

Despite her mood, a shadow of a smile crawled across Aimee's lips; but she wasn't finished being angry. Crossing her arms over her chest, she eyed him.

"Just when everything is falling apart, you have to say something romantic."

Then she turned and wandered toward the kitchen, wondering if they had an old box of Orville Redenbacher hidden in the pantry somewhere.

By the time Reagan arrived, Jack had ordered the girls a pizza, made sure they were in their pajamas, and readied them for bed with an old *Ren & Stimpy* rerun. Aimee had been granted the entire afternoon off and was slightly buzzed when Reagan turned up.

"Hi, Reagan," Aimee greeted from Jack's favorite armchair, nursing a beer.

"Hey, Aimee. Getting liquored up?" Reagan plopped himself down on the floor and put an arm around Abby while Charlie climbed into his lap with a goofy grin. "Hey, Charles. What's the word?"

"Nothing," Charlie said.

Abigail climbed onto the couch behind Reagan while Charlie poked a finger through the round spacer in his ear.

"I heard you were sick, man."

"I was," Charlie said. "I had to go to the doctor and everything."

"You did?"

"Yup." She sprawled out across him like a queen on a settee. "I had to go yesterday because Mom was totally freaking out, like…" She pulled at her hair and made a wild face.

Abigail giggled from behind them while playing with Reagan's hair, twisting it into tiny braids. Aimee smirked and took a swig of beer.

"So what happened?" Reagan asked.

"The doctor's incompetence happened," Aimee muttered from across the room.

"Clean bill of health," Jack corrected, hefting Charlie off Reagan's lap by her ankles. "Right?"

Charlie dangled upside down with a squeal, struggling to reach the ground with her hands.

"Oh God, Jack, put her down," Aimee said. "That's the last thing she needs. I mean, really."

"I'm gonna barf!" Charlie warned. "I'm gonna do it all over Uncle Reagan!"

"Do it," Reagan dared her. "If I show up to the show with barf all over me, I'd be totally hardcore."

Jack put Charlie down and she immediately crawled back into Reagan's lap.

"What's hardcore?" she asked.

"You don't know what hardcore is?" Reagan gave Jack a look of disapproval. "Jack, seriously, what aren't you teaching these girls?"

"I know what hardcore is," Abby said.

"You do, do you?" Aimee raised a curious eyebrow and waited for her eldest to define the term.

"It means awesome," Abby said.

Jack puffed out his chest with a grin. "See?" he said. "It means awesome."

"That's right." Aimee shook her head with a chuckle. "Because it's awesome to show up at a gig with vomit all over yourself. That's the definition of awesome. Abby hit that nail right on the head."

"What does it mean then?" Abby asked.

"It means awesome," Reagan assured her.

Charlie jumped to her feet excitedly. "Uncle Reagan, I barfed all over my room!"

"She did," Aimee said.

"That was hardcore, right?" Charlie asked.

"Wrong," Abby cut in. "That was totally gross."

"You should have seen it," Aimee muttered. "It was like *The Exorcist* in there."

"Impressive, little buddy." Reagan held his hand up for a high-five. Charlie slapped his palm and spun around with a laugh.

"I'll do it again too!" Charlie said, bouncing around.

"Over my dead body, kid," Aimee warned. "Next time you pull something like that, you're sleeping outside with Nubs."

"In the doghouse," Charlie laughed. "Like a dog. With fleas."

"And barf," Abby added from the couch.

"And dog food," Charlie said.

"And we should go," Jack interrupted, grabbing his guitar case out of the corner.

Reagan stood, dusting off the back of his jeans. "OK, ladies," he said, "the hardcore dudes must depart."

"Have a good time." Aimee forced a smile. She still wasn't thrilled with the idea of Jack leaving. Not after the fiasco with the doctor, and certainly not after what had happened two nights ago. With her luck, as soon as the boys pulled out of the driveway, Charlie would open her mouth and projectile vomit across the living room.

Jack put an arm around her and whispered into her ear. "I'll be home soon," he promised, then pressed a kiss to the corner of her mouth. She couldn't help a smile. He looked so handsome with that guitar case heavy in one hand.

"Bye, Daddy," Abby said.

"Bring me back a toy!" Charlie called after them. "Don't forget!"

And with the latch of the door and the slap of the screen beyond it, the house went silent save for the sound of *Ren & Stimpy*, and a faint scratching against the wall.

Despite his promise to come straight home, Jack decided to hit Bourbon Street for a few minutes after the show. It was tradition, and tonight that ritual seemed even more important to uphold than any night before. Every time he left home for a gig, he brought the girls a toy. It started out as guilt, but blossomed into a custom.

That wasn't to say the tradition was easy to uphold. Finding a toy for a kid on Bourbon Street was as easy as finding a nun in one of its bars.

Reagan stayed behind at the club, having a few drinks with the boys after the show, while Jack scoured the strip in search of an appropriate gift. Unless he was willing to settle on a T-shirt that read "My Daddy's Big and My Mommy's Easy," it would take some time to find. He had already bought them key chains sporting their names, and Charlie had already collected so much Día de los Muertos stuff that Aimee threatened to pack it all up and leave it at the Goodwill. Once he'd found her a tiny three-legged pig that, according to voodoo folklore, was supposed to bring the owner good luck. Aimee hadn't liked that so much either; she appreciated the sentiment, but she wasn't big on bringing voodoo into the house.

After a few minutes of stalking down Bourbon Street's uneven pavement—the music of various clubs crashing together in discord—he ducked down a crooked side street. It was strange how a single block of buildings could erase the tangle of sound that gave Bourbon Street its swinging personality, how a single alley could transform the scent of alcohol and sludge-filled gutters into something mouthwatering—a trace of freshly fried beignets, a whiff of a five-star restaurant he could never afford. Bourbon's brightly lit street gave way to wall-mounted gas lanterns and cobblestone beneath his feet. Rowdy clubs and trashy peepshows were replaced by French Colonial architecture, by breathtaking buildings with filigreed wrought iron and creeping ivy.

He found himself in front of an open door, its tiny shop window jammed with colorful odds and ends—candles and tarot decks and shrunken heads that claimed to be authentic. Inside, there was a wall dedicated to African masks, another lined with tapered candles of every shade of the rainbow, hanging two-by-two by an uncut wick. Small stickers were tacked beside each color, distinguishing which candles were to be used with which spells.

Despite Aimee's distaste for the knickknacks he'd bring home, Jack was drawn to these shops. He had voodoo sonar. As if by magic, he'd stray off Bourbon and end up in a cramped little store selling spells and herbs. He was comfortable among their overcrowded shelves, much like he had been comfortable among crumbling headstones. Despite the darkness these shops implied, for Jack, these were sacred pockets of silence among a sea of chaos. Jack was drawn to them, drunk off their mysticism. And tonight he was drawn to the back of that long, skinny shop.

He paused at a red curtain, a sign safety-pinned to the fabric: "Reading in session, quiet please."

"She's almost done if you want one," the girl at the counter told him.

"Sorry?"

"A reading." The girl nodded at the curtain. "She won't be long."

Jack looked back to the curtain. A framed price sheet sat at eye level, perched on a shelf. He'd gotten a reading a few years back. It had been on a Quarter visit just like this one; the band had an unusually late gig and had decided to shack up in New Orleans for the night rather than making the drive home. After a few too many Hand Grenades, Jack and Reagan stumbled across a tiny tarot reader's shop. The guy who took Jack's money was an awkward Dungeons and Dragons type. He wore a hooded blue velvet cape over an AC/DC T-shirt, and due to a few too many drinks, Jack and Reagan openly heckled the guy, calling him "Darth Bane," asking him to do an impromptu performance of "Back in Black." The guy nearly kicked them both out before they settled down, trying to be serious. Reagan's reading was what Reagan later called "standard bullshit," and he had insisted that Jack's was the same as his—just a bunch of mystical mumbo jumbo that you couldn't take seriously—a sham; they'd both been taken for sixty bucks a pop.

But Jack couldn't shake the reading he had received, and it appeared that the AC/DC guy had also been spooked by what he'd seen. Of his three-card spread, all of them were bad: the tower—a symbol of abandoning his past; the moon—signifying deception and trickery; and the last, the devil himself—two human demons flanking him, a man and a woman, chained to his perch. The AC/DC guy had run his fingers over that card, stopping over the man while giving Jack a weird look. He didn't have to say anything for Jack to know what that look meant: that man was him.

Standing in front of that red curtain, Jack felt a wave of vertigo rock him back and forth. He'd never considered the female on that card until now, never considered that if he represented the male, someone else had to represent the female.

"Thanks," Jack finally said, realizing that he was standing there, completely zoned out, very likely making the girl behind the counter completely uncomfortable. "I'm just looking for something for my kid."

The girl shrugged and looked back to her paperback.

"Any suggestions for a couple of girls, six and ten?" he asked, hopeful that this time he would be saved by a thoughtful customer service rep.

The girl stuck a bookmark between the tattered pages of what she was reading and motioned for Jack to come over, tapping the glass case beneath her elbow.

"Kids go nuts for these," she said, pointing to a display of mood rings. "They're made-in-China crap, but like a kid is gonna know."

"Do they work?"

The girl shrugged again. "I guess. They work off body heat, so they change color like they're supposed to. It doesn't have anything to do with mood, but like a kid is gonna know *that.*" She flicked a strand of dyed hair over her shoulder.

A soft jingle of a bell sounded behind him. A couple of girls pushed the red curtain aside, both of them flushed and giggling, eager to get out of the shop. Jack's stomach dropped when the reader followed them out. At first Jack was sure it would be the same guy, complete with robe and pudgy face. But it was a woman—a tiny African American woman with her hair pulled tight into a bun and her lightly freckled cheeks rosy above her smile. She adjusted the shawl around her shoulders, tiny gold bells tied to its tassels jingling with each move she made. She looked toward the front of the shop and gave Jack a warm smile, but it didn't last. Jack watched her expression shift from welcoming to spooked. She quickly looked away and ducked out of sight. Having witnessed the exchange, the counter girl gave Jack a weird look.

"I'll take three," Jack announced, fumbling for his wallet.

With the rings tucked safely in his pocket, he marched out of the shop. In his rush to get out of there, his shoulder crashed into a big guy trying to make his way inside.

"Shit, sorry," Jack muttered, holding out a hand to steady himself.

The big guy tipped the brim of a trucker cap at Jack in acknowledgment. As soon as he did, Jack was struck by a sense of familiarity—one that made every hair on his body stand on end. The trucker smiled a wide, toothy grin—a smile that seemed to crawl across his entire face.

"No problem, chief," the big guy said. "Good to see ya."

Before Jack could react, the guy stepped inside the shop. Jack stood frozen beside the shop's steps, then veered around and stepped back inside. When he did, there was nobody inside but the counter girl.

"That guy," Jack said, "did he go in the back?" He motioned to the red curtain.

"Um…" This time she was genuinely weirded out. Jack could see it written all over her face. Somehow, he had become the type of person who got Maced in the face by scared shop girls.

"The big guy," Jack clarified.

She continued to stare at him, a blank look plastered across her face. She didn't have to say another word. Jack knew what that look meant.

It meant that he was going crazy.

There was no trucker.

If he had existed outside the shop, he'd walked through the door and disappeared.

After the kids were asleep, Aimee popped a bag of popcorn, selected a flick she couldn't watch with the kids around—*From Dusk Till Dawn*, because George Clooney was sexy when he blew the heads off vampires—and decided to have her own girl's night in, just as Jack had suggested. With the lights off and the television throwing blue shadows across the room, she tried to relax and forget all that had happened in the past couple of days.

It was futile: her mind wouldn't shut off. That noise was getting louder, loud enough to force her out of her denial. Charlie had been telling the truth—there *was* scratching. And Jack had probably been right too; it was very likely some stupid backwoods animal trying to burrow its way beneath the house.

"Fantastic," she grumbled beneath her breath. She grabbed the remote and paused her movie, abandoning her bowl of popcorn upon the couch cushions, ready to track it down. Of all the nights this could have happened—because she'd know what to do about Ricky the Raccoon or Randall the Rat.

At first it seemed like it was coming from near the front door, but as soon as Aimee approached the area, the scratching shifted to another part of the house. What she was once sure was an animal clawing on the outer walls of the house suddenly became an impossibility. The noise was coming from *inside* the walls, creeping along the arteries of their home, burrowing its way into random corners.

Her search eventually led her to the kitchen. As soon as she pinpointed where the noise was coming from, it was back in the living room. If this was an animal, it knew it was being followed. It was playing games.

Eventually losing the noise's location, Aimee shook her head in exasperation. She had wasted a good ten minutes of movie time chasing rogue scuffing, as though finally cornering the noise would make it disappear. If she wanted that scratching gone, she'd have to knock a hole in the wall first. She grabbed a can of Diet Coke from the fridge and padded back to the living room, stopping short of the couch.

Her jaw fell slack at the mess. The popcorn she'd left on the couch was now all over the floor. Nubs was happily cleaning it up, crunching salty kernels with the wet smacking of his chops.

"Nubs!" she whispered with as much authority as she could. "Goddammit." Waving a hand to shoo him off, she snatched the metal mixing bowl off the couch and dropped to her knees, scooping up popcorn she'd eventually end up pouring into Nubs's bowl.

"Stupid fucking dog," she muttered to herself. "Last bag of popcorn too. I swear to God, if I was just a little meaner..." She looked up from the carpet to see Nubs sitting not more than a yard from her stripe-socked feet. "I thought I told you to get out of here," she said, waving her hand at him again. "Get."

But rather than skulking off into the shadows of the hallway, Nubs lowered his muzzle, looked at her with sad eyes, and whined. Aimee peered at him. It wasn't like Nubs to be so pathetic. He was an obedient dog—dumb, but not a troublemaker by any stretch. Some days it was almost impossible to move him from his napping spot, as though he hadn't slept in weeks when, in truth, he slept a good sixteen hours a day.

"What's wrong with you?" Aimee asked him with a scowl. Nubs answered by exhaling a sigh. He flattened himself out on the carpet, assuring her there was no way he was moving from that living room. Aimee continued to pluck popcorn off the floor.

"Do you need to go out?"

Picking up the last bits of mess, she slid the bowl onto the coffee table and got to her feet, moving to the front door to let Nubs into the front yard to do his business.

"Go," she told him after unlocking the door, holding open the screen. "You're a dog. Go find the stupid scratching animal. And eat it."

But Nubs, who was typically out-of-his-mind excited at the prospect of going outside to pee, didn't move from his spot. He didn't even lift his head, only following Aimee with his eyes. He watched her hold the door open, whined, and looked away.

Aimee furrowed her eyebrow and shook her head. "Whatever," she said, relocking the door. "If you pee in the house…" She paused, sighed. "I'm talking to a dog. I'm having a conversation with a dog on a Saturday night."

Collapsing onto the couch, she grabbed her soda off the floor, pulled her feet up, and unpaused the movie.

Less than thirty seconds later, a crash from the kitchen had Aimee on her feet in wide-eyed panic. Nubs jumped as well, growling at the darkness, his teeth bared. Aimee's heart slammed itself against her ribs like a bird trying to free itself from a cage. Her first thought was, *Someone's in the house. Someone's broken in and is going to kill me and the girls, and Jack will come back home to a gruesome murder scene.* Her eyes flitted around the room in search of a weapon. She lunged at Jack's old piano and grabbed a candlestick off its top.

"Hello?" she called out. She tried to sound imposing, but her attempt at confidence only made her sound that much more frightened.

Nubs backed up. He plopped his butt down on the rug and watched Aimee approach the dark hallway, double-fisting a piece of home décor. Despite the intensity of that crash, neither Charlie nor Abigail stirred, as though the noise that had nearly stopped Aimee's heart had somehow failed to infiltrate the thin walls of the girls' room.

She wavered at the border of light and darkness, scared to cross over even if it was only a few feet to the light switch.

"I have a gun," she warned. "I'll blow your fucking head off." But what was intended as a genuine threat sounded comical when it was whispered. Aimee eventually grew tired of her own apprehension and marched into the hall—suddenly a woman with no fear—and flipped the switch.

The hall lit up. Light spilled into the living room on one end and into the kitchen on the other. It was there, in the now hazy shadows of the kitchen, that Aimee spotted the culprit. Flipped over onto its top, the kitchen table rested on the floor with its legs pointing toward the ceiling.

She stared at the table for a long while, unable to look away from it as her mind tried to piece together how it could have fallen over. Every answer was improbable, every solution was ridiculous. Even if Nubs had taken a running start and jumped on it like a dog training for an agility contest, that table wouldn't have budged. It was an old relic, made of solid wood, heavy enough for Aimee to need Jack's help to move it. Sliding it across the floor, let alone lifting it and flipping it over, was impossible. Not to mention that Nubs had been at her feet, not in the kitchen.

She turned away, unable to look at it any longer. Squeezing her eyes shut, she tried to keep calm. Nubs watched her doubtfully as she stepped back into the living room. She stopped dead in her tracks for the second time, her breath wavering a bit, the fingers of her free hand trembling while the other continued to cling to the candlestick.

The mixing bowl was exactly where she'd left it—dead center in the middle of the coffee table. But it was empty. The popcorn was scattered across the room from wall to wall.

Aimee met Jack at the door the second she saw Reagan's headlights cut across the living room window. Trembling, she pulled him inside before he could say a word and grabbed the bowl off the coffee table, on the verge of tears.

"It won't stay in," she insisted. "I keep picking it up but it won't stay in. And this…" She caught Jack by the hand and led him down the hall, stopping at the mouth of the kitchen.

Jack blinked at the overturned table, confusion shifting to worry shifting to dread.

"Did you put the chairs back like that?" he asked after a moment.

She hadn't noticed it before. The table was upside down, but none of the chairs had been disturbed. They were all standing in their designated spots.

Startled, Aimee stood in the hallway with her fingers pressed to her mouth. Jack touched her shoulder, and she burst into tears.

CHAPTER SIX

JACK COULDN'T SLEEP AGAIN. HE TRIED TO STAY STILL AS he lay in bed, not wanting to wake Aimee and throw her into another fit of hysteria. It had taken hours to calm her down. Finally exhausted by her incessant tears, she had passed out while Jack stared up at the ceiling. It was the moment he had feared, the moment when Aimee started to realize that something wasn't normal. That something was terribly wrong. And the more he thought about it, the more that dread twisted his insides. The red curtain had reminded him of that card, overwhelming him with a helplessness he hadn't felt before. There were parts of his past he couldn't remember—chunks that he knew he had lived through, but they had simply disappeared from his memory as though they had never existed at all. He could recall specific instances of his childhood in vivid detail, could recall what he was watching on television, which pajamas he'd been wearing when certain things had happened in his life. He knew he had been wearing his *Transformers* slippers the Christmas he got a secondhand bike, and that his mom's favorite song was "Cherry Cherry" by Neil Diamond. He remembered that his dad never missed an episode of *Magnum PI*, and that even though he constantly made fun of Tom Selleck's mustache, he actually tried to grow his own the summer before Jack had finally cornered that cat. But his arrival in Louisiana was a blank. He assumed he had been picked up by a passing motorist, but why that motorist would have taken a fourteen-year-old over state lines without asking questions, without detouring to a police station, was a mystery.

And then there was Stephen and Gilda. Sure, they had been shitty parents, but they had been parents all the same. When things started getting bizarre, Jack began to see his mother in a different light: she really did care about him. If she hadn't, she wouldn't have tried to save him. She wouldn't have cried as much as she had—which had been more than he'd ever seen her cry in his life. She had tried to save him as hard as she could until she couldn't try anymore. So why wouldn't she have gone after him after Jack had left? Maybe he had pushed her too far. Maybe by the time he took off, she saw it as a blessing: the source of her biggest problem, her biggest heartache, had up and run away. She'd have been crazy to seek him out, and Stephen more than likely told her so.

Jack tried to put himself in their shoes, tried to imagine Charlie going crazy, tearing their family apart. At what point do parents back away from something they love more than their own lives, put up their hands, and admit defeat?

Aimee was scared by the things she had seen that night, but she had no idea that her reaction had terrified her husband. Jack couldn't get the image of his own mother out of his head, couldn't silence her wails as his father tried to comfort her, insisting that it was all in her head, that her mind was playing tricks. Offering the same argument to Aimee was to call her crazy, and Jack had seen the immovable kitchen table sitting flat on its surface with his own two eyes. If it had only been the popcorn it would have been different; it would have been easy to convince her that Nubs was stealing snacks. But that table—he and Arnold, Aimee's father, had struggled to get it inside the house when Aimee had brought it home. Jack had called Reagan for help, and even with three guys on the job, Arnold had still nearly managed to throw out his back. It was a refurbished relic, heavy as hell, made out of wood as dense as the Louisiana swamp.

Jack squeezed his eyes shut, tried to put it out of his mind, but minutes later he was rolling over, making sure Aimee was really asleep. Holding his breath, he sat up on their creaky mattress that was in desperate need of replacement. It was lumpy, and a couple of springs were starting to poke through the thin padding. It whined loudly enough to wake the dead whenever they got intimate—so bad at times that they had pulled the blankets off the bed and made love on the floor. Jack hadn't managed to fully sit up before the damn thing started making noise. He eventually got one foot on the carpet without those springs ratting him out, and he took another fifteen minutes to creep across the floor.

Finally making it into the hallway, he stood in a daze. After all that effort, he wasn't sure why he'd snuck out in the first place—something had pulled him out of that bedroom, beckoning him into the stillness of the house. He tiptoed down the hall to check on the girls. Abigail was on her side of the room, one arm jutting out over the side of her bed. Charlie, who was fond of odd sleeping positions, was pressed against the wall like a slug, her sheets pooled upon the floor like discarded snake skin. The coolness of the wall kept her from getting hot during muggy summer nights.

He took a step back and pulled the door with him, ready to fit it snugly into the jamb, and stopped short.

Something shifted in the corner of the room. It was a shadow, a squatting figure hiding in the darkness, waiting for Jack to leave the girls alone with it. Jack hesitated, his fingers tightly clutching the doorknob. Something twisted against the valves of his heart. It whispered to him: *Close the door. It's just your imagination. You don't want to see what you're afraid is here; and it's too late to do a damn thing about it anyway.*

He stood there for what felt like an eternity, an overwhelming sense of anger unraveling inside his stomach. He was a father, a husband, the protector of his family and his home, and here he was, afraid to stick his head back inside his daughters' room, allowing this thing, this shadow, to consume his children rather than facing his fear.

He took a breath. Shoved the door open. Looked inside.

Nothing.

Closing the door behind him, he was both relieved and sure he was wrong. He'd seen something crouched in the corner next to Charlie's bed. And while anyone else would have blamed it on too many horror movies, Jack couldn't blame it on anything but his own memory.

He had seen that very figure perched at the foot of his bed when he was a kid—black skin, scaly like a lizard's, small black horns poking out of its head. Its face, so eerily human, but yet so unearthly that it had certainly come from the very pits of hell itself. When it smiled, its crooked mouth curled all the way up to its eyes, displaying a maw full of long, jagged cannibal teeth. And those eyes—they were nothing but vacant hollows. The monster was real. The proof was etched into his skin, emblazoned across his back.

Jack stood outside the girls' door, chewing on his thumbnail. He needed a plan, a way to keep their lives from disintegrating into impossible chaos. It was what had happened with his own family, his mother convinced that he'd gone completely insane. In the end, despite her attempts to save her boy, Gilda couldn't look at him. Stephen tried to be strong, but during those last few days his eyes had betrayed him, radiating the fear he was so desperate to hide.

Jack and Aimee were headed down the same path. Aimee would eventually be too terrified to stay in the house. She'd lose her mind or run away, unable to take it anymore, and Jack would be left alone. *But never really alone,* that voice reassured him. *I've always been here, and I'll never leave.*

Jack woke to the sound of dishes clanging against the side of the sink. He blinked against the rectangle of sunlight that shone into his eyes, moving an arm to shield himself from the glare. The muscles in his neck had petrified during his night in the living room's wingback chair. It was his favorite, but it was a terrible bed.

Charlie ran into the room in her bare feet, twirling in a bright white sundress Jack didn't remember having seen before. In the morning light she looked like an angel, the light igniting her hair in a fiery glow. Smiling wide, she jumped into her father's lap, and pain shot up his neck. He groaned.

"What's wrong, Daddy?" she asked, surprised by the pained expression that seized his face.

"Just a stiff neck, sweetie." He tried to rub the frozen muscles loose, but the more he rubbed the more it hurt.

Charlie suddenly looked serious. "Daddy, did you sleep in here?"

"Just for a few hours," he answered through gnashed teeth.

"How come?"

"I don't know, baby. I came out here to read and fell asleep in my chair."

Charlie's eyes drifted across the room before returning to her father.

"What book?"

"A boring one."

"But you just woke up, and there's no book…"

"I put it back."

"But you said you fell asleep."

"I put it back before I fell asleep."

"Then how come you didn't go back to bed with Momma?"

There were cons to raising a smart kid.

Jack's patience was short. His nerves were frayed. He didn't respond to Charlie's question, kneading his neck instead.

"Daddy, did you put the table upside down?"

He blinked at the oversight. The kitchen table was still in its place, down the hall with its legs stabbing up into the air, unmoved. They hadn't bothered trying to flip it over, knowing their efforts would be useless. Jack would have to call Reagan for help. Probably Arnold too.

"Yes," Jack said after a moment. "Yes, I did."

"How come?"

"Because one of the legs was loose. I didn't want it to fall on top of you or your sister. What's your mother doing?"

"She's making breakfast. How come the leg got loose?"

Jack sighed. "I don't know, Charlie. Why don't you go help your mom in the kitchen?"

"Help her do what?"

"I don't know, honey. Just go ask her if she needs some help, would you?"

Charlie didn't move for a few seconds, sizing him up, before abruptly dashing down the hall to the kitchen. A second later she ran back into the living room with a message from Aimee.

"Momma says you better get ready."

"Get ready for what?"

"She says you gotta take a shower and get dressed because we're going to church."

Jack was completely caught off guard. Of the thirteen years Jack and Aimee had been married, they had gone to church all of three times. Two of those times were in the first year of their marriage—Christmas and Easter. Patricia, who liked to think herself a God-fearing Catholic, insisted that if he wanted to marry her daughter, he'd be attending church the way Aimee had her entire life. The third time was for Abigail's baptism two months after she was born—another one of Patricia's demands. Charlie hadn't been baptized. It had been Aimee's call, and by then Aimee was fed up with asking, "How high?" whenever her mother said, "Jump."

"You're inviting the devil into that girl," Patricia had warned. Six years ago, Jack called it bullshit. Today he wondered how he could have been so stupid.

Jack reluctantly pushed himself out of his chair and shuffled into the kitchen. Aimee stood over the stove in a blue polka-dot dress, an apron tied around her waist. She had curled her hair in 1950s style—June Cleaver poised over the stove in high heels and full makeup. Sensing his presence, she glanced over her shoulder at him, the crackle of bacon completing the morning's sound track.

"We're leaving in half an hour," she said.

"I heard." Jack still couldn't believe it. Aimee had been the one who had given up on the idea of religion in the first place, for no reason other than to declare war on her parents. For her to turn to God for answers—something she knew would overjoy her mother—was unlike her. And for Jack not to be vehemently opposed to the idea was unlike him. Aimee gave Jack a look—*Don't question it*—and turned back to the stove. Jack began to make his way to the bedroom but stopped when he saw Charlie sitting dead center in the middle of the overturned table.

"Daddy," she said. "None of these legs are wobbly."

"Oh good," Jack murmured to himself. "I must have fixed it in my sleep."

In towns as small as Live Oak, folks were tightly knit. They knew who attended church and who didn't, and those who didn't were in desperate need of saving. It was no surprise when all eyes were on Jack and Aimee as they stepped out of Arnold's Oldsmobile.

"This is a bad idea," Jack muttered, but Aimee was playing it cool, ready to march her family inside like they owned the place. Jack didn't think that was the best plan. Strutting into the wrong church with your nose in the air could get you crucified.

Jack pulled Charlotte out of her car seat and met Aimee and Abigail on the other side of the Olds.

"What's the point of this again?" he asked in a whisper.

"We need guidance," Aimee said, her voice low.

"Can't we get that somewhere else? You know, like therapy or something?"

"Therapy?" She raised an eyebrow at his suggestion. "What're you saying?"

"What? Nothing. I'm not saying anything," he backpedaled. "What I'm saying is…it's a little weird to ask God for help because our dog ate some popcorn. That's what I'm saying."

Churches gave him the creeps. They made him itchy, like something was digging its teeth beneath his skin. Standing barefoot in the wild grass in front of his Georgia home, Jack had been four years old when he felt a dull gnawing against his scrawny legs. When he looked down, he bore witness to a colony of fire ants crawling across his shins, trudging upward toward his knees and cotton shorts. He'd screamed bloody murder, scared to move, his arms outstretched toward his irritated father. He spent the rest of the afternoon in the bathtub, his legs burning beneath the water, red welts pocking his flesh. Churches made Jack feel a lot like that afternoon had, like he was being eaten alive.

Aimee slowed her steps, her children's hands firmly held in her own. She leveled her gaze on her husband and narrowed her eyes.

"What are you saying, Jack?" she asked again. "It was Nubs? Nubs scattered the popcorn all over the living room floor when I wasn't looking? I know what I saw. Next you'll blame the table on Nubs too."

She was right, one hundred percent. The table was an impossibility, but Jack didn't care. He wanted to leave, wanted to go home and wait for the evil to shake the walls, to open the kitchen cabinets and throw plates across the room. He'd face it—he wanted to *tell* her that he'd face it. But telling her that would mean telling her everything, and that was an impossibility as well.

"Nubs made the leg wobbly?" Charlie asked.

"He probably ran into it with his face," Abigail chimed in. "You know how he runs and can't stop on the floor?"

"Like ice skates," Charlie said with a bounce.

"I just think this is weird," Jack said. "What are we going to do here, tell the priest that weird shit is—"

Aimee's glare cut him off midsentence. His language was more than inappropriate, especially in the parking lot of the House of God. Jack glanced at the girls—of course they had heard him, but they knew better than to let their mother know. Jack rerouted.

"—weird *stuff* is going on?"

"I don't know what we're going to do here," Aimee admitted, releasing the girls from her grasp as soon as she spotted Patricia close to the front doors. The girls ran to their grandmother, and Aimee turned her full attention to Jack. "I don't know why I suddenly needed to come to church. I don't know anything. I don't know what to do, I don't know what's going on, and I don't know what to think or what to expect. So what do you want me to do?"

"I don't know," Jack confessed.

"Well then you know as much as I do."

"Aimee?" Patricia's voice cut through their conversation; the surprise in her voice was as soothing as a screeching violin. She bridged the distance between them, and Aimee gave her a quick one-armed hug.

"And *Jack*?" Patricia raised an eyebrow, making it clear that Jack's presence was truly unexpected. "To what do we owe the pleasure?"

"The girls wanted to see you," Aimee lied. "We figured it was a good time."

Sitting in a pew at the front of the church, Grandma kept her arms around both girls, Aimee kept her eyes on her hands, and Jack couldn't help but imagine Satan popping up from beneath the floorboards like a spring-loaded jack-in-the-box. When it came to dark forces, Hollywood had its typical formula—he searched for all the clichés he'd learned on the silver screen. Everyone knew demons didn't like the House of God. They couldn't stand the sight of holy relics, couldn't stomach being in the presence of a priest or a crucifix. But then there were flicks that challenged all of that. You hold up a cross to protect yourself from Satan and he laughs in your face; you serve a vampire a roasted garlic appetizer and he comes back for seconds…on your neck. If this were Hollywood, the priest would be the culprit. He'd turn to his congregation, hold out his arms as if to embrace them, and smile a demon's smile before pulling them all down to hell.

Jack sat beside Aimee, listening to the dull hum of the sermon that eventually became little more than background noise to his thoughts. He waited for Patricia's scream to cut through the silence as soon as Charlie fell victim to a fit of possessed convulsions. He waited for his youngest daughter to run down the center aisle toward the pulpit, her eyes black and her hair whipping behind her like Medusa's snakes; the priest splashing holy water in front of him, protecting himself, creating a barrier blessed by God and His angels; pictured him tearing the crucifix from around his neck and pressing it to Charlotte's forehead only to have her hiss in pain.

None of it happened.

An entire hour of sitting in a pew, waiting for the floor to burst open like an infected wound, but nothing; the monotonous droning went on without incident.

By the time mass was over, Jack was exhausted and Aimee was somehow assured that from then on everything would be OK, that sitting in church for sixty minutes would, in some way, cleanse them of any mysterious goings-on; that life would go back to business as usual. She felt so confident that she happily socialized on the church's front steps, laughing it up with old family friends she hadn't seen in years. But Jack couldn't forget one small detail: the kitchen table was upside down. He doubted that God had righted it for them.

The more Jack watched Aimee the more he remembered his own mother trying this same tactic. Stephen had protested, insisting that it was a ridiculous idea, that organized religion was nothing but a sham. But Gilda knew her son's problems weren't of this world: they were the work of something dark, something unspeakable, and only God could rid him of such a curse. Here, the tables were turned. Jack knew what was plaguing Charlie. He knew his mother was right in turning to prayer—at least right in a theological sense, because who else was there to turn to when you were battling evil? He wanted to believe that it could be that simple—just turn to the Big Guy, let Him do His thing, and all would be right with the world. Jesus loves you. He'll set you free. But Jack knew it was bullshit. It would have been nice to throw his hands up in the air, to throw his head back and proclaim that he was too small to handle this problem, that it was bigger than him, that he needed divine intervention and he needed it quick. God hadn't been able to help him—He hadn't even tried—and He wasn't going to help Charlie either.

On the way home, the Winters decided to stop at the girls' favorite place: a fifties-themed ice cream shop. The place specialized in sundaes, shakes, and floats and played Elvis Presley on a loop. The girls who worked the counter wore their hair in high ponytails and tied pink kerchiefs around their necks.

Climbing onto red vinyl-covered stools at the soda bar, Charlie ordered a strawberry shake and Abby got a scoop of vanilla with hot fudge, pink sprinkles, and a cherry on top. Aimee and Jack shared a banana split, and amid all of that sugar and syrup they were, for a moment, the perfect family fresh from Sunday mass.

But the moment didn't last long.

"Can I have your cherry?" Charlie asked her sister, muffling her words around the bright red maraschino in her mouth.

"No way," Abby said. She pulled her ice cream dish closer to her chest.

"You don't even like it."

"Do too. You already had yours."

"So? I want another one." Charlie shot her arm out, making a pass at Abigail's cherry stem. But Abby was quick. She jerked the dish away just in time, leaving her sister empty-handed with a sour look on her face.

"Give it to me," Charlie said flatly, her voice low.

Abby hesitated, looked over her shoulder at their parents sharing a round table a few yards away.

"What're you going to do?" Charlie whispered, her eyes narrowing into a squint. "Tell?"

"Why shouldn't I?" Abby asked.

"Because I'm your sister. So give me that cherry or I'll tell on *you.*"

Abigail wrinkled her nose at the threat.

"Fine," Charlie scowled, then abruptly slid her arm across the counter, knocking her strawberry shake to the floor. The heavy glass shattered with a wet thump, spraying the black and white floor tiles with bright pink and white while Elvis growled, *You ain't nothin' but a hound dog.*

Aimee jumped from her seat, nearly knocking her own sundae to the floor. "Oh my God." The words reflexively tumbled from her throat. "Charlie, what did you do?"

Abigail sat frozen on her stool, staring at the broken glass on the floor, unsure of what just happened.

Charlie's mouth hung open, feigning shock. Her bottom lip began to quiver. Her eyes went glassy with tears. A second later she let out a wail so pitifully wounded, anyone who hadn't seen exactly what had happened would have been convinced of the six-year-old's innocence.

"Abby did it," Charlie sobbed. "She wanted my cherry and I said no and I put it in my mouth and ate it, and she got mad and pushed my shake down."

Abigail stared at her sister, too stunned to react.

"Abby!" Aimee grabbed her by the arm, yanking her off the stool. "You're going to clean this up, you understand?"

"Ma'am, it's OK." The girl behind the counter forced a smile, having seen plenty of accidents like this before.

"No, it's *not* OK," Aimee said, her eyes never leaving Abby's face. "What's wrong with you?" She shook Abby by her arm. "You're grounded, young lady. And you better believe this is coming out of your allowance."

It was Abby's turn to burst into tears. She wrung her arm out of Aimee's grasp and ran out of the shop. Aimee pulled Charlie off her stool and pressed her youngest daughter's tear-stained face into her neck.

"Calm down," Aimee told her. "It's all right. Here." She plucked Abigail's abandoned sundae off the counter, holding it out for Charlie to see. Charlie wiped at her cheeks with the back of her hand and sniffed, staring mournfully at the cherry atop her sister's ice cream.

"Go ahead," Aimee said. "Take it."

Charlie fought through a sob-ridden breath, eventually plucked the cherry from its resting place, and popped it in her mouth with a meek little smile.

...and you ain't no friend of mine.

"All better?" Aimee asked.

Charlie nodded once, smearing tears across her face with the back of her hand. Aimee glanced over to Jack before stepping out of the shop, Charlie in her arms.

"I'm sorry," Jack said to the counter girl. "Seriously. This is..."

"It's all right," she said. "These things happen."

"You're telling me," he muttered, fumbling through his wallet for some money. He only had a twenty left, and while that was a pretty chunk of change on their budget, there was no way in hell he was about to ask the girl to make change. "For your trouble," he told her, forking over the bill.

"Oh." She shook her head with an embarrassed smile. "No, really, it's OK."

"This is going to take forever to clean up," Jack insisted. "It's a tip."

The girl hesitated, and for a second Jack was relieved that she was going to turn down his offer. But she finally relented and took it with a blush.

When Jack stepped into the parking lot, Abigail was being reprimanded for a second time. She sobbed into her hands while

Aimee scolded her, eventually pushing her into the backseat of the car.

"Hey, take it easy on her, all right?"

"Take it *easy* on her? You saw what she did," Aimee snapped. "You find that kind of behavior acceptable?"

"She didn't do it," Jack said under his breath.

"What?"

"I said she didn't do it," he repeated, enunciating his words.

"What are you saying? Charlie knocked down her own shake and then cried about it?"

Jack didn't say another word. He just got in the car and snapped his seatbelt into place.

By the time they got home, Aimee had gone deathly silent. Jack knew her mind was racing, trying to put it all together. He could tell by the way she was pulling on her bottom lip—a habit she'd had for as long as he'd known her. Anytime Aimee was deep in thought, her fingers would start to tug and pull. He had seen Charlie swing her arm across that counter, had watched that shake fly through the air in slow motion, hovering for half a second before gravity caught it by its heavy-footed bottom and pulled. He had witnessed the glint in Charlie's eyes, a glint he recognized. He had seen it among the grass and trees of his youth. Hell, he had seen it in the mirror. It would have been easy to say nothing, to let it play out, to let Abby take the fall, but Jack couldn't bring himself to do it. Seeing Abigail's face twisted with betrayal, forsaken by her little sister, all for something as trivial as a candied cherry—it turned Jack's stomach. He had suffered through his own stygian past as an only child. He couldn't imagine how hard it would have been for a sibling, someone who was, by default, a scapegoat.

The Oldsmobile crunched to a stop in the gravel driveway. Abby was the first one out of the car. It was obvious that she was embarrassed, ashamed, hurt. She didn't want to deal with anyone or be lectured about something she didn't do. When Aimee shoved the passenger door open to yell after her, Jack caught her by the forearm, seizing her attention.

"Let her go," he told her. "She needs some space."

Aimee opened her mouth to protest. He watched her eyes harden before she snapped her mouth shut. Instead of fighting his reasoning, she jerked her arm out of his grasp and climbed out of the car, slamming the door shut behind her. Jack watched her walk around the front of the car, leaving Charlie in her car seat, making a beeline for the house.

Jack glanced at Charlie in the rearview mirror. She sat silent as ever, staring at the mood ring around her finger.

"I don't like this ring," she whispered. "It doesn't even work."

He sighed, rubbing the bridge of his nose before speaking up.

"Do you want to tell me what happened at the ice cream shop?"

She looked up at her father, blinked once, and looked down again with a shake of her head.

"How come you didn't bring something else?"

"I know what happened," Jack interrupted her.

"Nothing happened," Charlie whispered.

"I saw what you did," he said. "And you blamed what you did on your big sister."

Charlie raised her shoulders up to her ears, refusing to speak.

"Do you remember doing what you did?"

She nodded faintly. She didn't want to admit guilt—but she had no other choice.

Jack looked out the side window. He could see Abigail's feet sticking out from behind one of the oaks in the front yard. The house was a piece of crap. There was no selling it. The plumbing was bad, and he didn't doubt there was mold growing inside the walls. Aimee had joked about it when Jack offered to fix the place up—to give it more "curb appeal." *This place doesn't need a facelift,* she had teased. *It needs a bulldozer.* Regardless of its shabby appearance, it almost always looked sunny—a happy home to a happy family. But today it looked positively dismal—a dry, empty husk of what it usually was.

"I didn't even want it," Charlie muttered. "And then I started crying because I did it, but when Momma looked I said Abby did it and I don't know why."

Jack let his head fall back against the seat.

"It wasn't me," Charlie whispered so quietly Jack was sure she hadn't meant for him to hear. He heard but didn't reply, deafened by his own thoughts—that faint whisper sing-songing inside his head.

It was you, it was me, it was us, it was we.

CHAPTER SEVEN

THE REST OF THE DAY WAS SILENT. ABIGAIL HID FROM the world in her room. Charlie watched *SpongeBob* on TV. Aimee retired to the kitchen, creating a new concoction for dinner. And Jack parked himself in his wingback chair, strumming his guitar, trying to work on lyrics to a song he'd been putting together for months, but he was doomed to fail. On top of the fact that he couldn't focus beyond that annoying cartoon voice, he kept zoning out every few minutes, music the furthest thing from his mind.

Reagan eventually arrived to help him flip the kitchen table over. He tried to break the tension with a few jokes, but after a look from Aimee he was quick to excuse himself.

By the time dinner rolled around they sat around the table without a word, none of them enjoying their spruced-up mac and cheese. The silence was eventually broken by the sound of something scurrying across the floor. All four of them stiffened. Aimee was the first to speak.

"What the hell was that? Was that a rat?"

The moment she suggested it, both girls squealed and pulled their feet onto their chairs.

Jack swept the kitchen with his eyes, searching for the intruder. A second later the sound of tiny nails running across the floor was heard again. Jack pushed his chair back and fell into action, searching the kitchen before someone decided to scream her head off. The girls got their phobia from Aimee. During the summer, when a field mouse had chewed through the screen door, it was a wonder they hadn't destroyed the house the way they leapt from chair to couch to coffee table—they may as well have been a family of Russian acrobats.

"I don't see anything," Jack finally announced.

"Well there has to be *something*," Aimee insisted. "We all heard it."

"But I don't *see* anything. I can't just wiggle my nose and have the damn thing come out from wherever it's hiding."

Jack returned to his seat, smoothed his napkin across his lap, and grabbed his fork.

"Let's all just keep quiet and eat," he said. "We'll trick him."

"Or he'll trick us," Aimee muttered.

Less than a minute later the sound was back, but this time it was in the walls.

"Great," Aimee said with a huff. "We're going to have rats making little rat families inside the house."

Jack narrowed his eyes at the noise. It didn't sound like an animal. It sounded more like someone scraping their nails across a surface, like claws being drawn down a plank of wood. Aimee's eyes grew wider the louder the sound became. Abigail sat petrified, her hands pressed over her ears. Charlie, on the other hand, didn't seem to be bothered by it. She still had her feet up on her chair but continued to eat her dinner.

After a few minutes, Aimee shot up from her chair and grabbed her plate.

"OK," she said, "that's it. Abby, get your books ready for tomorrow. Charlie, bath time in five minutes."

Abby bounded from her chair, anxious to get out of the kitchen. Conversely, Charlie took her time, stabbing another elbow macaroni with her fork.

"We need to call an exterminator," Aimee said. "I can't live with rats in the walls, Jack. Just the idea of it makes my skin crawl. How are we supposed to sleep with that scratching? What if they crawl into…oh God. What if they crawl into the beds?"

Just then, as though the source of the noise had heard Aimee's question, the room went silent. Charlie slid from her seat and padded down the hall, her fingers dragging along the wall. The scratching trailed her like a loyal companion.

That night, Charlie found herself standing beside Abigail's bed. She stood over her sister, her chest palpitating beneath her *SpongeBob* pajama top with short, birdlike breaths. She was leaning forward so that her hair hung in Abby's face; Abigail wrinkled her nose in her sleep, then swatted at her face. Charlie's breathing quickened, her mouth pulling into a tight grin. She gnashed her teeth and balled her hands into fists while watching her sleeping sister, unmoving, leering in the darkness. She didn't know why she was smiling. Her back ached from bending over the way she was; her feet hurt as though she'd been standing there forever. Puzzled by the fact that she was out of bed at all, she was tempted to run to her parents' room to tell her dad. But she froze when the closet door creaked on its hinges, gently swinging open. Charlie's eyes went wide. Her breath caught in her throat and she bounded for her bed, leaping onto the mattress to save her toes from the monster that most certainly lurked beneath it. Jerking the covers over her head, she huddled beneath the comforter. But no matter how hard she tried to get back to sleep, a tickle deep within her chest kept her awake, an itch she couldn't scratch. She knew there was only one way to get rid of the prickle that had burrowed into her heart: get up, stand over her sister again. Stand over her and wait until she stopped breathing.

Charlie had missed a few days of school due to her illness, and today would be her first day back to Robert Cavalier Elementary. To no one's surprise, it was nearly impossible to get her out of bed. Abigail was in the bathroom brushing her teeth while Charlie rolled around on top of her mattress like an ornery sea lion, emitting pitiful whines, pleading for mercy. After ten minutes of moaning Aimee lost her patience, yanked the covers off her daughter, and plucked Charlie out of bed.

"Enough," she said. "Get in that bathroom and brush your teeth right now."

Charlie exhaled another grumble, her arms hanging loose and boneless at her sides.

"I don't feel good," she protested.

Aimee hesitated, recalling what had happened the last time she sent Charlie to school when she hadn't felt well. But with a shake of the head she put it out of her mind and pointed to the bedroom door.

"March."

Charlie fell into step with another whine, dragging her feet to make sure her journey to the bathroom was a slow one.

Aimee set out the girls' clothes for the day and took inventory of what needed washing and what they could go without for another few days. By the time Charlie returned from the bathroom, Abby was already dressed and pulling on her shoes.

"You take as long as you are and you won't have time for breakfast," Aimee warned.

Charlie stuck out her bottom lip and grabbed her socks, defiantly pulling them on with a pout.

"I don't care," she said. "I'm not hungry. I don't want to go to school. I want to go back to sleep."

"Well that's too bad," Aimee told her. "It seems like you're going to do a lot of what you don't want to do today."

"I'm tired!" Charlie snapped.

Aimee blinked. She marched across the room from where she'd been tidying up Abigail's desk and caught Charlie by the chin.

"Did you just *yell* at me?" she asked, her nose mere inches from Charlie's. Abby watched the standoff in slack-jawed surprise.

"I yelled at you because you don't listen," Charlie said matter-of-factly. "You think you know everything, but sometimes you're just stupid."

Abby's eyes went wide, as did her mother's.

"You did *not* just call me stupid." Aimee straightened, staring down at her youngest.

"I couldn't sleep!" Charlie yelled again. "There were rats in here and they kept touching me!"

"There were no rats in here," Aimee said, her voice steady, trying to keep her composure. Her mother had warned her about this—about how kids who were typically angelic could turn on a dime into tiny monsters. Aimee had always rolled her eyes at the notion, but now she couldn't help herself; she wanted to run to the phone and call her mom for help.

"Then what was touching me?" Charlie asked. "If you know everything, what was touching me? Do you know?"

Aimee turned to a stock-still Abigail.

"Abby, were there rats in here last night?"

Abby slowly shook her head no.

"That's what I thought. Go eat your breakfast."

Abigail's tense expression relaxed when she was excused. She snatched her backpack off the floor and dashed out of the room, avoiding the general perimeter of Charlie's bed on her way out.

Aimee turned her attention back to the six-year-old. She leaned in close, peering into her daughter's face.

"Charlotte Marilyn Winter, if you ever yell at me or lie to me again, do you know what I'll do?"

Charlie didn't move. She rebelliously stared back at her mother, challenging Aimee to look away first.

"Remember Annie? How she had to scrub the floors at the orphanage?"

Charlie narrowed her eyes at the threat.

"Daddy would never let you," she said under her breath.

"Wouldn't he?"

"No." Her face went hard with anger. "Daddy loves me better than any one of you."

"Is that right?" Aimee crossed her arms over her chest. "Maybe we should ask Daddy if he loves you more than he loves your sister when he comes home from work today. We'll see if he tells you he loves you best."

"He won't say it," Charlie muttered.

"Why not?"

Sliding off her bed, her hands were balled up into fists. She glared down her nose at her mom, her sleep-tousled hair a chaotic tangle around her face.

"Because," she finally said, her voice taking on an unfamiliar heaviness, "he can't tell you. It's *our* secret. We have a lot of secrets, and you can't know any of them."

Once the girls were out the door and on the bus, Aimee collapsed onto the sofa. She stared at the blank TV screen, replaying Charlie's words inside her head. She needed to clear her mind, needed to get away from the chaos. Reagan had given Jack a ride to work that morning, and her daddy's old boat of a car sat in the driveway for the taking. She considered going to the local bar and getting shit-faced drunk; she hadn't done that since college. Aimee cracked a grin at the idea of wrecking her father's precious Olds *and* getting a DWI. They'd probably lock her up, and since Jack wouldn't be able to post bail, her parents would be forced to show up at the station, looks of disgusted outrage plastered across both their faces.

She shot a glance at the phone, tugged at her bottom lip while contemplating a conversation about Charlie with her mom, and eventually shook her head and shoved herself off the couch.

"No way," she told herself. The last thing she needed was Patricia breathing down her neck, insisting that she told her so, that she should have never married some weird musician from God only knew where. She had voiced too many opinions up until their wedding day as it was. *Who is he?* Patricia had asked her. *Do you have any idea where he comes from, what kind of father he would make?* She had made it clear to Aimee in the beginning, every fault was Jack's no matter what it was. Every shortcoming was his, and Aimee was marrying into a life of hardship, nothing else.

"I have to get the hell out of here," she told the empty house. "Before I lose my goddamn mind."

It took twenty miles to get to Mabel's Curious Curios, a small mom-and-pop place where she had found Jack's piano and wing-back chair. Mabel was in her eighties—a sophisticated woman who was as much a Southern belle as Scarlett O'Hara. She ran the curio shop with her husband, Phil. In Aimee's imagination, Phil flew B-29s in Korea; he took handsome photographs in his leather bomber jacket while posing next to the propeller of his plane. Phil wasn't much of an antiquer. She'd never seen him do anything but sit in his rocking chair, flip through the paper, and mutter to the old hound dog sleeping at his feet.

Phil and Mabel had come to be two of Aimee's favorite people. They never judged, never pried, and always had an extra cup of tea ready for anyone who needed it. Aimee had come to Mabel in the past after the fights, after the harsh words, after Jack had grabbed his guitar and stormed out the door for a rehearsal with the band when she needed him at home. She had spent hours among rooms of knickknacks, forgetting her troubles while Mabel related stories about her favorite items. She loved hearing stories of Mabel's time in Paris, something Aimee envied above all else. It was where she and Phil had met. He had proposed beneath the Eiffel Tower on a perfect summer day. Aimee hated herself for wishing it, but sometimes all she wanted was to start over again. If only she could transport herself and Jack to the Arc de Triomphe, rewind the clock by thirteen years. It was a terrible thing to pine for, but she couldn't help it. And Mabel was the only one who knew.

Aimee had talked to Mabel about the girls before. She knew about New Orleans, about the gigs and the conflicts. But today Aimee resolved that there would be no talk of family. Today she wanted to lose herself in Mabel's stories about her ancient artifacts, nothing more. The tiny bell that hung above the door marked her entrance with a fairy's chime.

"Aimee Winter," Mabel said, approaching her with open arms. "I thought you'd forgotten about us. Thank heavens…" She placed her hands on Aimee's shoulders with a smile. "I was wrong."

"How could I forget?" Aimee asked. She glanced over Mabel's shoulder and waved at Phil, who was slowly rocking back and forth, the dog still at his feet, unmoving, much like Jack's taxidermy collection.

"Oh, stranger things have happened," Mabel said. "Life gets in the way. Tea?"

"Please."

"Good." Mabel looked satisfied. "Then I trust you'll stay awhile."

With a cup of Earl Grey balanced on a delicate saucer, the two began their rounds of the shop. Mabel pointed out new items she'd acquired since Aimee's last visit, but the more they explored, the more Aimee's attention wavered. Her thoughts kept drifting back to that morning, to the anger in Charlie's eyes. Item after item, she tried to throw herself into exploration, will herself to forget the outside world, absorb the dusty magic of Mabel's store. But no matter how interesting Mabel's stories were, Aimee's mind was twenty miles away.

The old woman was far from oblivious. She stopped her story-telling and sipped her tea instead, watching Aimee with as much thoughtfulness as she gave the pieces she placed in her store.

"You didn't come to shop," she finally surmised. "You came to talk."

Aimee offered Mabel an apologetic smile, her eyes fixed on the floral design that circled the rim of her teacup. The fragile porcelain could have easily been a hundred years old. Perhaps out of a royal household, once used by the queen. Maybe off the *Titanic*—the only piece saved when all else was lost.

"I really just wanted to shop today," Aimee insisted, but she wasn't fooling anyone. Mabel shook her head and motioned for Aimee to join her at the front of the shop, where Phil continued to rock and that hound dog continued to snore.

Aimee reluctantly situated herself in a stiff-backed chair—reluctant not because she didn't love these visits, but because of what she might reveal—and forced a halfhearted smile.

"Now," Mabel said, "what's bothering you, sugar? You tell your old Aunt Mabel and we'll fix it up in a jiff."

"If it was only that easy…" Aimee exhaled a weak laugh.

"Well, how do you know it isn't? We've solved plenty of problems before, haven't we? You bring me the problem and I do the fixin'."

"It's true," Phil said from behind his paper. "May can't keep her nose out of anybody's business. She's had that nose in everybody's business since 1933."

"Don't listen to him." Mabel waved a hand in disregard. "He's gone and lost his mind since the last time you were here. All his marbles fell out, rolled under the tables and counters, and he's too old to bend down and find them."

"Throw out my back," Phil mused, rustling his paper.

Aimee smiled.

"Well, go on, then. What's got you distracted?"

"My girls," Aimee admitted. "Charlie's been acting strange these last few days."

"Strange?" Mabel asked.

"That's the problem with kids," Phil muttered to himself. "They're *all* strange."

Mabel rolled her eyes at him and urged Aimee to continue.

"Did something happen?" she asked.

"We got into an accident."

"Heavens!" Her hand pressed to her chest, perched there like a bird. "What sort of an accident?"

"A car accident. We were coming home from Charlie's birthday party. Jack was driving." Aimee shook her head. Trying to recall that night was difficult—nothing but a blur of panic. "I'm not really sure what happened because I dozed off, but the next thing I knew we were flying through the air. We landed on the roof of our car."

Mabel looked startled.

"Everyone was all right?"

"It seemed so. We all walked away without a scratch, which seems almost impossible for how bad the car was beaten up. The next day Charlie was sick, and now she's acting out."

Mabel sipped her tea as she mulled over the news.

"Well, children have mysterious ways of dealing with crises," she said. "She might have something pent up, something that was a result of the accident. Trauma."

"I've considered that."

"Well there you have it," Mabel said cheerfully, lifting her cup as though toasting the revelation. "Simple as that."

"Simple," Aimee echoed, but she didn't believe it.

"Sugar." Mabel leaned in and lowered her voice, like two girl-friends sharing a secret. "You take that little girl to one of them psychologists, have her talk it out with someone other than her own momma; she'll be right as rain."

With each passing incident, Aimee was starting to suspect her youngest was possibly disturbed. As a next step, a psychologist wasn't a bad idea.

"Either way, you never know until you try," Mabel assured her. "And you'll never try until old Mabel tells you so."

CHAPTER EIGHT

WHEN JACK CAME HOME FROM WORK, HE FOUND AIMEE on the couch with a glass of red wine held between her palms. She could have easily been unwinding from a rough day, but her posture betrayed her.

"Jack," she said, "we need to talk."

Jack hadn't taken more than a few steps inside the house when he stopped dead. Dirty from welding, his clothes smelled faintly of iron—a man who had crawled out of the pits of hell, the scent of brimstone following him home. Those four words were enough to make any husband seize up.

"I know I've said that before, but this is different. I think there's something really wrong with Charlie."

Jack said nothing.

"Well?" She peered at her glass, waiting.

"Well what?" Jack asked, not sure what she expected. He knew it would come to this; he just hadn't expected it to happen so fast. Standing in his own living room, he was no longer Jack Winter. He was Stephen and Aimee was Gilda—worried, tired, beginning to crack.

"You don't see it?" Aimee asked. "I don't believe that. I know you see it."

Jack's attention shifted. The house was too quiet.

"They're at my mother's," she said. "You should have seen her this morning. It was like she'd lost her mind. She refused to get out of bed, so I finally yanked her out and she started screaming about being tired and being touched and how stupid I am."

Jack took a seat on the edge of his armchair.

"Being touched?"

"Didn't you hear what I said?"

Jack didn't reply. He kept his eyes fixed to the floor instead.

"She called me *stupid*, Jack. That's not my daughter."

Pressing his lips together in a tight line, he didn't know what to say. In the back of his mind he wanted to ask what the big deal was, wanted to suggest all the ways it could have been worse. She could have grabbed a knife and cut out Aimee's heart; could have sat in the center of her room, playing in her mother's blood.

"And it wasn't just that," Aimee continued.

Jack blinked out of his daze.

"It was the way she said it." Aimee tugged at her lip. "There was this weird darkness to it, like she was making some unspoken promise."

It was definitely a promise, Jack thought. *But it wasn't hers.*

"What about the being touched thing?" he finally asked.

Aimee shook her head and raised a hand as if to dismiss it altogether. "She said it was rats."

Jack was familiar with the feeling of something crawling across his skin—like a spider or a beetle. He'd lost countless nights of sleep to it as a kid. Every time he dozed off, something would scramble across his arm or slither down his back. His eyes would dart open and he'd slingshot his head around, hoping to catch the shadow that was tormenting him. But try as he might, he never saw a damn thing, nothing but his room bathed in moonlight. He told himself he was crazy, that he was imagining things—but as soon as he'd start to fall asleep he'd feel it again. Whatever was doing it would wait until he was on the brink of sleep, then skitter gently across his skin and force him back to alertness once more. And that feeling had never completely gone away. Every now and again he'd sit up in bed, his eyes wide, knowing that he and Aimee weren't alone.

"I'll check the walls," Jack told her. "Maybe there's a hole in the girls' room."

"Jack." Aimee shot him a look. "There are no rats."

She was right. Their house, shitty as it was, wasn't infested by vermin. Jack wished it was, wished that he could call an exterminator and it would all be over. But Aimee couldn't know that. She'd think *he'd* gone crazy too.

"How do you know? You were ready to jump on top of the dinner table last night."

"You know what I mean," she said, then sighed. "Please, *please* let's not fight right now. I can't take it."

He chewed the inside of his cheek, clasping his hands together as if in prayer.

"I want to take her to see a doctor," Aimee confessed.

"A shrink." It wasn't a question.

"A psychologist," Aimee clarified. "I think the accident might have done something to her."

"Fried her wiring."

"Post-traumatic stress, Jack. It's a real thing and kids can get it."

Jack said nothing.

"First she got sick. Maybe the stress compromised her immune system. Then it was the thing at the ice cream place, which I thought was all Abigail..."

And she would have still thought it was Abigail had Jack not told her differently. He was starting to regret ever having said a thing about it. His repentance burned hot; one slipup was forgivable, but a second wouldn't be tolerated. That jagged-toothed shadow assured him of that.

"Now there's this outburst. I feel like she's veering out of control. What are we going to do if it keeps getting worse?"

"Worse how?" Jack asked. "You think she's going to take a gun to kindergarten?"

The gunshot echoed in his ears. Charlie stood over the body of a classmate, her smile bright red, misted in blood.

"Are you telling me that you'd let it come to that? You'd rather avoid the problem than address it early? Is that what you're saying?"

Pressing his fingers hard against his temples, he hung his face toward the floor. He squeezed his eyes shut, trying to make the entire conversation disappear. All he needed to do was convince her everything was fine. There was nothing wrong here. This was all completely normal. But he didn't understand why he wanted to do that at all. Wouldn't it have been better to tell her the truth? Maybe things would be different. Maybe his own parents failed to save him because they were simply bad parents, but he and Aimee weren't; he and Aimee were *good* parents, goddammit. This wasn't supposed to be happening. Not to their family. Not to them.

"Jack," Aimee snapped.

He looked up, met her eyes. "What?" he said with matching force. "You want to take her to a shrink? Fine, we'll take her to a shrink. If you think it'll fix the problem, great. Problem solved. Halle-fuckin'-lujah."

Aimee blinked at his hostility.

"Do you have any other ideas?" she finally asked, determined to keep her composure. "What, you suddenly don't believe in psychology?"

"I don't think there's anything wrong with her head," Jack murmured.

"Oh really?" She was incensed now. "So that's why you suggested we go to therapy instead of church? Then what *is* wrong with her?" Aimee asked with a snort. "Is she possessed by the devil? Want to call an exorcist? I have an idea: you hold her down while I scream Bible verses all night. You think that'll fix it? Probably a better idea than a psychologist."

It would have been so easy to tell her everything—the discovery of that hidden cemetery at the end of the lot; the set of eyes that stared at him from beyond the trees; the cat strung up for his mother to find; his own visits to Dr. Copeland's office. He could have told her everything, and instead of being horrified at *him* she would have been horrified at history repeating itself, at their youngest daughter being the victim of a genetic affliction—a curse. But Aimee didn't believe in things like that. She was the girl who rolled her eyes whenever a new movie about demonic possession was released, insisting it was all a bunch of crap because religion was just a figment of everyone's imagination—at least that was what she used to believe. But with their latest church visit, he wasn't sure anymore. Maybe she *would* believe.

Even he knew that if demons could exist, it meant there was real evil in the world, and if you believed in the devil, somewhere in the deepest fibers of your being you had to believe in God. He knew, firsthand, that the devil was real; he'd seen it with his own two eyes. But he'd never seen God. He'd never felt God. He'd never been helped by God. For all he knew, wickedness was strong enough to exist in a world without good.

"Jack." Aimee was tired. She rubbed at her eyes, drained, but still insistent. "If it isn't her head, what is it?"

"I don't know." The answer startled him. He heard the words, felt them vibrate in his throat, but the voice didn't belong to him. That was when he knew he would never tell her about his past, and he would never tell her that she was right about Charlie. He would never tell her because he'd never be allowed.

The morning after Gilda's bout of hysteria, she dug through the bedroom closet like a dog trying to sniff out a bone, and eventually she surfaced with an old Folgers coffee tin. She shoved the tin into her purse before grabbing Jack by the arm and tossing him into the back of their old yellow hatchback.

After a forty-five-minute drive, the car came to a stop in front of a three-story building. By most standards it was relatively small, but in their neck of the woods it was tall enough to be considered a skyscraper. Gilda gathered up her purse, her coffee can, and her kid, and marched into the office building with the confidence of a commandant. Stopped by a woman working the front desk, she trudged up to the secretary, grabbed the coffee can out of her purse, and dumped it onto the receptionist's counter. Jack had never seen so much money in his entire life. There were twenties and fifties, and he even saw a hundred-dollar bill crumpled up with the rest. It was his momma's life savings, and here she was, ready to give it all up.

"This is all the money I've got," she told the now stunned receptionist. "It's all my money and I ain't rich, you understand me?"

The secretary, who was blond and well dressed and had the reddest mouth Jack had ever seen on a woman, said nothing. She simply sat behind her protective barrier and tried to find the right words.

"There's something wrong with my boy," Gilda told her, her voice cracking, threatening another emotional collapse. "I need to see a doctor."

"I can schedule an appointment," the receptionist assured, but Gilda wasn't having it. She shook her head and swallowed her tears and looked that woman straight in the eyes, unrelenting.

"I don't think you understand me," she said, her tone deadly serious. "I'm not here to make an appointment. I'm here to see a doctor."

"Ma'am, you can't just walk in here and see—"

Gilda slammed her palm flat against the counter, loud as a gunshot. The red-lipped woman jumped along with Jack, her manicured hands flying up to her heart as if to protect herself from the crazy woman with a can full of cash.

"I just *did* come in here," Gilda told her. "So why don't you scurry your pretty little rear up to your boss's office and tell him he's got an emergency appointment with a boy who needs his help?"

The receptionist opened her mouth to protest.

"Just do your job, sweetheart," Gilda said under her breath, "and don't piss me off."

The blond woman snapped her mouth shut. She looked at Jack, then shuffled off in a hurry. Jack watched her disappear around a corner, sure the cops would show up any minute, then took a seat in the waiting area fancier than any room he'd seen in all his life. The walls were covered in striped wallpaper, soothing tones of muted gray and blue, perfect for lulling the deranged into a calm and peaceful state. A glass coffee table sat in the center of the room, covered with the latest magazines: *Time*, *Newsweek*, even *National Geographic*, which Jack had begged his parents to buy him each month, but they never did. Potted plants flanked the walls—wispy palms with delicate fronds that swayed whenever someone walked by, others bearing waxy leaves that seemed too flawless to be real. Pictures hung in a perfectly straight line along the wall, displaying images of glasslike lakes and peaceful forests.

It was a wonder the woman at the front desk hadn't called the police after Gilda's outburst. They may have had mercy for the good of her little boy, or it may have been that the waiting room was completely empty. It was just Jack and Gilda and an instrumental version of Air Supply's "I'm All Out of Love."

Jack grabbed a handful of *National Geographic* issues and flipped through them with speed that would suggest he wasn't really interested, but it couldn't have been further from the truth. Had there been people waiting to be seen before them, Jack would have been more confident in taking his time. But they were the only ones there, so his time frame was unclear; he was like a greedy, time-pressed tourist in a new and brilliant city, desperate to see everything in far too little time, visiting sites with reckless abandon, never giving himself the opportunity to truly take any of it in.

A door at the far end of the room opened, and an older gentleman filled its frame with his doughy girth. He was impossibly fat, and had he ever been thin, the shadow of that man had been wiped from every curve and every feature he possessed. His face was round, and his eyes had been pressed into its fleshy softness. His mouth was droll and puckered, as if the fullness of his cheeks had squished his lips together from the outside in. He looked like the guy who played Barf the "mog"—half man, half dog—in *Spaceballs*. Jack had seen that movie at least a dozen times—it was one of his favorites.

"Hi there, folks," he said. "Come on in."

To Jack's disappointment, the man's name was Copeland, not Barf, and he had gotten his degree in the faraway land of California, not the outer reaches of space. Jack found himself staring at the framed PhD hanging above Copeland's desk, the outline of California's shape embossed in a gold seal that some-how made the diploma official. He assumed getting that seal on a diploma was like getting a gold star on homework—it must have been a good thing, which probably meant Copeland was a good doctor, no matter how fat he was.

"Thank you for seeing us, Doctor. I…" Gilda hesitated, her hands wringing the top of her purse. "I really made a scene down-stairs. I'm real sorry about all that. You're real gracious."

Dr. Copeland lifted a puffy hand. No apology was necessary.

"Sometimes we do things we wouldn't normally do during times of stress," he said. Even at Jack's ten years of age, he knew that was true—and if Copeland knew it too, he probably deserved that gold seal after all.

"Now…" Copeland leaned forward. His chair groaned beneath his weight every time he moved. He looked down to a blank file. "You'll have to work with me here, Mrs.…"

"Winter," Gilda said. "Gilda Winter, and this is my son, Jack."

Copeland glanced at Jack and gave him a pudgy-faced smile.

"All right, then," he said, scribbling their names down. "What can I do for you?"

"Well…" Gilda hesitated. She glanced over at Jack, then back to the doctor, her expression a mix of reluctance and expectation.

"Jack?" Dr. Copeland turned his attention to the boy. "Do you know why you're here?"

Jack straightened in his chair, suddenly in the spotlight. He sucked his bottom lip into his mouth and bit down on it before lifting his shoulders up to his ears in a shrug.

Copeland furrowed his eyebrows at them. He scribbled something on a notepad, then tapped his pen against his desk before making an admission.

"Well, folks, I can't exactly help if I don't know what's going on. Mrs. Winter, maybe it would be best if you came to see me on your own."

Gilda continued to wring her purse, unable to look the doctor in the eye. Jack watched his mother's face tense in something that, to him, looked like a bad stomachache.

"Do you think that would be all right?" Dr. Copeland asked. "I'm pretty booked tomorrow, but I can squeeze you in. This is an urgent matter, is that right?"

Gilda managed a faint nod.

There was more scribbling, then the jarring sound of paper being torn from the adhesive spine of a prescription pad. The chair beneath Copeland creaked when he reached over his desk, handing her an appointment time.

"Tomorrow at ten," he said.

Gilda stuffed the square of paper into her purse. She stood, dared to look at Copeland for the first time since she entered his office, and exhaled a few breathy words.

"Thank you, Doctor. Thanks very much."

Gilda Winter wasn't one for appreciation. It had been one of the few times Jack had ever heard her say thank you and actually mean it. It was a red flag: this failed visit was more serious than he had initially thought.

Jack had been amazed when Abby was born. It was inconceivable to think that some part of him had created something so perfect—a tiny, flawless human being, born into the world with wide eyes and staggering innocence. But it hadn't taken him long to veer off the course of fascination straight toward a sense of foreboding.

For the first year of Abigail's life, Jack watched her every gurgle and burp with the intensity of an artist studying his muse, and this study of his baby daughter wasn't an open affair. Jack came to this disturbing realization of secrecy when, bent over Abby's crib, searching for signs of malevolence in those big eyes, Aimee stepped into the nursery only to send him reeling away.

After almost being caught searching Abby's face for wickedness, he made his study a private pastime.

By the time Abby turned two, his secret observations had started to bore him. Abigail was a happy, silly, giggly little girl who—if there was anything wrong with her whatsoever—was overly good-natured. It was ironic, then, that after spending so much time worrying about Abigail, he hadn't spent a single minute thinking about whether his second daughter would be "normal" as well.

But that was how the devil worked, making his appearance when you least expected it.

Sitting outside the Riley house in Arnold's Oldsmobile, Jack chewed on the pad of his thumb while the engine ran. His stomach was in knots and his heart felt like it was somersaulting inside his chest. He'd even stopped to check his own pulse, suddenly worried about dropping dead. He considered packing a bag and driving until he hit water, Pacific or Atlantic, it didn't matter which. He considered forgetting who he was, settling down in the town that ran his gas tank dry—start a new life and forget the old. But he'd already done that once before, and all it afforded him was a history of secrets nobody but a gullible priest would believe.

Aimee, much like his mother, would eventually lose her mind. Abigail would be scapegoated and scarred by the things she'd see and hear. And then there was Charlie—the six-year-old who loved to sing Warrant's "Cherry Pie" into a hairbrush, the little girl who loved classic rock and wanted to dress up as Ace Frehley for Halloween. Somehow he had managed to get away from the evil that had tried to consume him as a kid only to have it take his own child away.

He shuddered.

Eventually finding his way up Patricia and Arnold's front steps, he was greeted by Charlie vaulting herself into his arms as soon as he rang the bell. Jack hid his face in her hair and squeezed her tight while Patricia looked on.

"Daddy," Charlie squeaked out after a moment. "You're squishing my guts." Wriggling out of his grasp, she ran to the Olds. Abby was already waiting in the backseat, having crawled into the car during Jack and Charlie's embrace.

Patricia stared at Jack for a long while. She let the screen door slap closed between them, shuddering against the doorjamb.

"Arnold wants his car back," she told him.

Jack searched for an appropriate response, but he wasn't given much time. Before he could form a reply, Patricia cut in.

"Get off my porch, Jack," she said. "I'd quite appreciate it if you'd keep away."

Aimee noticed Jack's baffled expression as soon as he returned home with the girls.

"What?" she asked.

"Your mother just told me to get off her porch," he said. "She doesn't want to see me there again."

"What?" she repeated. "Jack, what did you do?"

"That's the part you're going to love," he said with a smirk. "I rang the doorbell."

Aimee stared at him.

"She's *your* mother," he said.

Admittedly, he was glad Patricia disliked him as much as she did. He hoped her contempt would distract Aimee from the real issue at hand...and distraction was a precious commodity Jack couldn't afford to waste.

Unfortunately, Charlie wasn't going to make it easy. Sitting around the kitchen table, Jack, Aimee, and Abigail quietly ate their dinner while Charlotte sat in her chair with her arms crossed over her chest. She looked like a tiny Buddha with her legs crossed, silent in her unexplained fury. Both Jack and Aimee shot each other a glance when Charlie took her position of defiance, but neither asked her what was wrong, deciding instead to eat as much as they could before the inevitable meltdown took place.

Charlie had always been a picky eater. Ever since she was old enough to sit in a high chair, she'd take as much pleasure in hurling food across the kitchen as she did in eating it. The initial search for foods she liked pushed Aimee to the brink of tears nearly every night. Thankfully, her pickiness subsided around age four. That's when she fell into her everything-like-Daddy phase and, during one memorable evening, choked down wads of steamed spinach because Jack was happily enjoying his own. This newfound mimicry resulted in Jack becoming a guinea pig. Aimee subjected him to weird foods so that their youngest daughter would grow up big and strong. The experiment had resulted in Charlie liking most of the foods that ended up on her plate, and by the middle of her fifth year she was eating along with everyone else without much complaint.

At least until now.

Charlie finally broke her silence, which she'd impressively kept for nearly ten whole minutes.

"I don't want it."

After what had happened that morning, Aimee was in no mood to argue. She gave in.

"OK," she said. "What do you want?"

"Not this," Charlie complained, making a face at her plate of pot roast. "This is gross. It looks like poop."

Jack kept his head down, his eyes flitting between Aimee and Charlotte as the battle commenced.

"That's enough," Aimee said, but her tone gave her away. She wasn't primed to fight; she was tired. Pushing her chair away from the table, Aimee wandered to the fridge and pulled open the freezer door. "Onion rings?" she asked. Onion rings were one of

Charlie's favorites. She'd stack them on her plate like the Leaning Tower of Pisa.

"No," Charlie said flatly. "I hate those."

Aimee rolled her eyes, and Jack knew she was at the end of her rope. "What about little pizza pockets?"

Charlie sat mute in her chair.

"Or chicken nuggets. I'll make you some of those."

"I don't like chicken nuggets," she said under her breath, but Aimee was through listening. She tossed the bag of nuggets onto the counter, then pulled one of Charlie's plastic *SpongeBob* plates out of the overhead cabinet. Charlie's expression went dark.

"I said I don't like those," she said with more force, her eyes fixed on her father.

"Whatever, kid," Aimee muttered as she tossed frozen chicken pieces onto the plate, crumbs of breading littering the counter.

Charlie narrowed her eyes at Jack. A strange smile played at the corners of her mouth. That's when she opened her mouth, held it open as wide as she could—waiting for Jack to stop her—before letting out an ear-piercing scream.

Aimee veered around, her hand pressed to her heart. Abigail jumped in her seat. Jack just stared at her, transfixed.

"Jack!" Aimee yelled.

The sound of his name was like a mental kick. He suddenly remembered where he was, who he was. As though he hadn't seen Charlie at all until now, Jack stared at his daughter before pushing away from the table, grabbing her by the biceps, and giving her a quick shake.

Charlie's mouth snapped shut.

Abigail stared at them both from across the table. She looked as if she were about to say something when her mother appeared on her right, retaking her seat, fitfully shoving a bite of pot roast into her mouth.

The chicken nuggets were left on the counter, their freezer-burned bodies glistening in the dull kitchen light.

A few blocks away, Patricia Riley considered calling her daughter and telling her what she thought of Jack once and for all. After what Charlie had told her, that Jack had told the child her grandmother was a "fat evil bitch," she never wanted to see that lousy bastard ever again.

Abigail slid onto the couch next to her dad while Aimee gave Charlotte her nightly bath. She folded her hands in her lap and focused on the television—a *Seinfeld* rerun.

"Dad?" She pulled her socked feet onto the couch, catching her heels on the edge of the cushion, her toes hanging over the edge. "Can I ask you something?"

Jack shifted his weight, sitting sideways to get a good look at the little girl sitting beside him. Abby looked worried. Her youthful features had taken on a maturity Jack hadn't seen before.

"Shoot." Jack offered her a reassuring smile, but rather than smiling back, she wrapped her arms around her legs and looked down at her knees. Jack furrowed his eyebrows. "Everything OK?"

Abby sat motionless for a moment, then slowly shook her head.

"What's wrong?" he asked. Abby pressed her mouth to her knees, her arms wrapped around her legs. When the television jumped to a brightly lit commercial, he caught the glimmer of tears in Abby's eyes.

"Hey…" He closed the distance between them, placing an arm around her shoulders. As soon as he touched her, her bottom lip began to quiver. "Abby, what's going on?" he asked quietly. Again, she shook her head.

"Charlie," she whispered, and that was all she said.

Jack sighed, holding her close against his side. He knew it would eventually come to this—Abigail buckling under her younger sister's behavior. After the ice cream incident it was just a matter of time.

"Charlie's just confused right now," Jack murmured.

"Confused about what?" She wiped at her eyes.

It was a good question—one that didn't have an answer, because Charlie wasn't confused at all. It had nothing to do with what Charlotte did and didn't understand.

"Oh, you know—just growing up in general," he said.

"Was I confused?" Abby asked after a moment.

Jack inhaled a deep breath. It was one thing to mislead Aimee, but lying to a ten-year-old… Aimee had a lifetime of beliefs behind her; she'd had enough time to form opinions and decide what she did and didn't believe in. Despite growing up with a strict religious background, she held her religious independence in front of her like a shield. The girls never had that opportunity. Abigail had set foot in a church a handful of times in her life, and Charlie had sat in a pew all of once. It seemed that those who spent lifetimes sitting in front of pulpits would be the first to believe in things like demons, but in Jack's experience it was the opposite. The devout refused to acknowledge the possibility that their God would allow such wickedness to exist, let alone get so close to those they loved.

"No," Jack finally said. "You weren't confused. But Charlie is."

Abby chewed on her bottom lip. She stiffened at the sound of bathwater draining out of the tub. Charlie and Aimee would be out of the bathroom soon. Turning to her father, she looked him in the eyes with a desperate expression.

"You saw it, didn't you?" she asked. "I saw you during dinner, right before she screamed."

Jack frowned, ready to deny whatever Abby was getting at, but the idea of someone else knowing, someone else suspecting what Jack knew for certain, was as alluring as a penny sparkling in the dirt.

"Saw what?" he asked almost inaudibly, not wanting Aimee to overhear.

"The darkness," Abby whispered. "The way she smiles."

He hesitated, afraid to admit it, afraid that as soon as he said yes their lives would collapse.

"Dad?" Abby's eyes shimmered. "I'm not crazy, right?"

Jack finally shook his head and pressed his lips to Abby's forehead. "No," he whispered. "You're not crazy."

"Can you maybe ask Mom if I can move into the attic?"

"The attic." Jack leaned away to get a look at her. "You don't want to have your room up there, kiddo." The attic was drafty and smelled of dust and mold. Both girls had been afraid of it for as long as he could remember. But Abby was nodding her head vigorously.

"I do," she insisted. "Please? I won't be scared, I swear." Her expression gave her away. She was terrified. Anything was better than sleeping in a room with someone who held darkness in their eyes.

Jack winced at the idea. Aimee would never go for it. But the anxiety in Abigail's eyes was enough to break his heart. She was on the verge of panicked tears. Her fingers clutched the hem of his shirt, hanging on for dear life, hanging on to her teetering sanity.

"I'll talk to your mom," he finally told her. "You need to give me a little time, though."

Abby nodded again and threw her arms around him.

"I knew you'd understand," she whispered, then slid off the couch and disappeared down the hall.

Jack couldn't help but wonder, why had Abby been so sure that he would understand? Why not her mother instead? Had she seen the darkness in his eyes as well?

CHAPTER NINE

THE BAR WAS A SEEDY JOINT—THE KIND OF PLACE WITH A front door that looked like it'd been kicked in one too many times. It was the electric heartbeat of Live Oak's insomnia, the midnight pulse of those too tired to deal with their problems without Jack Daniels there to listen. Jack felt his skin crawl as he sat in the gravel parking lot, considering whether he really wanted to go inside. Going in meant he'd need an excuse for asking Reagan to meet him, and having a reason meant either telling the truth or lying to his best friend. Sitting in the dark interior of Arnold's Olds, the cabin lit by garish red neon from a flickering Schlitz sign, he wondered if caring about lying to Reagan while having lied to Aimee for so long made him a bad husband. Aimee would have said so, and whose opinion mattered more than hers?

Sucking in a steadying breath, he shoved the driver's side door open and crunched his way past a rusty red pickup. Reagan was already inside, occupying a booth and nursing a Blue Moon, peering at a crappy old TV mounted in the top corner of the room. He lifted his bottle in a salute to the bar's choice of programming as soon as he saw Jack step inside.

"*Cheers*," Reagan said, then cracked a stupid grin. "No really, look."

Ted Danson sat at the bar on TV, chatting up Shelley Long.

"Ironic, isn't it? Playing *Cheers* in here? It just doesn't seem right. I don't know why," he said. "I just have this feeling like blasphemy is being...what would you say, performed? Is that right?"

A tired-looking waitress appeared at their table before Jack had a chance to settle in. She was gaunt. The weird lighting from the neon signs cast gruesome shadows across her face. If there was news of a zombie outbreak, this was one woman he'd steer clear of.

"What'll it be?" she asked. Her eye sockets looked like gaping holes, just like Charlie's Día de los Muertos figurines—skin and bones, like the woman was surviving off nothing but bumps of meth. Not that it would have been all that surprising. In places like these, addiction was as comforting as the bayou itself.

"What he's having," Jack said, motioning to Reagan's beer.

She didn't say anything, just turned and walked back to the bar, not giving half a shit about her patrons or their lousy two-dollar tips.

"So," Reagan started, "what's going on? Monday night? Must be serious."

He was right. They hadn't hit a bar on a weeknight since before Abigail was born. Jack had tried to be a responsible father and husband, and for the most part he had succeeded.

Reagan knew just as much as Aimee did when it came to his past, which wasn't much. Had he been more forthcoming with

Reagan all along, he could have spit it out: *History is repeating itself.* But that wasn't an option. Jack shook his head, hesitating.

"What?" Reagan asked. "Dude." He stopped peeling the label off his beer bottle and shifted his weight. Pressing his elbows against the table, he leaned forward to get a good look at his comrade. "Please tell me you aren't here to break up with me. My world will crumble."

Any other night, Jack would have laughed. Tonight he couldn't lift the weight off his shoulders for long enough to manage it.

"I hope it doesn't come to that," Jack admitted after a moment.

Reagan suddenly looked uncomfortable. "What're you talking about?" he asked. "What does that even mean?"

Jack sighed. He nodded at the waitress when she set his beer in front of him. His fingers wrapped around the bottom of the bottle, if only to give his hands something to do.

"Things aren't going all that well at home," Jack said. "I don't really know when going up to the Quarter would be appropriate."

Reagan's face twisted, a cross between worry and confusion.

"There's something wrong with Charlie," Jack heard himself say. It hadn't taken long to get to the point.

"What do you mean 'wrong'?" Reagan asked. "You mean how she's been sick?"

"Sort of."

It was Jack's turn to pull at the corner of his label. He carefully peeled it away, trying to keep it intact.

"Jack, come on, man. If you're going to ruin my fucking night at least be kind enough to be specific."

Jack actually laughed that time. It was a short burst, a knee-jerk reaction. Reagan stared at him from across the table. He was freaked out.

"OK?" he said, unsure of himself. "That was funny?"

Jack leaned back against the vinyl seat and shrugged. "Let me ask you something," he said. "What's your opinion on God?"

"God." Reagan continued to stare. "My opinion? Like whether or not I think God is a good guy? Well I don't know, Jack, we don't exactly run with the same crowd. But if I had to take a guess, I'd say he's probably a righteous dude."

"About that," Jack said. "Running with the same crowd." He paused, squinting at the bottle in front of him. "If you don't run with God's crowd, whose crowd do you run with?"

"Well, there's L. Ron Hubbard," Reagan quipped. "Imagine going to a party where there's one guy who can't stop talking about aliens and volcanoes."

"I'm serious."

"That's what's freaking me out. Serious about what? What are you asking me?"

"If you don't believe in God, what do you believe in?"

Seemingly stunned that he was having this sort of a conversation at a bar on a Monday night, Reagan gave Jack a *what the fuck* look. "I guess I don't know."

"Do you believe there's good in the world?"

"Well sure, there's good all over the place."

"So then, do you also believe in an opposite?"

"Like what, evil?"

Jack nodded.

"I guess." Reagan shrugged. "If there wasn't evil, we would be seriously lacking in the serial killer department. And child molesters. And those angel of death nurses who run around hospitals unplugging people's IVs."

Jack chewed on his bottom lip, his gaze focused on the torn beer label curled atop the table. "So are those people born evil? The serial killers and the child molesters and the crazy nurses? Are they just fucked in the head from square go, or do they start out like everyone else and become that way over time?"

"It could be the Kool-Aid. Who knows? Where is this coming from anyway? I mean, don't get me wrong, I don't mind existentialism, but you're asking me about whether or not people are born bad…in a bar. And you haven't even bought me a drink. This on the tail of telling me things aren't going well at home, that you might have to take a break from the band…"

"I'm trying to be open here."

"Well your openness is giving me a fucking heart attack."

"Do you believe there can be a devil if there is no God?" Jack pressed.

Reagan slowly leaned back in his seat, his expression wavering from confusion to full-blown concern. He pressed his lips together in a tight line as he stared across the table at his friend—a friend who looked dead serious about the question he'd just asked.

"I'm not really what one would consider 'worldly,'" Reagan finally said, "so my opinion on this might be completely full of shit, but…"

Jack looked up from the table. He met Reagan's eyes and waited, hoping the answer would be no, knowing it would be yes.

"I've never seen any miracles," Reagan said, "but I sure as hell have seen my share of darkness. Does God exist? I don't know. But I kind of hope he does. Because if he doesn't? We're probably fucked."

Jack came home well after the girls had been put to bed. Aimee was in the master bedroom with the comforter pulled up to her waist, the washed-out emblem on her mock football shirt peeking out from behind the spine of an old paperback. She'd given up on *Les Misérables* and picked up *The Stand*—another book she'd been trudging through for what seemed like the entirety of their marriage.

"You're still reading that?" Jack asked.

Aimee flipped the book over, a finger hooked between the pages to keep her place, and studied the cover. She had had it so long that the corners had rounded and softened.

"It probably makes me some sort of tasteless idiot," she said, "but I can't get into it."

"But you keep trying."

"It's King," she said. "Anybody who's anybody has read this."

Jack stood in the doorway of the bathroom, peeling off his T-shirt and kicking his jeans off his legs.

"I haven't read it," he told her. She rolled her eyes at him like that was supposed to mean anything.

"You also haven't read the Bible," she said. "Which, if my mother knew—I mean, I don't know…maybe she found out somehow and that's why she kicked you off the porch."

"Yeah, or maybe she's tired of pretending she doesn't hate me."

Aimee glared at the ceiling with a sigh. "She doesn't hate you. We've been over this."

"Well maybe you should go over it with *her* one of these days. Maybe filling her in on the details would cue her in to not act like a vengeful old…" He paused. Aimee watched him steadily, waiting for him to finish his thought. "…mother-in-law."

"Interesting," Aimee mused.

"What?" Jack looked suspicious.

"That you wouldn't call her a 'fat evil bitch' to my face, but you'd dare call her that in front of Charlie."

Jack blinked, shook his head.

"That's why she kicked you off the porch." Aimee fished her bookmark from the back few pages of the paperback and marked her place before slamming the book closed. "And quite frankly, I don't blame her." She shot her husband a look. "How *could* you?" she pressed. "To Charlie, of all things…"

Jack lifted his hands as if to protect himself from the oncoming onslaught. "Aimes…"

"Let me guess, it never happened?"

"It *didn't*."

Aimee closed her eyes.

"Oh come *on,*" he insisted. "Are you serious? How can you believe that? I would never."

"Then why would she say it, Jack?"

"Because she's fucking crazy? Hell, I don't know."

Tossing her book onto the nightstand, Aimee pulled the pillow beneath her head and yanked the covers up to her chin. "You ever heard the expression 'Kids don't lie'?"

Jack flipped the bathroom light off and slid into bed.

"We both know that's a bunch of bullshit," he told her. "Kids lie all the time."

Lying next to each other, Jack stared up at the ceiling and Aimee rolled over, her back to him, both of them stewing in uncomfortable silence.

"Is that what Reagan told you?" Aimee finally asked. "You two talked about kids over beers at that shitty bar? Did you talk about what a fat evil bitch my mother is?"

Jack sighed and changed the subject.

"Abby's ready for her own room. She offered to move up to the attic—"

"What?"

"I told her no. At least to the attic thing."

Aimee stared into the darkness.

"It's nasty up there," he said. "And it smells weird."

"That's because it's an attic. And what do you mean you told her no 'to the attic thing'? Does that mean you told her yes to getting her own room?"

"She's ten years old."

"So?"

"So imagine not having your own room at ten years old. Imagine having to share it with a younger sister who's obsessed with a yellow sponge."

"So we should let her move into the attic and cover the walls with posters of glittery vampires."

"Abby doesn't even *like* vampires…"

"Like we have the room, Jack. Like this house is big enough for four people as it is."

"You were expecting the girls to share a room until they were ready to move out of the house? They'll move out at puberty. Maybe the attic isn't that bad an idea."

"The way things are going?" Aimee said. "Moving out at puberty is a fantastic option."

"Cool," Jack replied, "it's settled then." He rolled onto his side to end the conversation.

It took her less than thirty seconds to pipe up again.

"I can't believe you'd get her hopes up like that. Now I'm going to have to be the bad guy and tell her she can't actually have her own room because Daddy doesn't think before he makes stupid promises."

"I didn't make her a stupid promise," he countered, his back still turned. "I told her I'd work something out to what I personally think is a reasonable request."

"Well, it's completely stupid." She turned her back as well, shoving the corner of her pillow underneath her head. "As soon as those two split up they'll live in the same house but never speak to each other again, just like every other dysfunctional family."

"Have you considered them hating each other if we *don't* split them up?" Jack asked the wall.

Aimee was silent.

"I'll fix it up," he said after a moment. "It'll be good to get it in order anyway. It needs to be insulated. It'll save us money."

Aimee threw her side of the covers off and sat up as if struck by lightning—but instead of lightning it was rage.

"No you won't," she snapped. "I don't care what you told Abby, and I don't care how disappointed she's going to be; she's not moving out of that room. Ever since the accident you've been taking everyone's side but mine, and I'm sick of it. I'm sick of being told what's going to happen, so now *I'm* telling *you*: Abigail isn't moving out of her room, we're not spending money to fix up the attic, and Charlie isn't going to be excused for her behavior because you swear there's nothing wrong with her. Because I think something *is*."

"Like what?" He watched her as she towered over him like the Fifty-Foot Woman, waited for horror to creep across her face, waited for the idea of fire and brimstone to breech her anger and sway her toward terror. But none of that happened. Aimee squared her shoulders and answered plainly:

"I think she doesn't spend enough time with her father. She needs your attention."

Jack opened his mouth to protest.

"You're too busy running around all of Louisiana with your buddies, playing bars and getting drunk and wandering up and down Bourbon Street doing God only knows what."

"What?"

"Oh come off it," she told him. "You've been distant. You voluntarily sleep on the couch..."

"You think I'm *cheating* on you?"

Aimee looked him square in the eyes, hers glittering in the moonlight.

"I don't know what to think," she confessed. "And quite honestly, I don't know if I care anymore."

His mouth snapped closed. His chest tightened. He watched her as she turned away again, pulling the sheets up to her chest. Aimee was wrong about it being his lack of quality time with Charlotte; no amount of father/daughter time would change what was going on. But she was right about one thing: it was definitely all his fault.

Dr. Copeland's oversized desk made Jack feel small. Even the chairs across from the desk, while comfortable, felt huge. It seemed odd to Jack that a doctor who was supposed to make people feel better would choose to dwarf them first.

"So," Copeland said, folding his hands on top of the varnished desktop. "Tell me what's bothering you."

Gilda had met with Copeland alone a few days before, and Jack could only imagine the horrors she had told him. For all he knew, she had recapped *The Exorcist*, having replaced the movie characters with their own family, exchanging that fancy brick house with their dilapidated trailer. Jack lowered his chin and looked down his nose at the doctor as if sizing him up, looking for signs of what Copeland did and didn't know.

"Is anything bothering you?" Copeland asked.

Jack held his silence. It was never smart to make the first move, in case you ended up giving yourself away.

Copeland frowned at this lack of participation, but he was prepared to fight. Leaning back in his squeaky chair, he folded his hands across the slope of his round belly and watched the kid with earnest curiosity.

"You aren't going to talk to me?" he asked.

Nothing.

"Are you afraid of what you might say?"

Jack narrowed his eyes, thinking it would make him look harder, tougher, but all it did was give Copeland a nonverbal answer.

"OK," Copeland said. "You obviously don't want to be here, but your mother won't let either of us off the hook until we get some work done, so why don't we cut to the chase? Tell me about the cat."

Jack stiffened.

"You know the one," Copeland said. "The cat you strung up in the tree."

Jack's fingers dug into the cushion of that fancy chair. He imagined his nails biting into the fabric, boring holes into the upholstery.

"Did that cat bother you?"

Jack flinched.

"Had it wronged you in some way?"

It had hissed and run. For no reason.

"Jack?"

He felt his breath catch in his throat. He felt hot.

"Jack, are you with me right now?"

He was sure that at any moment he'd lose the ability to suck in air, that he'd forget how to breathe.

"I didn't want to do it," he spit out. "I didn't know."

Copeland peered at him, contemplating Jack's revelation. Then he leaned forward and scribbled a note.

"That cat had it coming," Jack whispered. "He had it *coming*."

Aimee hesitated outside the girls' door the next morning, not wanting a repeat performance from the day before, but when she finally pushed the door open she was greeted by a sight that caught her off guard. Abigail was still fast asleep, but Charlie—the night owl—was wide awake, sitting on top of her *SpongeBob* covers, facing the bedroom door, waiting for her mom to come in.

Aimee's muscles went tight. "Charlie?"

"Good morning, Mommy," she said with a bright smile.

"Good morning," Aimee replied, but her words were less than sure. Charlie was notorious for sleeping in. The kid had the ability to sleep for twelve hours straight if she was allowed. Seeing Charlie awake, let alone cheerful at 7:00 a.m., was more than a little disconcerting.

"Is…everything OK?" she asked, giving her daughter a wide berth as she stepped inside the room. "Why are you up so early?"

"Because it's time for school," Charlie answered. "And it's time for breakfast."

Aimee turned away from her youngest, mouthing a silent *OK*, busying herself at the dresser. It was too weird—weird enough to send a chill down her back. When she heard bare feet hit the floor and scamper toward her, Aimee's breath caught in her throat. She spun around and shoved her back against the chest of drawers, the dresser shuddering from the impact.

Charlie stood a foot from her mother, looking up at her with an ear-to-ear grin.

"Good morning, Mommy," she repeated.

Aimee slowly opened her mouth.

"Yes," Charlie said. "Everything's OK." Her words were flat, but that wide smile remained. "It's time for school," Charlie said. "Better wake up. We don't want to miss the bus. Breakfast is on the table. Go brush your teeth."

Charlotte pivoted on the balls of her bare feet and bolted out of the room.

Aimee stood frozen against the dresser for several long seconds, her breath hitching in her chest. Abby rubbed her eyes, attempting to wake up across the room.

"Mom?" she said, her throat dry with sleep.

"It's OK, baby," Aimee croaked. Then she too excused herself. But instead of looking for where Charlie had gone, she rushed to the bedside table in the master bedroom and yanked the drawer out so fast it crashed to the floor. Searching through old receipts, random sticky notes, and a few hairstyle magazines she'd tucked away in case she ever felt like making a change, she eventually located her inhaler, uncapped it, and took a couple of puffs.

The prescription was expired by two years.

Aimee hadn't had an asthma attack in over three.

"Mom?" Abby stuck her head into her parents' bedroom and found her mother sitting limply at the corner of her bed. "Are you OK?"

Aimee swatted at the tears and forced a smile. "I'm fine, sweetie. Are you two done eating breakfast?"

Abigail nodded slowly, studying her mother. "OK," Aimee said, clearing her throat and gathering her wits. "Let's go." She got up and motioned for Abby to get moving, trying to fall into their typical morning routine. "Where's your backpack?"

Abby skittered down the hall to retrieve her things, and Aimee forced herself out of the bedroom. She paused when she stepped into the kitchen, her eyes snagging on Charlie, who was sitting at the table, her wide eyes fixed on a corner of the room, as if seeing something that wasn't there.

"Charlie," Aimee said as steadily as she could. "Chop chop, let's go."

But Charlie didn't move. Whatever lurked in that corner had her transfixed.

"Char?"

Nothing.

Aimee approached with slow, reluctant steps.

Charlie didn't respond.

"Honey, you're really starting to worry Mommy."

Regarding herself in the third person was one of Aimee's safeguards against vulnerability. Right now it made her feel removed, less in the line of fire of whatever decided to creep out of that corner and twist her once normal life beyond recognition.

She closed the distance between them, placing a hand on Charlie's shoulder—another move made with obvious hesitation, like putting a hand onto a stove that might be hot. As soon as she made contact, Charlie sprang from her chair and dashed after her sister like a spooked cat. Aimee was left alone in the kitchen, trying to push thoughts of childhood psychosis out of her head. But nothing she told herself convinced her that what was going on with Charlie was normal.

When Aimee appeared at the girls' door, Abby already had her backpack pulled over her shoulders. She stood at the opposite side of the room, keeping distance between her and her sibling.

As soon as Abby saw her mom appear, she pulled at the straps of her bag and fell into motion.

"I'll wait outside," she told her mother and brushed by her; staying in that room was clearly the last thing she wanted to do. Aimee was left alone with Charlotte yet again. She crouched down to help the six-year-old tie her shoes so she could join Abby at the bus stop.

Charlie began to giggle—a sound that had once been as airy and iridescent as bubbles floating through the sky, now oddly heavy with unidentifiable emotion.

"What's funny?" Aimee asked, looking up from her crouched position. That weird smile hung on Charlie's once-innocent face.

Aimee looked away, masking her panic by directing it toward the floor. Just as she finished securing Charlie's second shoe, she felt an exhale flutter a few strands of hair across her forehead. Charlie's crooked smile was less than an inch from Aimee's hairline. When Aimee lifted her head, coming nose to nose with her daughter, Charlie didn't lean back to give either of them more room. She remained uncomfortably close, her eyes glinting with wicked mischief—a glint that Aimee had seen before, but the malevolence was new.

"Good morning," Charlie sing-songed. "Better get up. Time for school."

"That's enough," Aimee said, surprised by the forcefulness that had jumped into her tone. "No more games. Mommy's tired of it."

"I know," Charlie said solemnly. "I'm sorry." Her apology was tainted by a grating babyish tone, making her insincerity that much more apparent.

Aimee turned away for a second, long enough to grab Charlie's backpack. When she turned back to the child, Charlotte was still grinning.

Suddenly, she wanted nothing more than to snatch her little girl by the shoulders and shake her as hard as she could, shake her until that smile was wiped from her face. Instead, she extended a stiff arm outward and handed Charlie her bag.

"You're going to miss the bus."

Charlie shrugged and sauntered out of the bedroom at a leisurely pace. Aimee followed, not to make sure she made it to the bus stop, but to make sure she simply left the house.

But Charlie wasn't one to make things easy. When she reached the front door, she turned to look back at her mother, that disconcerting smile still pulling her face tight.

"Don't be scared, Mommy," she said. "At least you still have Abigail."

CHAPTER TEN

When Jack saw Arnold's Oldsmobile ramble up to the boat shop he did a double take. In all the years he'd worked for Max, Aimee had come to the shop only once—delivering a sack lunch Jack had forgotten on the kitchen counter. Seeing her fumble with the seatbelt, he saw Reagan's *what the hell* look, dropped what he was doing, and met Aimee next to the car.

"We have to do something." Aimee's voice quaked. She pulled at her fingers as though trying to pluck them from her palms. "It's getting worse," she said. "There's something wrong, Jack. I know there's something wrong."

He glanced back toward the shop. Reagan stood beside the pontoon they'd been working on all morning, his welding helmet tipped up, watching both of them with genuine concern. Jack turned back to Aimee, put a hand on her shoulder, and led her to the back of the Olds.

"I think I know," she said.

"Know what?" He was trying to play it cool, but even the slightest hint that Aimee suspected the truth made part of him—the familiar him—want to run. The other half was already plotting out where to bury her: in the forest on the opposite side of the house, thick with kudzu and moss. When his mother had tossed aside her psychological explanations and finally saw the situation for what it was, it had sealed their fate as a family. He knew that as soon as Aimee did the same, it would be the end of them. Aimee began to pace. She was typically well put-together, but today her oversized sweater and sweatpants gave her a disheveled look. Jack knew that she wouldn't leave the house to grab a gallon of milk without fixing her hair and putting on something presentable. Seeing her this way worried him. She was a woman on the brink of something dangerous.

"We need that psychiatrist," she said, lifting her hands to silence Jack before he had a chance to protest. "I know, it's going to cost a fortune, but Jack…" She lowered her gaze to the ground, her fingers tangling themselves in the hem of her gray corded sweater. "I looked it up this morning; I think she may be schizophrenic."

Jack said nothing. The baleful smile that flashed across his face was so quick Aimee never saw it.

"She's scaring me," she said. "She gave me an asthma attack."

Jack remembered the sound of his own mother hyperventilating to the heavy screech of a bookcase being pushed across a cheap wood-paneled floor.

"OK," he said.

But Aimee didn't hear him.

"I look at her," she said, "but it isn't her. It's like I'm looking at someone else, like her eyes are vacant…"

It was the darkness. Soon, she'd see the same thing in his eyes too.

"I said OK."

Aimee stopped pacing. She blinked at her husband. Motionless for a moment, she threw herself at him like a girl overjoyed—but it wasn't joy, it was fear. As soon as his arms wrapped around her, her shoulders heaved in a sob.

"Oh God," she cried into the dirty cotton of his work shirt. "This cannot be happening. This isn't our family."

Inside his head, that little voice agreed with her sentiment.

This was never your family, it whispered. *It's always been mine.*

Dr. Copeland made Jack look at stacks of inkblot cards and asked him what he saw. In one, Jack saw a unicorn. In another, there was a bird. And the more intricate and complex the cards became, the more wickedness Jack seemed to see. The bird turned into a bat, the unicorn into a demon. As the cards continued to be laid out, Jack decided that if this was going to end, he would have to be the one to end it. Jack leaned away from Copeland's desk, took a deep breath, and outed himself in a desperate attempt at redemption.

"Dr. Copeland?" Jack began. "I haven't told you all there is to tell, sir."

Despite his backwoods upbringing, Gilda had raised a polite boy. She had insisted on it, explaining that manners made people more sophisticated; Jack's dad couldn't have cared less, but it made his mom feel more like they all belonged on planet Earth.

Copeland leaned back in his creaky chair and nodded at him in silent encouragement. He folded his arms across his globe-like stomach.

Jack hesitated. He knew this was risky, but he was tired of the questions and tests. All he wanted was a good night's sleep. He didn't want to be scared anymore. It made sense to him that if he was going to tell anybody about what was really going on, it should have been Dr. Barf. This was what his mom had spent her life savings for, and of all the ungrateful things he'd done in his life, letting her spend all that money on him like that without at least *some* result...well, it just felt wrong. It felt like she deserved for Jack to at least *try*.

"There's something living in my room," Jack told him. "It's what made me kill that cat."

Copeland's expression was pensive. He reached for his pad and pen. To Jack's dismay, the doctor didn't seem the least bit impressed with this revelation—a revelation that, in his eyes, should have answered all of the doctor's questions. Rather than Copeland's eyebrows shooting up in intrigue, the doc peered at his notepad with a vague look of concern before scribbling something down.

"What is this something?" Copeland asked. "Is it a person? An animal?"

"It's a shadow," Jack said, forcing the words outward. He didn't want to take too much time to think about what he was saying. He was sure that if he did, he'd change his mind. "It sits in the corner of my room, you know, like one of those stone monsters on top of big city skyscrapers."

"A gargoyle," Copeland said. "And how often do you see it?"

"Every night."

Copeland tapped his pen against his notepad.

"Sometimes it crawls up on the ceiling," Jack murmured toward his hands. It was an afterthought. Jack knew that if the shadow figure hadn't impressed Copeland by then, its movements would hardly interest him. But Copeland seemed to straighten in his chair, and a moment later he posed a question that caught Jack off guard.

"Jack, does your family live close to a road?"

They did. They lived right on a road, but it was just about as rural as a road could get. Their closest neighbor was a good half mile away, and neither Stephen nor Gilda had ever been all that neighborly. Stephen always said that the more neighbors you knew, the more people would come around asking you to do things you had no desire to do, like moving furniture or painting kitchens or lending sugar that they'd swear they were "just borrowing" like they were actually going to return it someday. They lived along a road, but they may as well have lived a million miles from it.

"Yes, sir," Jack said.

"And this shadow, you say you only see it at night?"

He gave the doctor a slight nod, a blast of moths' wings tickling the inside of his stomach. Was it good that he saw what he was describing only at night? By the way Dr. Barf was scribbling on his pad, it seemed as though maybe he knew what it was. Maybe his mom had been right—that glorious gold seal with the shape of California was going to save him. All he had to do was force himself to be honest, and there it was: success.

"Does the shadow stay in the same corner night after night?" Copeland asked.

"Yes," he replied, almost exuberant now.

"Jack, have you ever seen headlights travel across the inside of your room at night?"

"Yeah?" He blinked.

"Do you think that maybe what you're seeing are those headlights dancing across your walls?"

Headlights? he thought. *Are you kidding?* Jack frowned, feeling a surprising spark of anger, a spark that was heavy with betrayal. He'd told Copeland the truth, but Copeland thought it was a bunch of bologna—kid stuff, that was all.

"It isn't headlights," Jack insisted, an edge in his tone. "Nobody drives up and down that road hardly ever."

"Well, you and your family drive on it every day," Copeland reminded him. "Don't you think there may be other families that live along that road like you do?"

Jack looked back to his hands. He had put himself out there, he had told the truth—and all it had done was make him look stupid. Copeland wasn't going to help. Jack was never going to sleep again. And that shadow, it would never go away. It would sit perched at the foot of his bed, watching him sleep until the day he died.

"I'm *not* crazy," he whispered, sure that the doctor could hear. He waited for Copeland's obligatory reply, but the doctor didn't say anything. Jack's adolescent denial was left to hang heavy in the air until their session was over.

After Aimee's arrival at the shop, Jack took the rest of the day off. He put Aimee to bed, made a cup of coffee, and Googled psychiatrists near Live Oak. Part of him didn't want anything to do with a shrink—they'd do nothing but put his kid through a battery of tests and fill her up like a pill-stuffed piñata. Copeland had prescribed antianxiety meds, assuring Gilda that as long as Jack took them he'd be fine. But Jack didn't take them. He had wanted to, especially on nights when he knew he wasn't alone, when he could feel the rats crawling over him only to disappear when he opened his eyes. But every time he reached for that pill bottle, somehow, by some unexplainable force, he failed. The bottle would slip through his fingers and roll beneath the bed, or it wouldn't be where he had left it at all. The time he managed to swallow a pill, he choked on the water he used to wash it down, coughed so hard he ended up vomiting both the water and the pill all over his bedroom floor.

Jack wasn't a fan of medication as it was—he hardly took anything beyond a couple of Tylenol for the occasional headache. The idea of having a zombie for a daughter turned his stomach, but it struck him as better than the alternative: letting it get bad enough that Charlie would have to be put away.

It became his mission to find a psychiatrist who would, at least, prescribe a six-year-old a bunch of pills. He'd feed them to her himself if he had to. He'd turn Charlie into the walking dead if only to keep Aimee from fearing their daughter. Gilda's fear had been what had sealed his own fate. Letting Aimee fall into the same pattern would inevitably lead to the same result.

He called number after number, but in what seemed like a *Twilight Zone* scenario, he got a busy signal or a disconnect message for every single one. It was as though every doctor of psychiatry in all of Louisiana had closed their doors overnight. *We're sorry, the number you have dialed is no longer in service.* After a half hour, it was Dr. J. H. Markin's office who finally answered.

When the girls came home, Jack sat them down in front of bowls of mac and cheese, and after Abigail disappeared into her room to do her homework, Jack looked at Charlie from across the kitchen table, studying her as she read the back of a box of cereal that had been left out that morning.

"So you're still here," he said, unable to help himself, wondering if it would elicit some sort of response that didn't belong to his daughter, but to the thing he knew was buried inside her.

Charlie blinked at him, her little hand wrapped around the handle of the spoon jutting out of her mouth.

"I guess I should have known better," he murmured. "I always thought it was strange that I managed to outrun you. Now I know I was wrong to think I had."

Charlie's eyes darkened, but she continued to eat. But rather than looking back to her box of cereal, her gaze never left her father's face, fixed on him as intently as a dog ready to attack.

"So what do you want?" Jack asked. "What *did* you want? Or was I just the kid who sat in the wrong cemetery at the wrong time?"

A corner of Charlie's mouth curled upward. Her eyes flashed with acknowledgment. Jack wasn't the only one who remembered that graveyard tucked away among the trees. That twinkle assured him of that.

"I'd say 'take me instead,' but if that was an option you would have done it by now."

Charlie stared at him from across the table with a wide, blank stare. Without warning, her chair jerked backward, the legs screaming across the kitchen floor. It tipped rearward, then to the side, impossibly balancing on one leg. Jack sucked in a sudden breath, but he didn't move. Despite the chair's unnatural angle, Charlie was glued in place, grinning, her eyes as big as twin moons.

Jack regained his hold on reality. His mind unfroze, his throat reopened. Now he grasped at words he hoped would stop all of this. "You can do what you want with me, but leave my family out of this," he said.

Charlie's jagged smile turned into an exaggerated frown. That chair slammed onto its four legs and shot forward with such force that had it not stopped at just the right time, her ribs would have been crushed against the edge of the table. But it did stop, and that dark expression turned inhuman as she whispered across the table.

"I'll do what I want with you," she hissed. "And I'll take your family too."

Just as abruptly as it had come, that expression faded from Charlie's face. She went back to eating her mac and cheese, her attention fully focused on the picture of the prize she'd fished out of that box over a week before.

"Daddy," she said, "it says *collect all four.*"

And despite the fact that Jack knew she had meant something completely different, he couldn't help the foreboding that lodged at the back of his throat—like a sticky pill, too dry to go down.

The next morning, three of the four Winters found themselves sitting in Dr. Markin's waiting room. Aimee had screwed her face up in distaste the moment they had stepped inside. The place was like a bad seventies movie, complete with shag carpeting and outdated wood paneling nailed to the walls. It smelled stale, and Jack was sure that twenty-five years ago this was probably some sad insurance office where a guy in a cheap suit puffed away on cigarettes like the Marlboro man.

"Where did you find this place?" Aimee murmured out the side of her mouth. Before Jack could relate his story about how every other number hadn't worked, Dr. Markin surfaced from behind a door and Aimee forced a smile.

They were escorted into Markin's office—an office that lacked nothing but a velvet Elvis. Markin surveyed their little family like a hawk deciding which mouse to eat first.

"Well, first things first, I'm Dr. Markin," he said to Charlie, "and I'm here to help you figure out what's going on in that little head of yours."

Jack grimaced. Not only was the office tacky, the guy was also a pandering prick. But as long as the guy had access to a prescription pad, he'd keep his mouth shut and hope everything went according to plan.

"I'm Aimee," Aimee said. "This is my husband, Jack, and our daughter Charlie."

Doc Markin nodded once, then motioned toward Charlie the way someone would motion to a used car. "So," he said, "what seems to be the problem?"

Jack's stomach turned and he couldn't help but grimace.

"Charlie's been acting out a bit lately," Aimee explained in her most tender tone, pushing Charlotte's hair out of her eyes as she spoke. "We were all involved in an accident—"

"What kind of accident?" Markin cut in.

"A car accident…it was a little over a week ago. The car rolled. We were all fine, but ever since then, Charlie hasn't been herself."

"Probably just stress," he said. Aimee tensed visibly. The last time a doctor had told her there was nothing wrong with Charlotte, she'd gone off.

"Well, that's what we thought at first too," she countered. "But it seems to be getting worse."

Markin honed in on Charlie with his beady eyes. Jack marveled at how much the guy looked like an evil villain with his sharp features and thin lips—the total opposite of Copeland, with his doughy face and puckered smile.

"You want to tell me what's been going on, princess?" Markin asked Charlie. No dice: Charlie was smarter than that. She immediately pulled into herself and turned away from him, hiding her face in Jack's side. Markin let out a little laugh and walked around his desk, plopping into his chair. Aimee spun her wedding ring around her finger and watched Charlie. Jack could tell she was conflicted: part of her wanted a diagnosis, the other part wanted to get the hell out of there.

"Dr. Markin," Jack said after a moment—Aimee nearly jumped at the volume of Jack's calm, confident voice. "I think we just need to be straight with you."

"Certainly," Markin said, squaring his shoulders and folding his arms across his desk.

"We're concerned about a possible psychological condition," Jack said, choosing his words carefully. "Something that may have been triggered by our car accident."

Markin nodded. "That's understandable," he said. "Given the fact that the child has been displaying behavior that doesn't match her personality."

Jack nearly rolled his eyes at Markin's fancy footwork. His father had been the one to say it, and Jack was starting to believe it: head doctors are charlatans. You pay them to use fancy words and tell you what you already know.

"Aimee is worried that it may be schizophrenia."

Aimee blinked at his directness, nearly shot him a glare at the suddenness of his confession. Jack felt like an ass. Now Charlie would inevitably run around telling people her mommy thought she was crazy, but that was a risk he was willing to take. They needed meds. Medicating Charlie would treat the entire family. They were running out of time.

Markin was intrigued, but he didn't appear overly concerned.

"Mrs. Winter," he began, "you do understand that childhood-onset schizophrenia is extremely rare, correct?"

"I know it's rare," Aimee said, "but just because it's rare doesn't mean it's impossible."

"Well that's certainly true, but have there been signs? Voices or hallucinations? Imaginary friends—ones that seem to be real rather than imagined?"

Aimee furrowed her eyebrows in distress. "No," she said softly, the defeat in her voice sounding a lot like shame. "No, I suppose not."

"That's not true," Jack cut in, then hesitated. Charlie would certainly know they were talking about her now, but the detail had to be revealed. "There's someone living in the closet."

Charlie peeked at the doctor from beneath her father's arm.

"There have been personality changes."

"Monsters in the closet," Markin began, his attention now on Jack, "is all part of being a child, Mr. Winter. It's the inability to separate fantasy from reality that we look for. That's our big red flag. Now, that's not to say there isn't a problem."

There was the jackpot—the announcement that Jack had come for: Charlie probably wasn't schizophrenic, but maybe she was. Business was business, and everyone was a little crazy.

"I'd like to run a series of tests, check for things as pedestrian as attention deficit disorder—"

"No," Aimee said. "That's quite all right."

Jack blinked at his wife. He shook his head, not understanding her sudden change of heart.

Aimee leaned down and put her purse in her lap, ready to leave. "But thank you for seeing us." She stood, extending a hand to that sharp-featured man.

"Any time," Markin said with a tight smile.

"Wait." Jack hesitated. What had just happened? They couldn't just leave. "Aimee."

"I was wrong," she told him. "The doctor is right."

Jack swept Charlie up in his arms and rushed after her.

"He's *not* right," he insisted. "He never said you were wrong."

Just as they were about to make their exit, Markin stopped them with a final question.

"Mr. and Mrs. Winter, I didn't ask, but there wouldn't be a history of mental illness in the family, would there?"

Jack and Aimee looked at each other, and Jack was the one to glance back to Markin. This was his chance, his opportunity to paint an exaggerated picture of his own mother. He could make it all up, tell Markin that she was batshit insane, that he didn't know what they were, but she had been loaded up on pills. He'd seen enough movies to come up with a compelling argument. He could make Gilda Winter into a raging psychopath. Markin would be giddy with glee. Jack opened his mouth to speak, ready to insist that yes, there was a shitload of mental illness in the family, that maybe even *he* was crazy, that maybe *he* needed a diagnosis. But instead of sealing the deal, three words slipped past his lips that made his blood run cold.

"No," he said. "There isn't."

Just another lie to add to the rest.

Jack knew his mom had her share of problems in life. He'd heard bits and pieces of conversations long after his parents thought he was in bed. He knew that she'd grown up on little more than bologna and cheese while her mother—a grandmother whom Jack couldn't recall ever meeting—drank herself into a stupor, and her daddy—a man Jack had been told had perished in a mysterious accident—disappeared for days at a time. By the time she entered high school, she had an impressive list of issues: depression, alcoholism, and suicidal thoughts. She had confessed to trying to kill herself twice by the age of seventeen. Jack liked to think that getting pregnant was what saved her, that in some small way, he was the one who had turned his momma's life from bad to good. But once Jack was born, his mom's depression didn't lift; it got worse instead. The older Jack got, the more distant she became. Doctors prescribed her a bunch of pills—half a dozen tiny yellow plastic bottles that Jack would line up for her on the kitchen counter. He did it to help her remember, but she'd forget to take them anyway.

He hadn't been old enough to understand exactly what was wrong with her. All he knew was what his dad told him, and all Stephen told him was that "Momma had a nightmare," whenever she woke up crying. When Jack reached an age where he could better understand the workings of the human mind, Gilda's condition had been medicated away; that is, until Jack saw those soulless eyes.

She whispered her darkest fears to Stephen when she thought Jack wasn't within earshot: she'd passed on some genetic dysfunction, some mental illness that would ruin him just as it had ruined her. But after the tests were done and numerous doctors had been sought for second and third and fourth opinions, the consensus was that there was nothing wrong with Jack Winter—at least not as far as they could see.

For a while, his mom did nothing but yell, insisting they were wrong, that they were all missing something that she could plainly see. Jack couldn't help but to believe it, because normal kids didn't hang cats by lengths of fishing line from the branches of a family tree.

And then there were other signs, ones he kept to himself. He stopped sleeping. It wasn't that he slept for short periods of time; he simply didn't sleep at all. Whenever Gilda would stick her head into his room, she'd catch him staring up at the ceiling, wide eyed and unblinking. Then there was his zoning out. Jack, who was typically a bright and alert child, kept staring into random corners of the room without so much as moving a muscle. His parents were able to hold full-volume conversations around him, and yet he couldn't make out a single word, like they were a million miles away.

It was the fits of rage that did Gilda in. Out of nowhere, he'd go on tirades that included broken dishes and slammed doors, sometimes so hard they threatened to pop off their hinges. Stephen would be the one to give him a good whooping with his belt, but Gilda insisted it wasn't a phase. When she started going to church again, Jack knew his mom was familiar with the shadow that lurked in his room after dark. But she never asked, and Jack never told. And Stephen would never have believed it if either of them had brought it up.

Aimee was furious, and when she was furious she refused to talk. Silent as a deaf mute all the way back to the house, she kept her hands balled into fists on her lap, and while she let her rage boil without a word, Jack allowed his own shame to ferment in the pit of his stomach.

Arriving home, Aimee busied herself with emptying the dishwasher, purposely clanging plates together, testing the durability of their glassware by banging tumblers against the counter.

Charlie was in a mood after her meeting with Dr. Markin and insisted on an afternoon of *SpongeBob* reruns, which Jack happily obliged her with, then excused himself to the kitchen. His reasons for misleading Markin were confusing—he had set up that appointment to get Charlie pharmaceutical help, yet the minute Markin asked about his past he had fucked it all up. He wondered at the possibility of telling Aimee he hadn't been himself, that his own mother's issues—ones that mirrored both Charlie's and his own—had crossed his mind, but the ridiculousness of it only made him smirk at how insane it would all make him look, piling a psychotic husband on top of a psychotic kid. Jack was starting to consider changing their last name from Winter to Manson.

He paused in the kitchen, about to try his hand at comforting his angry wife.

"Let me do that," he told her, making a move to take over dish duty if only to keep her from throwing a plate against the wall. But Aimee continued to clang dishes like the Duchess of Wonderland.

"That man was ridiculous," she said with a snort. "Did you see him? Did you see his stupid little ratty face?"

Jack leaned against the counter and shrugged.

"What?" She stopped the clanging, a plate held dangerously in her grasp. "You didn't see his stupid ratty face? He looked like a rat, Jack. Probably like the goddamn rat that's scratching the insides of our walls. It's like that rat got out, morphed into a human, and dared to call himself a doctor." She exhaled an exasperated laugh. "One hundred fifty dollars, Jack. One hundred fifty fucking dollars down the drain, and for what?"

"Why did you walk out?" Jack asked her. "Because he looked weird?"

"He gave me the creeps," she muttered. "I wouldn't let a guy like that lay a finger on my daughter, let alone screw around inside her head."

Markin *had* looked like a dirty sewer lurker. Aimee shook her head as she stacked plates on the counter, precariously close to the edge.

"I'm not crazy," she said.

"Nobody said you are."

"Yeah, but I just took my kid to a psychiatrist, absolutely convinced there's something wrong, and then I just get up and walk out like, *Oh, never mind, everything is fine.* Why did I do that?"

With her palms pressed to the edge of the counter, she closed her eyes as if meditating.

"He was weird," Jack agreed, resting a hand on her shoulder. "Maternal instinct."

"But my maternal instinct tells me there's something *wrong*."

Jack sighed and took a seat at the kitchen table, propping his chin up in his palm. He wondered what she would do if he just came out with it. *It's the devil.* Maybe she'd stare at him for a long while before exhaling a snort and rolling her eyes. Maybe she'd grab one of those plates off the counter and chuck it at his head.

"I mean, I may as well prance around declaring my unshakable faith in the Easter Bunny," she said. "What difference does it make? I sit down in front of a shrink and the second my suspicion drops out of my mouth I feel like *I'm* the one who needs a diagnosis."

"We'll get a second opinion," he suggested. There had to be someone else they could see. Maybe all those disconnected numbers had been a fluke. Maybe there had been something wrong with his phone. But Aimee cut him off midthought before he could fish his cell out of his pocket.

"No," she said, catching the handle of the utensil basket, pulling it loose from the dishwasher door. "That slimy rat-faced creep had a point." She plucked spoons from the basket. "It's like a one-in-a-million chance, right? Especially without any family history.

Besides, I forgot to water the money tree out back. I'm pretty sure that one fifty was the last of it."

"We've got the money," Jack countered. "We've got the car fund."

Aimee exhaled a breath. She yanked the utensil drawer open and tossed the spoons in.

"That's a dumb idea. If Mom was being serious, Daddy wants the Olds back, which takes us down from four borrowed wheels to zero. It's hard enough as it is with one car. And I'm sure Reagan is having a grand old time driving out here every morning to pick you up for work. Not to mention that he probably hates me by now."

"You know that isn't true."

"Oh come off it," she said, tossing a handful of forks next to the spoons. "I know you've told him how pissed I get every time you drive into the city. He probably thinks I'm an idiot for marrying a musician. Surprise, surprise, there are actually gigs to play."

Jack frowned but didn't argue. Angry wives were a rocker's way of life.

"I'm sorry," she said, her back to him. "I've been a total bitch lately. I've just been so stressed out, so worried. And maybe that nasty rat is right—maybe there's nothing wrong with Charlie at all. Maybe I'm just...*imagining* things. Maybe it's a phase."

It was then, with perfect six-year-old timing, that Charlie appeared at the mouth of the hallway with a request for her mother. "Mo-om," she sing-songed. "Can you make me something to eat?"

Aimee turned from the counter to look at her daughter, and the look in her eyes assured Jack that Charlie was a child she was starting to fear. Aimee forced a halfhearted smile along with a nod. "Sure," she said, her tone unsure. "What would you like?"

"Nuggets!" Charlie said in her three-notches-too-loud inside voice. Then, as if she'd shouted some wizardly Harry Potter incantation, the plates that Aimee had stacked on the kitchen counter fell, a cacophony of breaking glass filling the house. Aimee yelped and jumped away from the counter. Jack leapt from his seat in alarm. All three of them stood in place, staring at the pile of broken dishware that had somehow found its way to the floor.

Charlie clamped her hands over her mouth, and when her parents turned their attention to her she wore an undeniable expression of guilt. "I'm sorry!" she yelled. "It wasn't me!" And then she ran away.

CHAPTER ELEVEN

ON A REGULAR SUMMER AFTERNOON, WHILE JACK SAT slumped on the couch watching *Scooby Doo* on the cheap JVC, a rage slithered into his blood just as it had in the cemetery. Gilda was in the kitchen frying up cheap skirt steaks she'd picked up at the Thriftway. The Winters didn't often have steak for dinner unless they were on manager's special, and his mom had bragged about how lucky she had been to walk by the meat counter at just the right time. They were the last ones left, and her luck had put her in a great mood while standing over the stove, cheap vegetable oil casting a thin veil of smoke across the interior of the trailer. She was singing the *Happy Days* theme song, except she didn't know the words somehow—it was like, what, ten words plus the days of the week?—and it was driving Jack crazy.

"Sunday, Monday, happy days." She sang right over an important part of *Scooby Doo* dialogue. Shaggy had always been Jack's favorite. He loved the way he called Scooby "Scoob" and swore that one day, when he finally had his own dog, he'd name him Scoob even if it was some girly poodle.

"Tuesday, Wednesday, happy days!"

He grimaced at his mother's singing and snatched the remote off the couch, mashing the volume button to drown her out, but the volume didn't go up. The batteries were dead again—that or the remote itself was fried. It was a cheap piece of crap his dad had picked up at a yard sale along the side of the road. When Jack had asked if it would work on their TV, Stephen insisted it was all about light waves and frequency, and maybe he was right because it worked half the time. But the other half, it was nothing but an ugly paperweight taking up room on their scuffed-up coffee table.

"Thursday, Friday, happy days!"

Scooby and the gang finally cornered the ghost they'd been chasing through the entire episode. Fred looked sure of himself, holding the phantom by its sheeted shoulders while Velma revealed its true identity.

"Saturday and Sunday too, all happy days for you!"

Right over the name of the bad guy.

Jack narrowed his eyes at the TV. He clenched the remote as hard as he could, imagining the stupid thing exploding into pieces in his hands. His mom kept singing as he twisted his head toward the kitchen. He could see her standing over the stove, her silhouette faint and hazy through the smoke. If she had been quiet, Jack would have known who the ghost had been. If she'd just stop singing, he could enjoy *The Smurfs* in peace as soon as *Scooby Doo* was over. They'd be on in a matter of seconds. Jack knew this because it was part of his regular scheduled programming; he knew this because during summer vacation, when he wasn't running around outside, he'd watch Hanna-Barbera. But his mom just kept singing. Normally, he would have been glad to see her in such a good mood; she was hardly ever cheerful anymore. But she was ruining everything. All he wanted to do was watch TV.

The Smurfs theme filled the living room and Jack's frustration skyrocketed. He glared at his mother, boring a hole into the back of her head.

And then she started to scream.

At first Jack thought that maybe he really did stare a hole right through her skull, that maybe she was screaming because her brains were oozing out of her head and into the frying pan. But then she moved and he saw that wasn't the case. Gilda jumped away from the stove, revealing a plume of fire as tall and deadly as the devil's finger. The pan was on fire.

"Oh my God!" she yelled. She grabbed for a dish towel, tossing it onto the pan in an attempt to suppress the flames—but the fire was too big for the likes of a cheap scrap of fabric. As soon as it hit the pan, the flames spiked higher. For a second they burned blue.

"Oh my God!" she kept screaming, scrambling around the kitchen, searching for something to douse the flames. In a panic, she grabbed the plastic handle of the pan and moved it from the stove to the sink. Something twisted in the pit of Jack's stomach—a pang that told him what his mom was about to do was a bad idea, maybe a lesson he'd half listened to at school, or something he'd seen on PBS. He opened his mouth to protest. Gilda twisted the kitchen faucet open. Her screams shifted from panic to terror.

As soon as the water hit the boiling oil, there was a hiss of steam. The oil jumped out of the pan and onto the counter, onto the kitchen floor, and onto her cooking apron and bare arms. That fire kept burning. Jack's eyes widened as he watched his mother spin around, her arms outspread like Jesus, her skin blistering before his eyes, like a vampire standing in the hot Georgia sun.

She screamed in pain while the Smurfs skipped and sang through their village.

She didn't sing.

She wailed.

It was Jack's turn to give Charlie her bath while Aimee caught up on a few of her favorite shows. Jack listened to Dr. Gregory House talk down to his patients through the open bathroom door while Charlie piled suds atop her head, turning herself into a giant soft-serve cone. When she wasn't piling bubbles onto her head, she was squeezing them out of a sponge and into an old plastic Big Gulp cup, which she'd then serve to her father as a milkshake. And if milkshakes weren't in season, she'd spend her time arranging foam letters along the bathtub wall.

Tonight was milkshake night. Charlie carefully squeezed a foamy stream of suds into her plastic cup while singing something Jack didn't recognize beneath her breath—probably off a new cartoon he had yet to catch. He lathered up her hair with apple-scented shampoo while she worked on a shake. Dr. House made a sarcastic quip, and despite her pensive mood, Jack heard Aimee laugh in the other room. Charlie served Jack his soapy confection, tilted her head to the side as if seeing her father for the first time, and posed a question Jack hadn't expected.

"Daddy, why did you run away from home?"

Poised to rinse the shampoo from his daughter's hair, he stared at the little girl before him with alarm. Neither one of the kids had ever been told about that part of his past. To hear it questioned so plainly, so innocently, as though she were asking whether tomorrow would be rainy or sunny, all but bowled him over.

"What do you mean?" he stammered, trying to shift his surprise to something resembling confusion, but he did a lousy job.

Charlie squinted at him, lifted a wet hand to rub at her nose, and then let it fall back into the water with a splash.

"You ran away from home when you were little," she told him. "Didn't you love your mommy and daddy?"

Jack felt his heart palpitate in his throat. He was found out. Exposed. Naked. Ready to deny it. The fact that Charlie knew his darkest secret assured him that she hadn't simply pulled it out of thin air; she hadn't just dreamed it up. No, someone had *told* her.

"Where did you hear that?" he asked as nonchalantly as he could, tipping her head back and rinsing the shampoo from her hair. But Charlie didn't reply. She sat quietly while he rinsed, and once he was done she went back to making her milkshakes, squeezing the sponge with pruny fingers.

"Charlie, honey?"

Charlotte avoided his gaze, purposefully busying herself the way kids did when they didn't want to answer a question. But Jack wasn't about to let it rest; he wasn't about to let his secret walk out of that bathroom and, potentially, into Aimee's lap.

"Charlie." Jack caught her hands in his. "I asked you a question."

She frowned and mumbled under her breath. "What?"

"Where did you hear that?"

Jutting her bottom lip out like a dock over a lake, she huffed.

"You brought it up, so now you answer my question."

"No," she muttered. "I don't want to."

"I'm not giving you a choice. Now, you tell me where you heard that before you get yourself into trouble."

Charlie shook her head.

"Why not?"

"Because he'll be mad," Charlie murmured.

Jack's mouth went sour. He tasted blood.

"Who?" he asked.

Again, Charlie shook her head in denial. Jack dropped the rinse cup into the water.

"Fine. No more 'Don't Stop Believin.'"

Charlie's mouth fell open in an O-shape. Her eyes went wide in disbelief. Jack pulled the stopper to the tub and the water began to drain, swirling into a siphoning whirlpool of soap and shampoo. He grabbed Charlie's towel off its holder, dropped it onto the toilet, and caught Charlie beneath her armpits. As soon as her wet feet hit the bath mat her eyes were welling up with tears.

"No 'Don't Stop Believin'"?" she asked in a whisper. Her bottom lip trembled.

Jack stuck to his threat and said nothing more about it despite her puppy-dog eyes. It was the old Charlie, his little stinker, the kid who made his life complete. He wanted to wrap his arms around her and hug her as hard as he could, knowing that he very well may never get to do it again. But he stuck to his guns, toweling Charlie off with silent discipline.

"Fine!" she yelled. "It was Mr. Scratch. He's the one who told me. He knows everything, and now he knows I told you and he's not going to let me sleep ever again."

Jack's heart dropped. An involuntary sob welled up in his chest and tried to punch through, but he swallowed it down. He watched her expression shift. She was upset with herself, as though asking her dad about his running away had been against the rules in the first place, whatever those rules may have been.

Jack didn't need to ask his daughter who Mr. Scratch was. He already knew the answer. He'd seen Mr. Scratch the night he had popped his head into the girls' room—he'd seen that shadow perched in the corner of the room. It was the same shadow that had balanced at the foot of his bed when he was a kid—the shadow with needle-point teeth and a jagged smile. The shadow that was etched into his skin, burning at his back as if to remind him that no, Mr. Scratch had never left—that he was so permanent in Jack's life that he'd tattooed himself into Jack's flesh.

"He says he knows you," Charlie whispered. "He says you guys are friends."

A shiver shot down his spine. He felt his skin crawl with the memory of pulling his sheets over his head, hiding from the demon that watched him while he slept.

"What does he want?" he asked, suddenly ten again. *Tell him to get out of here,* he wanted to tell her. *Tell him to leave me alone.*

Charlie shifted her weight from foot to foot, weighing her options, considering her answer. Finally, she looked up at her dad with a sad sort of smile.

"He's here to play," she told him. "He said you never finished the game."

After Gilda's cooking accident, she gave her son a wide berth. Even though Jack had been in the living room when the fire started, she knew it had been him. She saw something lingering behind the gray of Jack's eyes. It swirled beneath that stormy hue, like ink coiling through water, like fog crawling across the marsh. Her insistence that doctors diagnose his condition faded into silent defeat. And when she dared tell Stephen that she was afraid of their only child, she was sure she appeared insane. She was the one who saw the darkness, who battled fires and found cats swinging in trees. Stephen, for the most part, only heard the stories, and there was only so much he was willing to believe.

By the time Jack turned fourteen, his mother hardly spoke to him. The woman who had once been content to stay home and watch talk shows was now working sixty hours a week just to keep herself out of the house. She couldn't bear spending time at home, especially when Stephen was at work and Jack was home.

During one of her late-night waitressing shifts, she looked out the window while refilling a customer's cup of coffee and saw her son standing in the parking lot. Staring at the diner, he was waiting for her to finish her shift, waiting for her to walk outside so he could finally do away with her. At least that was what she told herself. She snuck into the stockroom and tried to call Stephen. When she couldn't reach him, she peeked back out into that lot. Jack was gone.

Stephen insisted she had hallucinated the whole thing. It was the only logical explanation, after all. The diner was a good dozen miles from the house. Jack didn't have access to a car, let alone have a license. But she just about had a heart attack when she spotted him standing under the same light post the next night. To assure herself she wasn't losing her mind, she asked a big guy in a John Deere cap if he saw the kid in the parking lot too.

"Yep," the trucker said. "Looks like a loon to me."

And he was right—Jack looked insane. He stood in that sickly yellow lamplight with his arms straight down at his sides. His chin was tucked against his chest, and the ridges above his eyes cast an eerie shadow across his face—more like a skull than a boy.

Jack appeared the night after that as well. One of the girls nearly called the police before being stopped by a fellow waitress.

"Better not call the cops," she said. "That's Gilda's boy."

"Well what's he doing just standing there like that?" asked the other. "He looks like he's thinking about shooting up the place."

The cops eventually got called, but not by the girls at the diner. The Winters received the call at 3:00 a.m. on a Sunday. Jack had been found standing on the town pastor's lawn looking ready to slit someone's throat. Worried for his wife and kids, the pastor called the police. Jack had lashed out at them when they finally arrived. The sheriff had explained to a groggy Stephen that his son had been "acting crazy." *Like a wild animal,* he had said. *Like nothing I've seen in all my days.*

Stephen arrived at the police station and found his son in a cell all his own. They'd locked him up by himself to protect the few town drunks, afraid he would have twisted their necks the wrong way round.

"I know it sounds crazy," the sheriff told Stephen, "but that boy of yours didn't seem human. He looked like the devil had gone ahead and eaten his soul right out of his body."

When Gilda caught wind of what had happened, she refused to sleep under the same roof.

"I don't care what you do with him," she told him. "That isn't my son. Look at his eyes, Steve. That isn't Jack. That's something else."

That night, Stephen boarded up Jack's bedroom window from the outside. He secured the door with two-by-fours and kept vigil by sleeping in an old recliner he'd dragged into the hall. Gilda tried to sleep across the house, but all she could do was cry. They had agreed it would be best for Stephen to drive Jack to the psych center in Moultrie. Stephen planned on leaving him there, whether they took him voluntarily or not. It was the last night Jack would be beneath their roof, and Gilda couldn't spend it with him, too afraid to hold him the way a mother should.

After Charlie's revelation about Mr. Scratch, it had taken Jack hours to slip into a restless sleep, battling demons even in unconsciousness. He pulled the sheets over his head when the sunlight crept across his pillow through the blinds, but the smell of sizzling bacon yanked him out of bed like a fish on a hook.

Aimee was standing at the stove, humming under her breath. It should have comforted him, but her humming did little more than shoot a chill down his back. He pictured her turning to say good morning only to see his mother's face—red and scorched and melting, torched by boiling oil. Jack grimaced, and Aimee turned at the perfect moment to catch his expression.

"What?" she asked. "You don't want breakfast?"

Jack forced a tired smile and slouched in one of the kitchen chairs. "Breakfast sounds good," he told her, pressing his face into his hands as exhaustion crept in.

"You were tossing and turning all night," Aimee said. "Did you get any sleep?"

"Hardly."

"Maybe you should call in," she suggested, and Jack found himself considering it. He never missed work. Skipping out on the shop sounded far more appealing than welding on zero sleep. But he'd cut out of work early just a few days before. Reagan had been pulling double shifts just to keep them on track with repairs, determined to keep Max happy, determined to not let Jack lose his job.

"I was thinking…" Aimee set his breakfast in front of him before taking her usual seat. "Maybe we can do some grown-up stuff today, just the two of us. You know, like normal people."

Jack plucked his fork off the table and dug into his breakfast.

"I thought that maybe we could go to some dealerships, check out a few cars."

Jack hated using Arnold's Olds and Aimee knew it. Yet, amid the recent chaos, visiting the car salesman had been put off indefinitely. Letting someone try to swindle them out of their money would be a refreshing change of pace.

"And then we could go get lunch in town somewhere," she suggested. "Maybe Bijou?"

It all sounded fantastic. They'd be a childless, worry-free couple for a handful of hours. For half a day their problems would be pushed to the background, and maybe that's all it would take— half a day to reestablish their sanity, to regroup and refresh and find their way back to the life they used to have. Before Jack had a chance to protest—it wasn't fair to Reagan, he *had* to go to work regardless of how little sleep he'd gotten—the phone rang and chaos found them again.

It was Charlie's school.

The principal was a stern-looking woman—the kind of woman who was born to discipline small children. Mrs. Hutchins sat at her desk with her hands folded in front of her. She eyed Charlie's parents—a gaze heavy with judgment—before she finally spoke.

"Mr. and Mrs. Winter, we've had an incident."

Incident—Jack hated that word. It made him think of worst-case scenarios. He pictured Charlie burying schoolchildren in the sand beneath the monkey bars, or poisoning the school lunch by sprinkling rat poison into the mashed potatoes.

"What kind of an incident?" Aimee asked, tugging on her bottom lip.

"Charlotte interrupted an exam this morning," Mrs. Hutchins explained. "The children were in the middle of taking a vocabulary test when Charlie began to shake her desk."

Jack and Aimee glanced at each other.

"I know what you're thinking," she continued. "And I'll admit, the idea of a child as small as Charlotte being able to shake her desk while sitting in it is, well, a bit like a magic trick. But her teacher insists it happened. She said the desk was shaking like an old washer on its spin cycle."

"How can that be possible?" Aimee asked. Mrs. Hutchins shook her head, unfolding her hands to show Aimee that she didn't have a solid answer.

"Mrs. Winter, I'm not a physicist, I'm an elementary school principal. All I know is that Charlotte disrupted an entire class, and when she was asked to stop she continued, which resulted in my calling you here today."

"Did anything else happen?" Jack asked after a moment. "Other than the desk?" *Like spinning heads and homicide?*

Mrs. Hutchins cleared her throat and raised an eyebrow. "Funny you should ask," she said. "Shortly after Charlotte was told to come see me she had an outburst."

"An outburst," Jack repeated.

"She called her teacher a name," Mrs. Hutchins explained. "A vulgar name…one that I'd rather not imagine her learning at home."

"What did she say?" he asked, but Mrs. Hutchins snorted at his question.

"Mr. Winter, I'm not about to repeat profanity, even if it came out of a six-year-old girl."

"She's been having problems," Aimee explained. "We've taken her to a therapist."

"I see." Mrs. Hutchins sounded less than interested. "Mr. and Mrs. Winter, under advice from Charlotte's teacher, we feel that she should take a few days off."

"A few days off?" Aimee shook her head. "Charlie just missed a day last week. She can't take any more time off school. It's just—"

"Unfortunately, the decision has already been made."

Aimee's eyes lit up with defiance. "Are you suspending my daughter?" she challenged.

"We don't like to call it a suspension," Mrs. Hutchins explained. "It's just a break until Monday."

Incensed, Aimee stood with a glare. "She needs normalcy," she said. "Something that you're about to deny her." Mrs. Hutchins opened her mouth to offer a rebuttal, but Aimee cut her off mid-breath. "If my daughter's condition worsens because of this little *break*…" She paused, considering her words carefully. "I'll hold you personally responsible."

Again, Mrs. Hutchins was about to speak, but Aimee persisted.

"We may not have a lot of money, and maybe that's where you get off," she said. "I'm sure you have a picture-perfect house built off stolen milk money, but let's make one thing perfectly clear."

Jack blinked at his wife. He was stunned into stillness.

"If this affects Charlotte badly, you'll be hearing from my lawyer—and I don't have a lawyer, Mrs. Hutchins, but believe me when I say I'll hire one. I'll pay one just to help me dig your grave."

Aimee turned on the balls of her feet and marched out of the office, leaving Jack to stare at a wide-eyed principal left speechless in Aimee Winter's wake. Jack slowly rose from his seat, cleared his throat, and offered Mrs. Hutchins a slight nod.

"Have a nice day," he told her, then rushed to follow after Aimee, desperate to get out of that office before Mrs. Hutchins suspended him too.

Aimee was livid, and her anger didn't stop with the principal. As soon as Charlie was strapped into her seat and the Oldsmobile was rolling along the street, she launched into a tirade that extended to both her husband and daughter.

"What were you thinking?" she snapped. "During a *test*, Charlie? Are you serious?"

"I didn't do anything!" Charlie insisted, but Aimee was too angry to listen. She turned her attention to Jack instead.

"And you," she began. "You just sat there and took that woman's bullshit."

"Um," Jack blinked. "Language."

"Oh shut up," Aimee muttered.

"You handled the situation like a champ," he told her, but it just made Aimee more upset.

"That isn't the point and you know it. The point is that I shouldn't have had to handle the situation. *You're* the man. *You're* the one who's supposed to stand up to that...that *tyrant*."

"Charlie interrupted the entire class," Jack reminded her.

"I didn't do it!" Charlie yelled from the backseat.

"Are you taking that woman's side?" Aimee looked flabbergasted. "You think this is the right course of action?"

"I'm not saying it's the right course of action..."

"It certainly sounds like that's what you're saying."

"What's done is done. Maybe this is a good thing."

"A *good* thing? Charlie missing more school is a good thing? Please explain to me how that's possible."

"I don't know how it's a good thing," he told her. "I'm just trying to be optimistic."

"Well thank you for that bit of sunshine, but your optimism isn't going to fix things," she told him, and she was right. He could hope for the best, he could convince Aimee and maybe even himself that Charlie was simply having some sort of mental break, he could even tell himself that it was all in his head, that *he* was the one who was imagining things, replaying his own childhood nightmare like some TV rerun. But none of that would change anything. Nothing he did would save Charlie from what he knew was torturing her. Nothing would save her because nothing had saved him.

The realization hit him head-on, like a bullet train on a one-way track. Steering the car toward the house, he was suddenly overtaken by a wave of nausea that threatened to choke him. The cabin of the Olds became claustrophobic. He felt a scream claw its way up his throat, threatening to punch its way through his teeth. His heart threw itself against his ribcage, desperately trying to escape the prison of his chest.

He drove the rest of the way home in a fugue state, not sure how he managed to get them there in one piece, not sure how Aimee hadn't noticed the cold sweat that had bloomed across his forehead. Charlie sprinted across the lawn and into the house. Aimee followed shortly after, leaving Jack alone in the car. He couldn't bring himself to step outside. He was going to lose his daughter. He couldn't do anything to stop it.

CHAPTER TWELVE

AFTER ABBY HAD COME HOME FROM SCHOOL, JACK SAT on the front porch steps of the house and watched the girls play with Nubs on the front lawn. Jack was walking a thin line between panic and defeat. His mind was racing, trying to pick apart a situation that hardly anyone would believe. There was one option left—one that he could hardly bring himself to acknowledge. Calling an exorcist would not only mark his daughter as disturbed, but also mark his entire family as crazy, insane, out of their minds...the kind of backwoods hillbillies who believed in witchcraft and the end of the world. He hadn't considered it before, but maybe exorcisms really worked. Maybe, for once in his life, God would step up to the plate and help, if not him then at least Charlie. Charlie hadn't done anything wrong. It wasn't possible for a six-year-old girl to deserve the devil's attention. If there was a God, he would certainly help a child, wouldn't he? Jack was sure his own parents believed Jesus would walk the earth one day, but even they had counted demonic possession out of the equation. They were poised to send him to an institution, to lock him up in an asylum for the rest of his life—they were ready to make him a prisoner of the state before they would ever lash him to his bed and sprinkle him with holy water. But what if they had tried? Could it have been possible that things would have been different? Could he have been saved?

The last thing he wanted to do was send Charlie away. Despite their reasonable fear, he'd never forgiven his own parents for turning their backs on him. They had given up and chosen the simplest solution: to get rid of the problem, you get rid of the kid.

Charlie and Abigail raced across the lawn in a bubble of laughter, Nubs dashing after them with his tongue sticking out the side of his mouth, his ears pulled back as though he was racing through a wind tunnel. They were playing hide-and-seek, and despite Nubs's inability to grasp even the simplest concepts, he had somehow learned the rules of the game. Abigail had taught him how to hide behind trees, plopping his butt down on the grass and waiting patiently to be found. In that sense, he was the perfect dog—always ready to play, his tail wagging as gaily as it had when he was nine weeks old.

It was Charlie's turn to be the seeker. She stood against the side of her grandpa's car and covered her face, counting as loudly as she could while Nubs and Abby searched for a hiding place. Abby was particularly good at finding random nooks and crannies to squeeze herself into, like a contortionist squeezing herself into a tiny box.

She'd once managed to get herself stuck beneath the front porch. Jack and Aimee had wiggled her out into the open right before Aimee was set to panic, ready to call the fire department.

Nubs, on the other hand, while good at hiding, was bad at finding new trees to hide behind. Predictably, he dashed to the same tree every time and sat wagging his tail.

Charlie reached fifty and yelled the well-known childhood battle cry of "*Ready or not,*" and then dashed across the lawn. She searched the front side of the house, scouring all of Abby's usual spots. When Charlie didn't find her, she moved to Nubs's tree. She let out a little yelp as soon as she saw him and ran at him, determined to tag him on his furry butt and disqualify him from the game. Nubs pressed his front paws to the ground, his hind-quarters pointed skyward—a position that assured Charlie he was ready for the chase. She darted toward him and he sprinted away, stopping a few yards down the lawn, taunting her with that puppylike pose. She ran at him again, and Nubs dashed around her. Jack was impressed by how agile the old dog still seemed to be, and relieved by how utterly normal Charlie appeared.

Charlie stopped to catch her breath. With her hands on her knees, she peered at Nubs from across the yard. This time, when she looked at him, Nubs's tail stopped wagging. Instead of running, Charlie strolled toward him, sing-songing, "*Here puppy, puppy, puppy.*" At first the call was innocent, but Charlie's tone changed when, a few feet from her target, Nubs dashed away yet again. Nubs's body language had also shifted. Rather than his typical puppylike jaunt, he ran away with his tail between his legs. Charlie stared at him from across the yard, her hands balling up into fists. Nubs laid down, his nose buried in the cool blades of grass. He exhaled a whine from deep within his throat.

The game had turned dark. Jack watched Charlie's mouth curl up into a sneer, but he didn't move. He wanted to leap from that front step and put an end to it, but something held him in place. A part of him knew the game would end badly, and that part—the moral part—was ready to sprint into action and stop the whole thing. But he simply sat there. Despite his desire to jump up, he simply sat there and watched the hunt with a sick sense of fascination, glued to the top step by an unseen hand.

This time Charlie took her time moving across the grass, taking step after slow step, as though trying to fool the stupid dog into thinking she was standing still instead of moving toward him. Nubs held his position; Charlie continued to inch closer. When she was only a few yards away, she lunged like a predator. Nubs scrambled to his feet, almost comical in the way his legs bent and wobbled beneath him. But Charlie showed no sympathy for her loyal companion, running after him despite Nubs's palpable fear. Suddenly, Charlie stopped as if giving up the chase, but her expression gave her intentions away. She glared at Nubs while he panted in the sun.

She leaped forward abruptly. Nubs gave a yelp, running from her the way an animal runs from a bigger, stronger opponent. Had it not been Charlie, he would have bared his teeth and dared her to come closer. But in his confusion—attacked by someone who he thought was his friend—he could do nothing but run. His nails clacked against the asphalt as he ran into the street. Whatever was holding Jack down released him then. His eyes darted to the approaching truck—once distant, but now hopelessly close. The sound of tires skidding on pavement made him cringe, but he was unable to tear his eyes away from the carnage.

Charlie stood along the side of the road while the delivery guy bounded from a UPS truck yelling, "*Oh my God!*" with a heavy Southern twang. Abigail erupted from her hiding place, running at the truck with a strange sort of garbled scream, as though the scream was unsure of itself—as though reality was, for the briefest of moments, too horrible to be happening. Jack was off those steps right along with her, but Abby had become the fastest runner in all of Louisiana. She outran her father and reached the truck first. That's when a genuine scream tore loose from her chest.

Stopping just shy of the pavement, Jack saw Nubs wedged beneath a tire, his bottom half crushed, nearly torn in two by the impact. Surreal as it was, his top half was untouched. He looked as though he could have still been alive if you didn't look at him from the waist down. He was dead before the truck ever came to a complete stop.

Abby wailed like a Greek at a funeral. Jack reached for her, but she shoved him away and ran back to the house, pushing past Aimee, who must have come out when she heard Abby's screams and stood stunned on the front porch step. Jack stared at Aimee for a moment before she disappeared inside, rushing to their daughter's aid. Charlotte was unmoved by her sister's tears. She stood expressionless in front of the truck, watching the delivery guy freak out as though Nubs had been his dog instead of hers.

"I'm so sorry," the guy kept saying. "Oh my God, I'm so sorry, mister."

He eventually ran back inside the truck and grabbed a cell phone with a shaky hand, probably placing a call to his dispatcher. All the while, Charlie stood motionless, staring at the remains of a dog four years her elder without a scrap of despair in her eyes. Jack wasn't sure she knew he was standing next to her—he wasn't sure she remembered that anyone else existed at that moment at all. She was in a trance, a tiny zombie examining her handiwork. And as if it couldn't have gotten any worse—that delivery guy yelling into his phone, Abigail screaming inside the house, Nubs torn in half with his guts spilling onto the road—the corner of Charlie's mouth twitched, not into a frown, but a smile. And the voice whispered:

You sat there and watched her do it. How good does that feel?

Walking back inside that house was terrifying. Jack could hear Abby wailing long before he pulled open the screen door. Her sorrow was immense—powerful enough to seep through the walls and into the yard like vapor. Her despair twisted his heart into a knot, pulling so tight that his heartstrings creaked. As he stood motionless in the doorway, Abigail's weeping slithered from inside her room and tied itself like a noose around his neck. The backs of his eyes burned. His sinuses sizzled with the sting of saline. All at once he was sure he was about to lose it—about to suffer the emotional breakdown he had feared since he had seen those dark, empty eyes a split second before their Saturn had flipped through the air.

He turned away from the house, ready to sneak away until the sound of Abby's tears was something he could handle. Then he saw Charlie standing on the top porch step, and he stopped short.

"What's wrong, Daddy?" she asked, her eyes round and inno-cent, ignoring her sister's cries—weeping so loudly it drowned out every other sound in the world.

Jack suddenly wanted to snatch her off her feet and throw her down those steps. He wanted to shake her so hard the devil would scramble away in search of a place to hide. The little girl who, six years before, had redefined his entire life, now made his blood run cold. Everything about her, from her little-girl voice to the artificial innocence she wore across her face, made Jack hate her. At that very moment, had Charlotte turned and run across the lawn into the trees across the road, he wouldn't have followed her. He would have turned away and pretended he hadn't seen a thing.

But Charlie didn't turn, and she didn't run; and Jack didn't make a move to grab her the way he had imagined a second before. She remained on the front porch step, her eyes wide, glittering with childlike virtue. "Poor Daddy," she told him, her expression as chaste as one of God's angels. "So sad," she whis-pered. "Sad about a dead fucking dog."

Jack didn't tell Aimee what he had seen—not the way the girls had been playing hide-and-seek, not the way Charlie had lunged at Nubs just as the delivery truck passed by. He was sure Aimee suspected the worst, but she hadn't been there; it was his word over hers. For all intents and purposes, it was a horrible accident. Nubs had run out into the road on his own.

He knew it couldn't go on for much longer. He was at his limit, sure that if things continued to escalate he'd be barring the girls' windows, just as his father had barred his own. He'd blockade their bedroom door with his crappy piano until he could figure out what the hell to do. And yet, in the same instant he knew that would never happen. The longer it went on the less he did to stop it. The moment an exorcism had crossed his mind, he was assured by his motionlessness upon that front step that he wouldn't be doing anything of the sort. He was nothing but an enabler—a facilitator of his own daughter's demise.

He left the house, burned rubber across Live Oak until he arrived at Reagan's place—a house even shittier than their own. Jack didn't bother to knock. He burst inside like a serial killer thirsty for blood, catching Reagan completely off guard while he sat in front of his computer. A photo of a topless chick bent over a Trans Am was speckled with program icons.

"Holy shit," Reagan half laughed, half yelped. "You scared the fuck out of me. What..." He paused, the look on Jack's face making his own expression go cold. "Jack?"

"Nubs is dead," Jack announced, marching past his best friend and into Reagan's kitchen. "She ran him into the fucking road."

Reagan sat motionless, stunned into silence as Jack yanked the refrigerator door open. He was searching for beer, but Reagan must have been drinking the last one.

"Wait, what? *Who* ran Nubs into the—"

"Charlie," Jack cut him off. "Fucking *Charlie* did. She ran him under a delivery van."

Reagan lifted his arms, pushed his hands through his hair, his expression frozen in disturbed disbelief.

"I don't know what to do," Jack confessed, slamming the refrigerator door closed. He slid down the kitchen wall, his head thrown back, his eyes focused on the moth-filled light fixture overhead. "It's over," he whispered. "It's done."

Reagan cautiously rose from his computer desk. He carefully approached Jack, squatting in front of the man he'd grown up with.

"Jack, why are you here, man? Why aren't you at home?"

Something tore loose inside him then. All the pent-up emotion, the anger and the fear, it ripped itself from where it had been stuck for decades—a scab viciously torn away, an open wound hissing with pain. Jack's head lolled forward into his arms and a sob echoed up from the linoleum floor.

That was when the last viable option for Charlie's deliverance came to him. He could think of one last possibility.

Why aren't you at home?

Go back and face the demons he'd run from nearly two decades before.

Go back.

Go to Georgia.

"I don't understand," Aimee muttered, gathering a few of Nubs's chew toys off the floor. She had been furious when Jack had up and disappeared. He had left her to console a heartbroken child, but her anger dissipated when she saw the expression on Jack's face. He was just as upset as Abigail. She wiped at her eyes, still not having fully recovered from what had happened that afternoon.

"First you take off, you *leave* me here with…" She paused, shaking one of Nubs's toys at the girls' room as if not wanting to speak Charlie's name. "And now you want to leave again? Are you *kidding* me? No. Absolutely not."

Jack had lied again. He told her that Max, his boss, had dropped the name of a child psychiatrist, one of the best...one that just so happened to be in Georgia instead of Louisiana.

"It can wait," Aimee said. "It's waited this long, so it can wait a little longer."

"I already called," Jack told her.

"So call again and reschedule. What do you want me to do, leave Abby at my mother's? After what just happened? We can't make it."

"*We* can't," Jack agreed, "but *I* can." It was the heart of his argument. There was no doctor, no appointment. There was only Jack's old house—a trailer out in the middle of nowhere that may very well have been gone for years. All he knew was where it had been. And if it was gone? Well, the town wasn't much bigger than Live Oak. It would take but a handful of hours to ask around, to find someone who knew Stephen and Gilda Winter. He needed to speak to his mother. He needed to ask her what she knew.

Aimee grabbed a half-eaten squeaky toy off the living room rug. Destroying stuffed toys had been Nubs's specialty. He had once eaten all of the polyester filling out of a stuffed hot dog. It had clogged him up for days.

"That's what doesn't make sense," Aimee said. "What's the point of you going by yourself?"

"It's just a consultation. You can't get your kid in to see this guy before you meet with him first. Even if we all were able to go, he wouldn't see Charlie anyway."

Aimee looked down at the torn yellow duck in her hand. She frowned at it.

"And we'll have to drive to Georgia to see him," she said. "What, every weekend? How are we going to afford something like that? If he's so good, how are we going to afford to see him at all? You have to work. And what about the band?"

"Reagan knows," Jack confessed. "He's the one who encouraged it. Listen, don't worry about that stuff, OK?" Jack exhaled a breath and lifted his shoulders in a shrug. "I have to do this."

Aimee narrowed her eyes in a flash of suspicion, and Jack realized it had been an odd thing to say, that *he* had to do it instead of *they* had to do it.

"For Charlie," Jack added. "As her dad."

"And leave me here with the girls."

"Just for a couple of days."

"When Abigail is a wreck, Jack. And Charlie…" She hesitated. "I thought this was an accident. I thought Nubs just ran out. Isn't that what happened?"

Jack stared down at the floor. It was too late to deny the obvious.

"Jack?" Aimee's eyes went glossy with tears. "Isn't that what happened?"

"We need to get her help," he said softly.

"Oh my God." Aimee's tears began to flow. "I knew it. I was hoping I was wrong, but I *knew* it." She pressed her free hand over her eyes. "Everything is falling apart," she whispered. "Everything is completely fucked up."

CHAPTER THIRTEEN

THE DRIVE TO ROSEWOOD WAS A LONG ONE—OVER EIGHT hours one way—but Jack decided to get an early start and leave that night instead of waiting until morning. Getting there early would give him an extra half day of daylight, and though Aimee didn't like the idea of Jack driving at night on his own, she was too tired to argue.

The Louisiana darkness was oppressive. If the night sky had torn itself open and bled ink onto the earth, it still wouldn't come close to the depth of shadow that swallowed the levees and live oaks. It was liquid darkness, a darkness so heavy it blotted out the brightest headlights. But the weightiness of night was, for Jack, more than appropriate. It was the perfect backdrop to a battalion of unwanted memories, the perfect color for the nightmare that had become his life.

He remembered being locked in his room, he remembered police lights and standing on someone's lawn, but he didn't remember exactly what had pushed his parents over the edge. Something had happened to reduce his mother into an emotional wreck of a woman, weeping, trying to talk around the hitching in her throat. He could hear them yelling at one another outside his door, but everything was muffled, underwater. Jack made out a few words, words like "safety" and "away" and "not right" and "no choice." Otherwise, all he could recall was that their argument was stop-and-go. One minute they were yelling, and the next minute there was nothing but silence—off and on like a blinking streetlight.

Beyond that memory, he had no idea how he had escaped his bedroom. He had been lying on his bed, staring up at the ceiling, and suddenly there was damp grass beneath his feet as he sprinted across the lawn. He had been absent, maybe asleep, but as time had gone on he had grown used to losing time.

At first it had been just minutes. Then, eventually, inevitably, those minutes had grown into hours. Sometimes he'd wake up in random places—parking lots, his mom's diner, the football field behind the high school gym. The idea of his condition being passed down chilled him as he drove. Maybe it had gone dormant, but he'd been infected all along. He was almost positive that his mother had been suffering from the same thing—it was why she'd gone crazy when Jack started acting out. He'd caught the disease from her, but who had infected her? The grandparents he had never met? Was that why he hadn't met them? Was she hiding her past the way Jack had been hiding his?

He shot an arm out to Arnold's stock stereo, desperate for some noise to quiet his thoughts. Nothing but talk radio riddled

with static. Out in the middle of nowhere, nothing survived—
not even rock and roll. He could have pulled the car over and
blown his brains out if he wanted. Nobody would be there to hear
the gunshot. Nobody would call the cops. He'd just lie there, his
brains oozing out of his skull, dead and waiting for the animals to
drag him away.

He blinked.

Suicide had never crossed his mind before, and now he was
picturing himself mouthing the barrel of a gun.

"What the fuck, Jack?" he murmured, glaring at the road. He
punched the gas, challenging the ridiculous thought by blasting
toward Georgia's border faster than before. But speed didn't keep
those thoughts from slithering into his ear like a parasitic worm.
There was a story he hadn't thought of in God knew how long,
a story every kid knew—the tale of the phantom hitchhiker sitting in the backseat of a dark car, waiting to be discovered in the
rearview mirror. But instead of it being a rotten-faced ghost in
the back of Arnold's Olds, Jack imagined a razor-toothed shadow
wearing an ear-to-ear grin.

Mr. Scratch.

That's what Charlie had called him. Twenty years ago, it
hadn't had a name.

He fought the urge, but his eyes jumped to the rearview. The
backseat was empty—nothing. Mr. Scratch had more important
things to do than take a road trip back to Rosewood. Mr. Scratch
was busy with a six-year-old girl who, for all Jack knew, would no
longer be his daughter by the time he got back home.

A few minutes past 3:00 a.m., the bang of the screen door jerked
Aimee awake. Someone was in the house. That serial killer she'd
been waiting for had finally found her, and now he was going to
murder her in front of the girls.

She heard a quiet bleat slip through the bedroom. Had it not vibrated in her throat, she would have sworn it had come from someone other than her.

"Think of the girls," she whispered, psyching herself up. If Jack had been home, she'd have sent him out into the hall to investigate, sacrificed her own husband so she could make her escape. But Jack wasn't there. She was left as the protector.

As she grabbed a framed photograph of her and Jack on a trip to Charleston as a weapon, a ridiculous thought came into her head: Would she beat the serial killer over the head with it, or show him what a nice family she had? As she crept into the hallway with the picture clasped in her hands, she was sure there was something wrong with her maternal instinct. All the things she'd read about mothers protecting their children, yet her first impulse was to run out of the house screaming bloody murder.

Finally making it to the living room, she nearly choked on her heart. The front door was wide open. She veered around, her eyes as wide as possible to help her see in the dark, but she didn't see anyone. She told herself there couldn't have been anyone in the house, because Nubs would have gone ballistic.

And then she remembered that Nubs couldn't warn them, because Nubs was dead.

With the picture frame pressed to her chest like a shield, she crept toward the door. Outside, the wind had picked up. She could hear the branches of the oaks groan and complain as they swayed back and forth. They were the kind of trees you wanted on your property because they were ancient and mystical, but that you regretted having when the rain fell sideways and the wind howled through the leaves.

She stopped at the threshold of the door, her toes brushing the frame of the screen door as she looked out into the yard. Out on the road that ran in front of the house, in the exact spot where Nubs had expired, a shadow lurked in what looked to be a crouch, hunched over something unseen. It looked like an animal—maybe a wolf that had crawled out of the trees to sniff at the blood-soaked road. But when it moved Aimee knew she was wrong. The shadow shifted its weight with jerky, unnatural motions, like an old movie reel hitching on its sprockets. She drew in a breath—silent beneath the whisper of wind and shivering leaves—but the small sound of drawing in air did something to that blotch of darkness. It froze as if listening. Aimee's eyes went wide when the shadow stopped moving, knowing that she'd been heard. The idea of this thing, whatever it was, knowing that she was standing in the doorway made her blood run cold. She pressed her hand over her mouth to muffle her breathing, but the shadow liked that even less. It bristled when it sensed movement. It reeled and shot a stare across the lawn, its black eyes unspeakably dark—twin black holes, devouring light.

Aimee's breath caught. Her heart ceased to beat. She stared at the thing that was leering at her and stumbled away from the door. It had fangs—cannibal teeth as sharp as the points of her best kitchen knives. As soon as it saw her step back, its mouth twisted, those jagged teeth shining red with blood. Beyond its shoulder she could see the remnants of what could have only been Nubs's body, torn to pieces, glistening against the asphalt.

She exhaled a yelp and shoved the front door closed, throwing the dead bolt into place. As soon as the door slammed shut, she ran to the window to see if the shadow was still out there, still eating her dog.

It was gone. So was Nubs—Jack had buried him in the backyard before he had left. Aimee squeezed her eyes shut.

"You're seeing things," she whispered, pressing her forehead against the cool glass. But the longer she stood there, the more reality drummed at her brain. *The door,* she thought. *That wasn't my imagination.* The door had been open; she knew this because she had just slammed it shut. Her body went tense at the thought;

she had assumed someone had come in, but the more she put it together the more it seemed like someone, or something, had gone *out*.

Jack pulled over at a gas station just shy of the Georgia state line, drawn to the place by its cold fluorescent glow. The place looked out of business, like a photo out of a ghost town picture book—the kind of place you put behind you as fast as possible because the vibe is wrong; the kind of place that, if you ever caught a flat, would be the last place you'd want to stop to ask for help. But Jack stopped. He didn't need gas—he had a half tank that would take him well beyond Rosewood—but he stopped anyway, drawn to the place by some unexplainable pull.

Fluorescent lights buzzed over two rusty gas pumps in the middle of the cracked parking lot, flickering and popping, giving the place that classic horror movie vibe. There was something cinematically surreal about it, something that matched his situation to a T.

Loose gravel crunched beneath his shoes as he walked toward the building he hoped at least had a working soda machine. He was fiending for a Milky Way but doubted he'd get lucky. Passing a grungy window, he spotted a guy sitting behind a counter—mangy beard, bushy eyebrows, wild eyes, and a trucker's cap. A bolt of anxiety shot through his veins. Something clicked inside his brain, told him to run. It was the guy from the voodoo shop, the one who had disappeared seemingly into thin air. *Go back*, he told himself. *Don't go in there. Bad fucking idea.* But he went inside anyway. He went inside despite the screaming inside his head.

The guy didn't say anything when Jack entered, but he did move a hairy arm to tip the brim of his hat in greeting before spitting a wad of black tar into a plastic drink cup. Unease churned in the pit of Jack's stomach. He turned to search the barren shelves for a snack and found nothing but lukewarm bottled water and a pack of pink snowballs, half-crushed and two years beyond their expiration date. He grimaced and slid his hands into his pockets. He'd have to drive through half of Georgia on an empty stomach.

Just as Jack turned to shuffle out of the place, the guy behind the counter stopped him with a few gruff words.

"What'cher lookin' for?"

"Just a candy bar." Jack focused his full attention on the guy. He was huge—probably towered close to seven feet.

"You're drivin' down this road at four in the mornin' lookin' for a candy bar?" The guy spit another mouthful of black saliva into his cup. "Must have a hell of a sweet tooth."

That dirty trucker cap gave Jack the creeps. Something about the guy didn't sit right, like maybe he didn't actually work at the station at all. Maybe he just had a key and he flipped on the lights every now and again, waiting for a car to pull into that shitty parking lot so he could sink a knife deep into a stranger's belly.

"Thanks anyway," Jack murmured. He wanted to ask the guy if he had seen him somewhere before, wanted to know how he'd react, but he didn't dare. Jack continued to the door.

"You might better watch out," the trucker said, bringing Jack to a halt. At first he wasn't sure whether it was a warning or a suggestion. The jolly green giant spotted Jack's confusion and continued. "You bein' followed, chief, and you done know it too."

"I'm being followed," Jack repeated. He had meant for it to come out as a question, but it just sounded like an echo.

"You're runnin', but you're runnin' from something you've been runnin' from all your life, aren't ya? Runnin' like it's gonna make some sort of big difference this time round."

Sourness crept into Jack's mouth. He stared at the bearded giant, said nothing.

"I've seen your kind. I see you all the time, drivin' down the road like the devil can't chase ya if ya step on the gas."

A shudder shook Jack from the inside out—a tiny earth-quake of the heart. He swallowed the spit that had collected in his mouth.

"Ain't no use denyin', chief. I've seen your kind plenty of times. Seems like the ones runnin' are the only ones that ever stop on in here, lookin' for an excuse to turn right around and head back to where they came from. They just tell themselves, 'Naw, I'm just stoppin' for a Coke. I'm just stoppin' for a Hershey's or a HoHo, or maybe they got them one of those slushie machines.' But we don't got none of that, do we?"

Jack cleared his throat. "Doesn't look like it," he said.

"Don't look like it because we don't got none of it, that's why."

Shifting his weight from one foot to the other, Jack contem-plated making a run for it, sure that the giant behind the counter would lunge at him if he tried. But the longer he stood there the more his curiosity began to itch.

"Why is that?" Jack asked. "What's the point of being open if you don't have anything to buy?"

"Maybe I do got something to buy," he said. "Maybe what I'm sellin' you just can't see yet."

Jack chewed on his bottom lip. Part of his brain urged him to crawl back into that Oldsmobile and continue to Rosewood as planned. But another part of his brain, a bigger part, was con-vinced this guy knew things, that he was fated to meet this enor-mous man, a man who could have easily been a mass murderer, if only to prepare himself for the next round of his trip.

"You go to N'awlins quite a bit, don't ya?"

Jack tensed.

"I can smell it. That place gots the smell of ghosts, chief, and that smell don't wash off easy."

"Why does that matter?" Jack asked. The guy exhaled a laugh.

"It matters cause you found answers there, but you brushed 'em aside, ended up drivin' in the middle of the night instead.

You're lookin' for a way out and you don't know which way to look."

Jack went silent for a long while, then eventually confessed, "You're right. I don't know what the fuck I'm doing."

"I already told ya. You're runnin' like you've been runnin' for your whole damn life."

"Except I'm running toward something this time," Jack assured him. "I'm running straight toward the thing I've been avoiding, so that's a start, right?"

"A start to what, chief?"

"A solution," Jack said. "At least I hope it is. If it isn't, I don't know what else to do."

The trucker took on a thoughtful look before offering Jack a knowing nod.

"I suppose that *is* a start," he said. "But ya aren't gonna like what ya find."

Jack opened his mouth to speak. The trucker cut him off with a chuckle.

"Let me guess, that's a risk yer willin' t'take, right? People always think they've got to be riskin' something to get to the end of the story. But let me tell ya: it's *your* story. The end of the story is gonna get ya whether you want it to er not. You think you gotta go chase fate? Fate is chasin' *you*, chief. But *you* know that, right? Better than any old body."

Jack stared, frozen in place.

"I'm sayin' it don't matter," the trucker said. "You want to turn right back around and go home. Ya do that. It ain't gonna make one bit of a difference. The end is gonna find you no matter which direction ya drive. And if I'm right about what's chasin' ya…" He lifted his big shoulders in an almost childlike shrug, his expression shifting toward apologetic. "You ain't gonna outrun it—at least not by my experience. I've been around for a long time, been sittin' here watchin' people roll in and out for my entire life, and

I gotta tell ya…" He leaned forward on the stool he occupied, its rusty metal legs whining beneath his weight. "I ain't never seen anyone, not *anyone* outrun the devil."

Jack's mouth went acrid, like someone had cracked open a battery and poured the acid onto his tongue. He took a step back, one of his hands drifting to his chest, pressing against his sternum, where his lungs had gone tight and raw.

"What do you know about the devil?" Jack asked, but his inquiry was nothing more than a dry whisper. He was about to tell the guy that nobody knew more about the devil than him, but when his eyes snagged on the guy's face, his heart seized. The giant laughed, and when he threw his head back to chortle toward the stained ceiling, Jack caught a glimpse of needle points glinting inside that gaping mouth.

Jack bolted for the exit, flinging the cracked glass door open so hard it hit the outside of the station and shook. Sprinting across that cracked parking lot, he nearly lost his footing on some loose gravel, the pebbles rolling beneath the soles of his boots like roller skate wheels. Regaining traction, he bounded toward the Olds, all the while hearing that laughter boom behind him—laughter that seemed to be less and less human with each passing second.

After what she'd seen outside, there was no way Aimee would be sleeping anytime soon. But instead of staking out in the living room to make sure nothing came in, she checked on the girls before she locked herself in the bedroom and pulled the covers up to her chin. The wind was picking up. The walls of the house groaned with each gust. She imagined the roof being peeled off the top of the house like a lid off an aluminum can. That shadow figure was probably lurking out there in the storm, peering through windows, licking panes of glass with its long serpent tongue. After half an hour of lying in bed with her eyes wide open, she rolled over, grabbed the phone off the bedside table, and punched in Jack's number. There was no answer. Jack was out in the middle of nowhere, no civilization, no reception. And even if he had answered, what would she have said? That she was spooked by something she wasn't sure was real?

"Get a grip," she muttered, kicking the comforter from her legs, trying to reestablish herself as the owner of her space. Not the whole house—not yet. But at least the master bedroom was hers.

With sleep out the window, she tossed Victor Hugo's beat-up paperback onto the bed. She might as well start a pot of coffee. She padded across the room to the closet and threw open the door, peering at clothes that hung from a badly sagging rod before snatching her favorite sweater off a hanger.

There was a thump across the house.

Aimee pulled her sweater on, then crossed her arms protectively across her chest. Taking slow steps to the bedroom door, she pressed an ear to the wood and listened.

The skittering of feet.

She felt herself go wobbly. What if it was the thing she'd seen outside? What if it had gotten inside the house? Pressing her forehead to the door, she pulled on her bottom lip, scared to open the door, imagining herself jerking it open to see that shadow perched over one of her daughters, intestines pulled taut in its teeth.

She jerked the door open with a yell, no longer caring if she woke the girls. Shooting a look down the hall, she saw a set of scrawny legs ducking into the girls' room. Charlie was up.

Aimee's first reaction was that of absolute dread. Charlie was the last person she wanted to deal with in the middle of the night. She was completely freaked out as it was. A second later, Aimee was stomping down the hall, her hand jamming itself against the light switch to kill the darkness around her. This was ridiculous. This entire night was out of control. And now Charlie was running around in the dead of night like she owned the place. If anything, Aimee felt the need to remain somewhat in control of the situation. The moment she let Charlie run the show was the moment that kid would be assured she could do anything—and after Nubs, God only knew what that anything would be.

"Charlie?" Aimee spoke into the silence of the house, flipping lights on as she moved through the house. By the time she reached the girls' room, the place was lit up brighter than the Superdome. She pushed the bedroom door open, half expecting to see Charlie standing a foot from the entrance, grinning that terrifying *Hello, Mommy* smile. And that would have more than likely scared her less than what she did see: a dark room, both of her daughters fast asleep.

She backed away from the room, her heart thumping beneath the wool of her sweater. Veering around, she glared at the front door, waiting for it to burst open of its own accord. She waited for a crash from the kitchen to rattle the walls, the kitchen table flipping back on its top. She waited for *something* to happen, but nothing did.

Wandering back to the master bedroom, she stopped dead in the doorway. She'd left the closet door open, and it appeared that a hurricane had torn through it when she had gone to chase Charlie down. But rather than being terrified at what she saw, she stepped into the room in a disconcerted sort of way, squatted down, and began collecting clothes in her arms as she quietly cried. She was exhausted by the unexplainable. Every scenario sent her mind reeling back to the one movie that scared her when she was a kid—the one with the pretty little blond girl and the static-filled TV. All she needed was for Charlie to appear in the doorway and sing-song, *They're here.* It would have been the perfect ending to an impossible situation.

She plucked clothes off the floor, her tears intensifying with each passing second. She all but reeled back when she revealed an uprooted shoebox beneath one of Jack's work shirts. They didn't keep shoeboxes. Aimee always threw them away, insisting they took up too much room—but here one was, lying on its top, waiting to be picked up, waiting to be discovered.

Frustrated, she threw the clothes in her arms onto the floor next to the closet. If she'd told him once she'd told him a thousand times, throw the shoeboxes out, for God's sake. But leave it to Jack not to listen, leave it to him, forcing her into repeating herself over and over again like a fucking parrot. He was probably hiding something in it, having stuffed the box in the farthest corner of the closet so she wouldn't find it—love letters from another woman, or worse—maybe drugs. She snatched the box off the floor, expecting the worst.

The lid gave way and photographs spilled onto the floor.

She blinked at them as she collected them off the rug. They were family pictures. The topmost was of Jack and the girls standing on top of a levee, the Mississippi glistening behind them like white fire. In the second, Jack pushed Charlie on a tire swing, Charlie's expression one of sheer joy while Jack laughed behind her. There was one of Jack and his bandmates in someone's basement, and one with Jack and Reagan throwing up devil horns outside the Red Door on Bourbon. At first she couldn't fathom why he'd hidden them. They were wonderful photos, old memories that she would have happily filed away in a photo album. She shoved them back in the box, ready to shove the box back into the closet, when something unsettling occurred to her: she'd taken half of those pictures herself. She frowned, picturing Jack sorting through them in the pharmacy parking lot before bringing them home, squirreling certain ones away like a hoarder.

She peered at the photos, knowing that her discovery would end up as an argument. She'd accuse him of keeping secrets; he'd accuse her of invading his privacy. She'd yell that in marriage, privacy didn't exist; he'd snap back that maybe they shouldn't be married at all. And then they'd get bored, the argument would fade, and they'd quote each other for a few days with stupid smiles and gentle teasing.

Aimee grabbed the box lid, ready to abandon it on top of the pile of clothes at the foot of the closet, when something caught her eye. Narrowing her eyes at the photograph on top of the pile, she scrutinized the backdrop behind Jack as he stood in Jackson Square, a greasy bag of sugar-covered beignets in one hand, a fresh fried Louisiana doughnut in the other; his grin of utter indulgence had distracted her the first time around. But what caught her attention now was something hiding behind a tree— a shadow much like the one she'd seen outside in the darkness peering out from behind the trunk of an oak, glaring at the photographer while Jack mugged for the camera.

Aimee examined the image for a long while. She was just about ready to dismiss it as a trick of the light, when she flicked down to the next photograph in the pile. There, practically staring her right in the face, she saw the same thing. In the picture of Charlie on the tire swing, the same shadow—greasy, almost serpentine—lurked in the background.

The third photo was harder to spot. Jack and Reagan posed in front of the Red Door beneath a neon glow. Aimee held the photo a few inches from her nose, searching the details of that street scene for what she hoped she wouldn't find.

But she found it. Half-hidden by a doorframe, it lurked across the street, hiding behind the shoulder of a bearded guy in a John Deere cap.

Her heart hammered against her rib cage. She suddenly realized what that shadow reminded her of: Jack's tattoo. It was the same creature, the same malevolent grin.

Her vision wavy through a sheen of tears, she saw a picture of Charlotte standing in the front yard in her white summer dress, Nubs sitting obediently at her feet. And there, in an otherwise perfect background, the darkness lingered yards away. She shook

her head, refusing to believe this was the root of Charlie's problems, refusing to acknowledge that Jack knew—that he'd known
all along. But it was impossible to deny. The proof was etched into
his skin like a calling card. She swiped at her tears and looked
back to the photo in her hand, only to drop it and scramble away.

The picture had changed. Charlie stood in the front yard in
her white summer dress, smiling with razor-sharp teeth, Nubs
dead at her feet.

CHAPTER FOURTEEN

JACK HADN'T BEEN BACK TO ROSEWOOD IN NEARLY twenty years, but as soon as he crossed the city limits, an air of familiarity wrapped itself around him. He drove along Rosewood's main street, passing locations he hadn't even thought of since he was a kid. There was the old Pizza Hut, where he had attended his first all-kid birthday party and learned how to play Pac-Man on a flat-top arcade table. There was the mini golf course where he had scored a hole in one, an achievement he had bragged about for days before Stephen lost his temper and told him it wasn't that big a deal. The Superette where he'd swiped a Pez dispenser was still standing. He doubted his parents would have cared even if they had caught him red-handed, but Jack still managed to feel pangs of guilt for an entire week before deciding to return it during the following grocery store trip. He stashed it between a few boxes of cereal and walked out empty-handed.

The farther Jack drove the more spread-out things became. Rosewood's main street ended in a fork—a right turn would take him to the rural road where their trailer sat, hiding the secret cemetery behind it like some sort of blight. Jack came to a complete stop at the junction, hesitated, and then veered right, the giant's howl of laughter echoing inside his head.

That rural road hadn't changed. The pavement was still as bad as ever, monster potholes playing their part as permanent roadside obstacles. The tall grass and weeping trees were what he remembered from his youth, only twice as big. He'd walked up and down this road during summer vacations a hundred times over, making the long and humid trek from the trailer to the drive-in for a cherry-flavored slush so cold it froze his brain every time. Some of the trailers that had been parked along that road were gone, and the spots they'd sat on were long overgrown. A few of the houses were still there—some spruced up with new paint and upgraded roofs, others fallen into disrepair. A few looked like they'd been torn down either by the county or a tornado, faint signs of remaining foundations the only clue that a house had ever stood there at all. Rosewood wasn't a place people wanted to raise their kids. It was nice and quaint and humble and had that air of classic Southern hospitality, but it wasn't the type of place where you wanted to spend your whole life unless your whole life was already behind you.

Jack passed the ghosts of his childhood at fifteen miles per hour, going slowly to take in the scenery, to delay the inevitable. The road leading to where he grew up eventually gave way to nothing but sagging trees and a locust hum. As Jack crept along, he eventually caught sight of what he'd come back to Georgia to see—that trailer, still sitting far within no-man's-land. Alone. Washed out. Nothing but a bad memory.

Something about seeing his childhood home afforded him a strange sense of disappointment. The front porch had dislocated itself from the front of the house and sagged into the yard like a broken limb. The porch steps were destroyed—half of them missing, the other half on the ground, rotting into the soil. The corrugated metal that had covered their roof had been peeled back, most likely the work of an unforgiving storm. The majority of the windows were broken, and the screen door hung outward on a single hinge like a loose tooth. The next storm that whipped through Georgia would take it clean off. The siding that his dad had put up to make the trailer look "nice" was rusted over and had come loose, jutting into the wild grass like an outstretched hand asking for help. The place had never been in the best of shape, but it had been livable. Seeing it now, Jack was sure his parents had long moved off the property. He could only hope they were still somewhere in Rosewood.

Jack guided the Olds onto the spot that used to be a gravel driveway, now overgrown with weeds. He approached the trailer with caution, his hands shoved firmly in the pockets of his jeans. It was like a bad accident along the side of the road—he didn't want to look, didn't want to remember, but those dingy broken windows called out to him. *Come look inside*, they said. *Come see what you left behind.*

Avoiding the destroyed front deck, he stepped around back where his bedroom window had been, pausing when he spotted the collection of holes that decorated the paneling there. It was where his father had nailed two-by-fours to the outside of the house. Jack took a forward step, his curiosity getting the best of him, wanting to get a peek at the room that used to be his.

He was surprised to see his bed in place. His old sheets were there, tossed back as though someone had just recently gotten up. His eyes went wide as he took in his old desk, still piled with books and broken toys, a few old records, even a Styrofoam cup from the drive-in he used to keep for loose change. It was as though the world had stopped the night Jack had stepped out of his old life. The room he was sure his parents would have gutted for extra space was preserved, blanketed in a thick coat of dust. He hadn't expected the twisting in his chest, the pang of sadness that dug its way into the center of his heart. Despite all the bad memories, he was struck by an overwhelming loneliness. He missed his mother, the way she laughed when his dad told a particularly bad joke; he missed his dad and the afternoon out in the yard where he taught Jack how to use the slingshot.

"Can I help you?"

Jack veered around, his heart in his throat. A man in tattered jeans and a faded T-shirt stood not five yards from him, shielding his eyes from the early morning sun.

"Um…hi." Jack lifted a hand in greeting the way they did in space movies, cautiously greeting an alien race.

"Howdy," the man replied, then rephrased the question Jack had failed to answer. "What can I do you for?"

Glancing over his shoulder, Jack hitched a thumb at the trailer. "I used to live here."

"That right?"

"Long time ago. Just came back to see if it was still here."

"It's still here, all right." The guy stalked over and stopped in the thin strip of shadow that ran along the length of the mobile home, hiding from the sun. He pulled a handkerchief from his pocket and wiped down his face. "I've been meaning to haul this old bitch out of here for years now, but I just haven't been able to justify the cost."

"You own the land?"

"Bought thirty acres out here about fifteen years ago. It's out of the way but still close to town. Good for farming."

"Is that when the people who lived here moved out?"

The guy folded his handkerchief, careful to match the ends to one another, then slid it into the back pocket of his jeans.

"This place was empty when I got here. From what I know, it was empty for years before. Looks just about the same now as it did when I showed up."

Jack hesitated, considering whether he actually wanted to ask the question that was poised at the tip of his tongue. It was unlikely this guy would have the answer he was looking for, but he'd driven hundreds of miles—the least he could do was convince himself that he hadn't driven to Georgia for nothing.

"Do you know where they went?"

It was the landowner's turn to pause. He gave Jack a once-over, then turned his attention back to the dilapidated trailer taking up space on his land. His eyes crinkled at the corners as he peered at it, then glanced back to Jack with a curious expression.

"I moved to Rosewood a year before I bought this property, so I'm no expert in local history," he explained. "People told me I was crazy buying this land. People in town say it's cursed."

Jack tried not to react. He stood motionless, concentrating on keeping his expression as unreadable as possible. But his heart was thumping in his ears.

"Why do they say that?"

The guy shrugged.

"Those folks," he said, motioning to the trailer. "The rumor is they were found dead in there."

Jack's jaw clenched. His stomach somersaulted, cramping with queasiness.

"They say it was bad, like someone went ballistic on them— real dirty, like the person doing the killing didn't just want them dead, but wanted them *good* and dead."

Jack felt like he was floating, like his chest had closed up and forced the air from his lungs. He lifted a hand to steady himself against the house, trying to keep his composure, but the guy beside him raised an eyebrow as Jack swayed like a reed in the wind.

"But that's all just rumors," he said, offering Jack an unsure smile. "For all I know, it could be a bunch of hogwash…someone making up stories, trying to swipe a good land deal out from under my feet when I was buying. If you want more information on those folks, you should see a gal named Ginny. She lives in town, works up at the bowling alley. She calls herself Rosewood's historical expert. If anyone knows about what happened around here, it would be her."

Jack nodded. "OK, thanks," he said, but it was the last thing he wanted to do. If the story was true—if Stephen and Gilda had been murdered—he didn't want to know about it. He didn't want to even consider it.

He turned back to the Olds, unsteady on his feet, and paused beside the front wheel when he thought of one last thing.

"Do you mind if I walk around a bit?" he asked. "Just to take it all in?"

The landowner furrowed his eyebrows but eventually shrugged. "Be my guest."

The guy excused himself, wandering back to where a truck was parked a few dozen yards away, half-hidden by a line of oaks. Jack trudged through the wild grass and weeds, his heart hammering in his chest. He made a beeline for the trees at the back of the lot, ducked through the branches, and stopped when his eyes snagged on a half-buried slingshot handle. Reaching down, he pulled it out of the dirt, a crude JW etched into the wood of the handle having all but vanished after years of being outside. When he looked up, he expected to see a handful of headstones, the rusted iron gate that had always been there, protecting the secret cemetery from trespassers.

But it was gone.

Other than the weatherworn slingshot in his hand, there wasn't a trace that the cemetery had existed at all.

As the girls entered the kitchen for their breakfast, Aimee's nerves buzzed. She turned, saw Charlie standing beside her, and immediately sidestepped away from the girl. Her heart fluttered in her chest as Charlie stalked around the kitchen, and she was able to catch her breath only when the girl finally took a seat at the table and waited for her hash browns. Aimee was scared of her own child, and she wasn't sure whether to be disgusted with herself or feel justified.

Still somber about Nubs, Abby sat at the table with her head in her hands. Charlie, however, didn't seem the least bit fazed by the sudden absence of their pet. Aimee delivered the girls' plates to the table, took a seat, and placed a hand on Abby's back.

"What would you say if we went down to the animal shelter today?"

Aimee wasn't particularly motivated to look for a replacement for Nubs, but if it got her out of the house after the night she'd had, it was as good an excuse as any.

Abby didn't respond to her mother's offer. She gave Aimee a blank look, then peered at her breakfast as if waiting for it to crawl off her plate. Charlie was the first to react, bouncing up and down in her chair with a grin.

"To get a new dog?" she asked.

"Well, maybe not right away," Aimee said. "Maybe we can just look and think about what we want to do."

"I don't want another dog," Abigail murmured into her hands. Charlie went quiet and cast a look at her mother, as though searching for assurance that they would, in fact, get a new pet. Aimee kept quiet, and Charlie frowned at her sister.

"Why not?" she asked. "Dogs are cool."

"Don't push," Aimee warned.

"I just don't," Abby said. "I don't ever want another dog again."

"But we're going to get one," Charlie told her, self-assured. "So when we get one, I guess you're going to hate it."

"I guess," Abby told her plate.

"We can get another dog, can't we? Not getting another one would be stupid, right, Momma?"

"Charlie…"

Abigail pressed her palms against the lip of the table and shoved. The legs of her chair screamed against the linoleum. "I said I don't want another dog!" Abby snapped. "I don't want another dog! *I don't want another dog!*"

"You're just an idiot!" Charlie yelled back.

Abby stared at her sister with giant eyes, tears shimmering in the sunlight that filtered through the kitchen curtains.

"I just want Nubs back," Abby whispered, then pressed her hands to her face and began to cry.

Charlie's expression went hard at her sister's breakdown. She shoved her breakfast away, got up from the table, and stared at Abby while Aimee struggled for something to say. But Charlie beat her mother to it, hissing out her words.

"He was just a stupid dog. He got what he deserved."

Then she turned on her heels and stomped out of the room.

Shock stalled Abby's tears. She stared down the hall after her sister, her mouth slack. Aimee sat frozen as well, her own tears—ones of panic—slowly bubbling up her esophagus, clawing at the backs of her eyes.

Jack couldn't recall ever going to the bowling alley when he was a kid, but that didn't mean he didn't know where it was. Turning down a few streets and pulling into a rough-looking parking lot brought him to Top Pin, its sign rusted and its paint job fading.

Inside, the scent of buttered popcorn mingled with the smell of old bowling shoes and dingy carpeting. Jack followed a trail of cartoon pins etched into the carpet. They brought him to the main counter, where an acne-plagued teen sat on a stool reading an old *Mad* magazine, a giant wall of cubbies stuffed with clown shoes towering behind him.

"Hey," Jack said. The kid looked up, forced a fake smile, and stood out of obligation.

"We aren't open for another fifteen minutes," he said. "But I can get you your shoes at least. You with the league?"

Empty bowling lanes flanked the far wall of the establishment. The place was abandoned save for the kid in front of him and another popping popcorn at the snack bar.

"I'm actually looking for someone. Ginny?"

The kid squinted at Jack, then pursed his lips in a pensive sort of way.

"Ginny doesn't really deal with customers," he said. "She's more of a back office type of person."

"But I'm not a customer."

"Same goes for noncustomers." The kid settled back onto his stool and flipped a page of his magazine. "She just does the books, you know? Tax stuff. You want the manager?"

"I was told that she's a Rosewood history expert."

The kid didn't budge, unimpressed.

"Listen," Jack said, "I need her help. I've driven all the way from Louisiana. I left my wife and kids alone and drove eight hours just to revisit this shithole town."

The teen raised an eyebrow.

"So please," he continued, "cut me some slack."

Motivation didn't come easily to the pimply faced teen, so Jack threw out one last bone. The landowner had mentioned that the old trailer was the stuff of legend. If anyone followed stories of local ax murders, it was kids like this one.

"Tell her I'm here about the trailer out on Route 17."

Like a dog with a steak dangled before his nose, the kid sat at attention.

"That place?" he asked. "Man, what do you want with that place? That place is evil."

"What do you mean?" There was another unwelcome word: evil. The answers he was looking for grew darker at every turn.

"People don't go out on that road after dark," the kid confessed. "Those who do only do it on a dare. If you drive past that trailer at night, your engine cuts out and you end up stranded, and the thing that killed those folks...it still wanders up and down that strip of land, waiting for its next victim."

Jack wanted to laugh, wanted to slam his palms against the counter and tell the kid he was full of it—just some stupid teen who believed any idiotic story made up by a handful of bored Rosewood kids. But he said nothing.

"Maybe it's just made up." The kid scratched his chin, barely missing a swollen zit. "But you know what they say about urban legends: all legends are based on at least a little bit of truth."

Jack felt his stomach twist.

The kid hopped off his stool and motioned for Jack to follow. "Ginny's in the back," he said. "I'll take you to her."

Ginny wasn't what Jack had expected. He had pictured a homely woman, the kind who lived with a hundred cats. But Ginny was nothing like that at all. She must have been a good sixty years old, but she looked young for her age. Her hair was a luxurious red without a spot of gray—red like a summer sunset after a storm, and momentarily Jack swore he remembered her from years ago. There had been a woman in Rosewood—hair as red as fire—whom he'd seen at the grocery store a few times. She had been older than his mom; he remembered that because his dad had found it amusing that Gilda was jealous of the mysterious woman. But his mom had been right about one thing: the woman with the fiery hair had been beautiful. All the men noticed her, even his dad. And all the women noticed her because of exactly that.

The pimpled kid left Jack in the back office, and Ginny greeted him with a wide smile, extending a hand. She was still beautiful.

"Well aren't you a handsome young man?" Her cheeks flushed with a touch of pink. "Please tell me you're Rosewood's newest resident."

Jack forced a smile, and Ginny motioned to a pair of chairs in front of her desk. She took a seat next to him, folding her hands in her lap.

"I actually live in Louisiana," Jack explained.

"Oh, wonderful. If I could pick up and move away, I'd live there too. Beautiful place, really. Not that Georgia is anywhere near an eyesore," Ginny teased. "We're all peaches out here." She waved a hand at herself and playfully rolled her eyes.

"You're the Rosewood historical expert?" Jack asked, and Ginny chuckled, pressing a hand to her chest, flattered.

"Is that what they're saying? I suppose I *do* know a thing or two about this little corner of the world."

"I'm here about the trailer out on Route 17."

Just as expected, Ginny's smiling face went hard.

"Do you know anything about that?" Jack asked, but she didn't have to answer. Her expression gave her away. Suddenly, the Southern hospitality that she couldn't help but exude vanished as quickly as a roach in a brightly lit room.

"Oh, I know plenty about that," she said. "But that doesn't mean I want to spend any time talking about it."

Jack nodded slowly. He hadn't considered the possibility of Ginny not wanting to discuss it, and maybe it was for the best. He hadn't wanted to visit that bowling alley, hadn't wanted to ask to speak to this woman at all, yet there he was, asking anyway. He kept his mouth shut, hoping his silence would bore her, that maybe all it would take was slight disinterest to turn her off. He waited for her to wave him off, to ask him to go away, but as soon as he stopped asking questions, she was giving him answers.

"That trailer wasn't always there," she told him. "One day that field was empty, and the next there's that trailer, come out of nowhere like someone had dropped it out of the sky. And the folks who lived in it…" She clucked her tongue against the roof of her mouth. "Strange people—the kind of folks that don't really talk to anyone. Sure, we'd see them out and about. It's hard not to in a place like this. You can't fart without half the town knowing about it."

Jack attempted a smile.

"I didn't know them personally, but I do remember their names. There was Steve and there was Glenda."

Close enough, Jack thought.

"They had a little boy. Cute little kid, as I remember. Always friendly, always smiling…seemed like a happy child despite his oddball parents. At least that's what everyone thought at first."

"At first?"

"You know the saying, 'He seemed like such a nice boy'? That didn't come from nowhere. The craziest of them all seem nice and normal and happy until some vital part of their brain fries like bad wiring. Granted, nobody really knows what happened that night," she assured him. "But we all have our hunches, and most of those hunches point to that nice little boy not being so nice after all. That cute, smiling face was nothing more than a disguise."

Jack shook his head mutely.

"Like a wolf in sheep's clothing," she said. "A mask."

"For what?" he asked, his skin prickly with hypersensitivity. It felt like someone had stuck a live wire into his shoes and turned up the electricity just high enough to rattle his teeth.

"Well, if you go by what happened in that trailer on Route 17—if you go by what most of Rosewood *believes* happened—I'd say it was a mask for whatever evil was lurking behind that kid's eyes."

Jack had heard enough. He sat there, trying to convince himself that there was nothing left to learn. And yet he heard himself ask a question, detached and far away.

"What happened?"

She shook her head, and for a moment he was relieved. He'd reached Ginny's limit, the invisible line that she wouldn't cross. But as soon as he began to relax, she started up again.

"There was a murder," she told him, and every hair on Jack's body stood at attention. "But you wouldn't be asking about that trailer if you didn't already know that."

He went silent once more, wondering how it was possible that he wanted to get up but couldn't. Something was holding him down, pressing him into that chair. Just the same as there had been an invisible hand guiding him to that dilapidated gas station. Just the same as how someone had put the landowner out on that property. Just like how something had led him to this woman.

Something wanted him to sit and listen and not move.

"Since those folks were loners, it took the police a good four or five days to find them. The man, Steve, had some sort of job lined up in town—construction or something like that. When he didn't show up to work and nobody could find him, the cops were sent out to make sure everything was all right out on Route 17."

Ginny shifted in her seat, obviously not comfortable telling this story—but just as something held Jack in place and forced him to listen, it seemed that something was pushing her to keep talking.

"When the police arrived, everything looked fine. There was no sign of a break-in. It didn't make much sense, but details like that took a backseat to what they found inside. I could talk all day and I still wouldn't come close to describing what those officers unearthed inside."

"Can you try?" someone asked. The voice sounded suspiciously like Jack's.

"Those folks were torn to pieces," she told him. "And I don't mean figuratively. It looked like what they did to criminals a long time back, when they tied a rope around each limb and tied each rope around a horse, sending them in different directions. They couldn't figure out how a person could manage to do something like that. Well, they just couldn't put two and two together."

She paused, took a breath.

"And then the little boy came into question. The boy was gone, so the first thing we assumed was that he'd been abducted, that whoever killed those folks swiped the kid and snuck off into the night. But the more the police looked around the more it looked like nobody had broken in, but that someone had broken *out*."

Jack could taste vomit curdling in the back of his throat. He wondered if he'd be able to get out of that chair to grab the small trash can in time, or whether he'd projectile vomit across the expanse of Ginny's desk.

"Regardless, the police called up a manhunt. They called about six or seven different states to keep an eye out. Not like it would be difficult to spot a stray that young, especially one without any experience of being out on his own. They were sure they'd find him within a matter of days…but they didn't.

"After a few months with no leads, they left it on the assumption that the boy was to blame. At first everyone thought it was a mistake. How could they be so sure such a gruesome crime could have been committed by a child? They eventually revealed the detail that had led them to their conclusion, and that's when all of Rosewood—all of Georgia, really—stopped doubting and started believing. Looking through that trailer for clues, they found some old boards lying in the grass outside the boy's window. They found holes around the window on the outside, like those boards had been nailed there to keep the kid in his room. And I guess that's where it gets really scary." Ginny frowned.

"There's only one reason to board someone up in a room like that, and that's because you're afraid of them. Those folks were scared of their own boy, and they must have had a reason. They knew there was something wrong, that there was something dangerous about that child, so they locked him up like some animal, never expecting that he would get out of that room not just to escape, but to avenge his incarceration. Or maybe he did what he did to confirm their suspicion."

"Suspicion?"

Ginny nodded. "That he wasn't human: that he was a demon."

A shudder rang through Jack's body like a bell. Every nerve hissed. His fingers bit into the armrests of his chair as though he were being electrocuted—like an epileptic on the cusp of a grand mal.

Ginny's sudden laughter nearly made him jump out of his chair.

"Superstition," she said with a chuckle, waving a hand to dismiss the whole thing. "Leave it to a town like this one to blame the devil for everything. It's ridiculous. That case was never closed," she told him. "I suppose if you went down to the station the folks there could fill you in more thoroughly than I can."

Jack stood.

"I can't thank you enough," he told her, but his tone told a different story. Ginny's narrative had set him on edge. All he wanted to do was bolt for the door, to run as fast and as far as he could to the point of collapse, and then maybe crumple in front of a big rig as it blew past, too close for the driver to slam on his brakes, torn apart...limb from limb.

Ginny watched him walk to the door, then spoke just as he pulled it open to make his exit.

"I'm Rosewood's local historical expert. You said it yourself," she said. "That isn't a story I like to tell very often, even if it's just an old wives' tale. But you asked, and I did. So now I have a question for *you*."

Jack already knew what it was. His mouth went dry. He felt his legs wobble, and for a moment he was sure that if she asked what he knew she was going to ask, he'd turn on her, tear her to pieces.

"Jack Winter," she said. "Did you kill your parents?"

His heart drained of blood. For a half second he couldn't catch his breath, sure he'd never breathe again. A spark of rage fired in the pit of his stomach, but it subsided quickly, and he managed to form a reply.

With his hand on the doorknob and his back to the woman who had destroyed his entire world, Jack eventually answered.

"I don't know," he croaked. "But I think I probably did."

The night had been silent save for the furious padding of his feet and his breath, which came in waves. Jack fled that trailer in the dead of night, and while he couldn't remember how he had gotten out without being chased by his father, he knew he had to run as fast as he could. His lungs burned as he sprinted down Route 17. Eventually he stopped, his hands pressed to his trembling knees, his head hanging limp between his shoulders. It was then, gasping for air, that he realized he wasn't wearing any shoes.

His legs were bleeding. From what he could see in the pale Georgia moonlight, he'd somehow managed to get some of that blood on his hands and feet. But that didn't matter. After catching his breath, Jack took on a brisk pace toward Rosewood, where he'd jog out to the highway and hitch a ride out of Dodge. Stephen and Gilda would never see him again.

He bypassed Rosewood as much as he could, not wanting anyone to spot "the Winter boy" stomping his way out of town.

When he hit the highway he thrust his skinny arm out into the road and jutted his thumb into the sky. Childhood optimism assured him that someone would stop. Someone had to. Only a heartless bastard would pass up a scrawny, barefooted kid. Violent psychopaths didn't even enter Jack's mind. In his head, he knew some nice couple would pull over, toss him in the backseat, and get him a fancy dinner at the Huddle House or Waffle King. They'd tuck him into a hotel bed and kiss him on the forehead and swear they'd protect him forever. Jack was running away, but it wasn't because he didn't want parents. He just didn't want *his* parents. Anyone who yanked him off the highway would be better than Stephen and Gilda. He was never going back to that run-down trailer on the outskirts of town.

"They'll miss me," he muttered as he marched ahead. His arm was growing tired, but he kept it stuck out to the side even when there weren't any cars coming, sure that as soon as he let it fall some phantom sedan would scream out of an invisible vortex and pass him by.

"They'll be sorry when they find out," he said. "They'll see that I'm gone, and they'll be so sorry they won't even know what to think. They'll cry until they're dead."

A pair of headlights appeared in the distance. It was an old pickup, its rusted red hood rattling on the latch that held it down, threatening to release its grip and toss that metal sheet into the windshield like a drunk girl flashing her tits at Mardi Gras. Those headlights were cockeyed. The left one pointed too far to the left like it was searching for roadkill, while the right pointed down a bit too sharply. When the truck's skewed headlights caught Jack's silhouette, it came to a stop dead center in the road.

Jack stood on the shoulder while the truck rumbled like a tyrannosaur. He kept his arm out and his thumb pointed up even after locking eyes with the giant inside the cab. The guy's teeth gleamed in the darkness. He leaned across the bench seat and pushed the passenger side door open. The door hinges creaked.

"Hey there, chief, need a lift?"

Jack climbed into the truck without a word, dazed, not knowing what he was doing, not seeing the driver at all. Jack didn't care where he ended up—he just wanted that big driver to drive. And the giant wearing the John Deere cap didn't ask where the kid wanted to go; he just eyed the fourteen-year-old boy sitting next to him and grinned.

He grinned because Jack Winter had been in the exact spot he was meant to be in that night. He grinned because, judging by the dazed expression on the kid's face, Jack Winter didn't realize he was covered from head to toe in blood.

CHAPTER FIFTEEN

JABBING THE END OF A STICK INTO THE SOFT EARTH, Charlie brooded as she paced the lawn. It was hot and she was bored, and Abby was just sitting there reading some stupid book. She narrowed her eyes. Had Abigail not been such a crybaby, they could have been at the animal shelter picking out a new dog. But instead, they were stuck in front of the house with nothing to do. It was all her stupid sister's fault.

Charlie threw the stick across the road as hard as she could. It spun through the air like a helicopter blade and disappeared into the trees that flanked the other side of the street. She exhaled a little gasp to garner her sister's interest. It worked. Abby looked up from her book.

"Did you see that?" Charlie asked, wide-eyed with mock surprise.

"See what?"

"A possum!" Charlie said. Abby made a face. She looked less than impressed and glanced back to her book a moment later. Charlie squeezed her hands into tight little fists at her sides. "It was across the street," she continued. Her tone was animated with childlike excitement, but no expression touched her face. "I think it had babies on its back."

That got Abby's attention immediately; she was a sucker for baby animals.

"Babies?" She blinked at the news. Closing her book, she dropped it beside the trunk of the tree and met her little sister next to the road. They both peered across the street, searching for a possum that didn't exist.

"I bet Momma would let us adopt one," Charlie said. "We just have to catch up to it."

Charlie smiled to herself while Abby toed the edge of that road. They stood there like lawn ornaments, searching the trees. Even the rumble of an old pickup didn't distract them. A rusty red Ford approached, and Charlie's fingers twitched. She gritted her teeth, her eyes narrowing to dangerous slits. The truck rambled closer, a good ten miles over the thirty-mile-per-hour limit.

Charlie lifted a hand behind Abigail's back. She pulled her arm backward, waiting for the perfect moment.

The truck grew louder as it approached, its engine sputtering beneath a peeling hood. It was close enough for Charlotte to make out the driver's face—a bushy beard hung on to the driver's chin, a tangle of hair stuffed beneath a brimmed cap.

The truck was screaming now, loud as a locomotive. Charlie reared back, but Abby turned toward her sister just as the pickup bounced by.

"Should we go look for it?" Abby asked. Life was trickling back into her face. For the first time since the accident, she looked genuinely excited.

Charlie's arm dropped to her side when Abby turned, and while rage simmered in her veins, she made her expression enthusiastic—an expression a normal child was expected to wear when adventure called.

"Maybe we should go ask Mom," Charlie suggested, but it was the last thing she meant to do—like she'd ask that bitch for permission to do anything. Abby shook her head at the idea.

"We've probably waited too long as it is," she said. "If we wait any longer there's no way we'll ever catch up to it." That was when Abby grabbed her hand and pulled her across the street. Charlie dragged her feet, putting on a show of little-sister jitters. Had Abby glanced over her shoulder, she would have spotted a sinister smile spread wide across Charlie's mouth.

Jack flew down the highway toward Louisiana. His foot mashed the gas pedal against the floorboard. The engine rumbled with a surprising amount of muscle, like a sleeping Formula One car that had been disguised as a boring family sedan its entire life. Jack was doing one hundred and ten along a two-lane road, the double yellow line blurring into an arrow, pointing him in the right direction. Driving as fast as the devil himself, he wondered how the car managed to stay on the road, how it hadn't veered off onto an embankment where the police would find him, collapsed skull and ribs poking through his chest like the flayed bones of a fancy roast. The faster he drove the more clearly he could see the twists and turns ahead of him. It was like some sort of high-speed intuition, a racer's third eye.

His thoughts were spiraling out of control—thoughts about his parents, his mother, the grandparents he hadn't met. He didn't want to believe it, didn't want to even consider the possibility that the reason he'd never met Grandma and Grandpa was because his mother had killed them; he couldn't stomach the idea, the possibility that this was nothing but a wicked game, an endless cycle that was destined to end in death. But the longer he had to think about it, the more he could remember. His mother screaming, his father already dead at his feet, a butcher's knife glistening red in Jack's hand.

He pressed his foot hard against the gas, but the car was at its limit. His knuckles went white against the steering wheel. He gripped it tightly and tried to shake it loose, a moan of frustration rising above the engine's hum. The scream of his cell phone made him jump. He snatched it out of the cup holder and fumbled to answer the call.

"Jack." Reagan's voice was strained with anxiety—he sounded just like Jack felt: panicked, unnerved. "Where the fuck are you, man?"

"Driving home," Jack said. "Why? What?"

"Dude." Reagan paused as if bracing himself. "Man, I don't know. Aimee," he said. "Aimee is losing her shit."

Jack's heart stopped. The worst-case scenario spun through his mind like a helicopter blade, threatening to behead him before he ever got home.

"The girls are gone, man."

He couldn't speak.

"Jesus, are you fucking *there*?" Reagan yelled. "Did you hear what I said?"

Jack had heard. He'd heard so well that Reagan's announcement skipped inside his head like a broken record. *The girls are gone.*

How was he supposed to respond to that? What was he supposed to say? What was the correct reaction? Screaming? Throwing the phone against the windshield? Pulling onto the shoulder and running down the road like a lunatic? Jack wanted to do it all. He wanted to yell back at Reagan to fuck off, to cut him some slack. He wanted to lash out, because if Reagan was in his shoes he sure as fuck wouldn't be doing any better than Jack was. He wanted to call the house, wanted to scream at Aimee for letting those girls out of her sight. What was she thinking? If Charlie was capable of running Nubs into the road, wasn't Aimee the least bit concerned what she could do to Abigail? He wanted to call the police. *Save the older one*, he'd tell them. *Save the one the least like me.* But he didn't say or do any of those things. Rather than freaking out and losing his mind, he replied to Reagan's question, countering his best friend's alarm with a matter-of-fact statement.

"I'm on my way."

He made it back to Live Oak in five and a half hours instead of eight—all done without passing a single police officer or filling up the gas tank. When he pulled up to the house, the tank had been dry for a good thirty miles, but the Olds kept rolling. The street was lined with Louisiana State Troopers, their lights flashing red and blue in a surreal sort of silence.

Jack parked the Olds halfway on the lawn and left the driver's side door open, running up the porch steps and into the house. Aimee was on the couch, a box of tissues balanced on her knees. Her face was swollen, as though she'd just climbed out of a boxing ring. When she saw Jack step through the door, she abandoned the officer asking her questions and jumped off the couch, exploding into a fit of choking sobs. But rather than running to him for comfort, she held up her hands and backed away.

"Don't come near me," she shrieked. "Don't you dare come near me!"

The police turned their attention to Jack, their expressions both suspicious and concerned. They flocked to him like mosquitoes to stagnant water.

"Mr. Winter?"

Jack blinked, looking away from his hysterical wife. She sat back down and settled into quiet whimpering, fisting handfuls of tissues against her eyes.

"Mr. Winter, are you aware of the situation?" the officer asked. His name was engraved on a shiny gold nametag clipped to the pocket of his starched shirt: Officer Marvin.

"Yes." Jack paused. "Sort of. I got a call."

Reagan stepped out of the kitchen and into the hallway, his own expression dazed. He stared at Jack, offered him a shake of his head as if to say he didn't understand—couldn't comprehend the situation, let alone Aimee's reaction to Jack coming home.

"Mr. Winter, your wife has informed us that both of your daughters are missing," Marvin told him, shooting for a tone between sympathetic and professional. He wasn't very good at it, and he looked a little unsure of himself as he stood there, rehashing what he knew. "It's my understanding that the girls are six and ten years of age, is that correct?"

"Yes," Jack replied.

Cops wandered around the house, taking notes, chatting in low tones. Jack felt like a guy on a tiny island, sharks circling his little patch of land. His thoughts drifted to his own crime; he was worried that someone would recognize his name. Why hadn't the police ever found him? He had been a stupid kid, not hiding, not even knowing he had done anything wrong save for running away. It didn't make sense.

It doesn't have to make sense, he told himself. *It doesn't have anything to do with you.*

"Your wife—she's understandably beside herself," Marvin said. "We've had a time getting her to cooperate with us."

He waited for Marvin to ask about Aimee's demand for Jack to stay away, but the question never came. It seemed as though Marvin had seen one too many hysterical women in his day, and that was good. Because the last thing Jack needed was cops questioning him, realizing who he was—a murderer, a guy who'd hacked up his parents like cheap meat for a dog's dinner. He was a psychopath. A lunatic. He'd be put away for life.

"Mr. Winter?"

For life.

"Mr. Winter, I understand this is a difficult situation, but the more information we get about your daughters, and the faster we do it—"

"Sorry." Jack shook his head. "Sure, you're right...I'm just freaking out."

Marvin nodded, motioned for Jack to join him at the kitchen table. Reagan hovered next to the sink while Jack took his usual seat and Officer Marvin took Charlie's chair—the chair that had skidded across the kitchen before tipping sideways, Mr. Scratch smiling a jagged smile, wearing Charlie's face like a mask.

"Do you have any recent photos of the girls?" the officer asked. There had been plenty of photos around the house when Jack had left—pictures of the girls playing in the yard, the girls sitting at the base of a Christmas tree at their grandparents' house. His favorite had always rested atop his piano. It was a photo of Charlie dressed in her rocker wear, singing into a pink plastic microphone. Officer Marvin's question assured him that those pictures were no longer where they used to be.

"Give me a minute," Jack said and excused himself, stepping into the master bedroom, assuming it was where Aimee had tossed all of those framed photos in a fit of panic. But rather than finding a bed piled with family photographs, he found an empty shoebox instead. Beside it were the photos he'd been squirreling away over time, the photos he didn't want Aimee to see. Those secret photos were scattered across the bed, mere shadows of what they had been, torn to shreds by an inconsolable mother who was spiraling into the depth of maternal despair.

Seeing his secret uncovered, rage boiled up within him, immediate and inconsolable, just like the rage that stray cat had sparked twenty years before. Aimee had crossed the line. *She knows,* was all he could think. And Aimee knowing was against the rules.

"Jack?" Reagan ducked into the bedroom, closing the door behind him while taking in the disaster atop the bed. "Man, what the fuck? What's Aimee's deal?"

The torn photographs, the way she had reacted when Jack stepped inside the house—it was undeniable that there was something more to the nightmare than the girls having disappeared.

"She said it's your fault," Reagan confessed. "I told her she's crazy. I mean, that's fucking crazy, right? You weren't even here."

"I really don't have time to explain," Jack muttered.

"What do you—"

"I really don't, Reagan," Jack cut him off, his tone hard, unrelenting. "Don't fucking push, OK? This isn't the time."

Reagan held his hands up in surrender as Jack pushed past him. Leaving Reagan in the bedroom, Jack returned to the kitchen table and drew out his wallet. He plucked a small photograph of the girls from the plastic sleeve that held his driver's license and handed it over. Marvin hesitantly took it before posing another question.

"Anything bigger?" he asked, thumbing the tiny snapshot.

"We have plenty bigger," Jack confessed. "But they all seem to be missing."

Marvin looked confused, and Jack nodded toward the living room, signaling that the whimpering woman in the opposite room was the culprit. Marvin hesitated but nodded anyway, placing the photo on the table next to his clipboard.

"Mr. Winter, your wife…she's in a bad way," Marvin said, then paused, weighing his words. "She has, however, had her lucid moments." Again he stalled, puckering his lips. "The first thing she told us was that your daughter, Abigail, had been abducted."

Jack said nothing. He simply offered the officer a faint nod of his head to continue.

"Then it turned out that it wasn't just Abigail who was missing, but also your youngest, Charlotte." Marvin was hitching like an old pickup with a bad spark plug. The words trickled out of him with painful reservation. Eventually, he exhaled a sigh and leveled his gaze on Jack, leaning forward, closing some of the distance between them to speak under his breath. "Mr. Winter..."

"Jack."

"Jack, can I level with you?"

Jack nodded again, and Marvin glanced over his shoulder before proceeding.

"When we showed up, it appeared that from what your wife told us, she was convinced that Charlotte was the one who had abducted Abigail. Do you..." He shook his head. "Do you have any idea why she would have come to that conclusion?"

Jack leaned back in his chair and sucked a breath in through his nose. For a flash of a second he considered tearing the seam on his dark secret, considered telling Marvin and his band of merry men that Charlie wasn't Charlie anymore, just like he hadn't been Jack on that fateful summer night in a nowhere town. He pictured Marvin's face while calling out its names: devil, Satan, Lucifer, demon. He imagined the officer's expression twisting in silent disgust before his cheeks turned red like a drunk's. That's when Marvin would throw his head back and exhale a boom of laughter, dismissing the entire thing as a hoax.

"Officer Marvin," Jack said, "Charlotte is six years old."

Marvin nodded, and Jack sat there for a moment, staring at the cop across from him.

"She's six years old," he repeated himself. "She can't even tie her own shoes."

"I understand," Marvin assured him. "But you also understand that, as it was said, it's my job to question all possibilities." When Jack didn't respond, Marvin rose from his seat and tucked the tiny photo of the girls into his front shirt pocket. "Obviously, we'll keep in touch. Would you like an officer to stay at the house with you while the situation pans out?"

"We'll be fine," Jack told him.

Marvin scissored a business card between his fingers, holding it out to Jack. "If you think of anything or if you find a larger photo…please call me."

Jack took the card and offered the policeman a tight-lipped smile.

After the troopers had filtered out of the house, he was left listening to Aimee's whimpering. It took all his strength to stay in the kitchen instead of storming into the living room, ending her then and there.

The hours ticked by with the slowness of a hundred years. Reagan eventually left, and Jack and Aimee kept to their separate rooms—her in the living room, Jack in the kitchen—making time inch by that much more slowly. There was a sickening tinge of finality to their division, as though they'd reached the end of something.

Jack had already pushed through four cups of coffee when he decided to try for a peace offering. Part of him wanted nothing to do with her, but the other half—the half that had loved her for so long—pushed for reconciliation. He fished a mug from the cupboard and poured Aimee a cup of coffee.

When he stepped into the living room, Aimee tensed. She was in the same spot he'd left her hours before: her feet were pulled up onto the cushions of the couch, her shoulders wrapped in a faux cashmere blanket Patricia had given her as a last-minute birthday present one year—the kind of gift you pick up on your way to a party, an afterthought. Aimee's eyes were still swollen. Her skin was sallow. She was coming down with a bad case of heartbreak. Jack stepped across the room and offered her the mug. She didn't take it, and he placed it on the coffee table before silently taking a seat next to her. As soon as he did, she pulled into herself, creating as much distance as she could.

It was hard to know what to say. They couldn't talk about normal things because nothing was normal anymore, and they certainly couldn't talk about the girls because the girls were gone. Jack pressed his lips together in a tight line and finally found a suitable inquiry. Not "Why are you scared of me?" Because he knew the answer to that question. The torn photos on the bed said it all. She'd put the puzzle together, and now Jack was no longer her husband. He was a monster.

"Did you call your mother?"

Aimee didn't answer. Jack stared at his hands for a long time, trying to decipher a puzzle of his own. Despite the gut-wrenching anxiety of having both their children missing, he couldn't seem to fit one of the pieces in its rightful slot. It seemed that they should have been closer than ever while dealing with something so incomprehensible. When they had met, banding together had been one of their talents. They were on the same side of every argument, shared the same opinion on nearly every subject. But now, just when they needed each other most, Aimee wasn't there at all. She was vacant. Missing, just like Abby and Charlotte. And Jack was half-gone, his soul being eaten away by the darkness of his past.

"I'm sorry," he finally said. "For everything."

Aimee kept her silence, her eyes glittering with fresh-sprung tears. Jack looked back to his hands. He tried to sit there, to give her time, but after a handful of seconds, waiting became pointless. This was the grand finale. The waiting was over. It was now time for action. Jack got up and pointed himself down the hallway. Aimee spoke just as he rounded the corner.

"You're a liar," she said flatly. "You brought evil into this house."

He stopped where he stood, his hand pressed against the hallway wall, his eyes fixed on the floor.

"What is it?" she asked. "That *thing* on your back? Do I deserve to know yet? Or will I only deserve it when the police call and ask us to meet them at the morgue?"

Jack retraced his steps into the living room. The man who loved her wanted to tell her. Telling her would lift the weight of his terrible secret; it would free him from the burden of looking over his shoulder every day, half expecting to see a razor-toothed monster standing behind him with a snarling grin. Any other time, he would have felt paralyzed, unable to tell her the truth because of something beyond him—some force that kept him from ruining the game, keeping Mr. Scratch from calling checkmate. But the game was lost. There was no longer anything to protect. For the first time in his life, Jack felt free. But the look on her face, it stopped him from revealing the truth. Her expression was bitter, twisted in muted betrayal. He could see the shimmer of loathing behind her eyes. Those big doe eyes that used to smile at him were now filled with nothing short of confined disdain. He could handle a lot—losing Charlie, facing his darkest fears…but seeing Aimee fall out of love with him right before his eyes was something he hadn't counted on.

"So you aren't going to tell me?" she asked.

Jack shook his head. He was defeated. Their fates were sealed. Telling her now would do nothing but assure her that it was over. Their marriage. Their family.

"No," he said, then turned down the hall.

Aimee followed him into the bedroom, caught him pulling on his jacket. She blocked the door by pressing her hip against the jamb.

"You're leaving?" she asked, her tone growing more defiant. Jack didn't look at her. He slid his arms through his sleeves and shoved a few supplies into his backpack—a flashlight, some extra batteries, a bottle of water he'd grabbed out of the fridge.

"I'm going to look for the girls."

This time Aimee didn't recoil when he approached her. She continued to block his way, and he had to physically move her aside to get into the hall. Aimee watched him stalk down the hallway, and suddenly panic set in. It was her turn to get that sense of finality, to realize that this moment would forever change her life.

"Jack." His name warbled in her throat. When he turned, she hesitated, not knowing what to say.

She looked down at her feet. The familiar burn of saline flared in her sinus cavity. When she looked up again she was crying.

"I don't want to be alone," she confessed.

Jack shifted his backpack from his shoulder to the floor and met Aimee at the threshold of their bedroom. His hands drifted to her shoulders as a sob rumbled deep in her throat.

"You won't be alone for long," he assured her with a whisper. "I'll see you soon," he said, then leaned in and pressed a kiss to the top of her head.

She tried to whisper "*I love you*," but it caught in her throat. The screen door slammed behind him, and she slid down the wall to the floor, sobbing like a girl who'd just lost everything.

CHAPTER SIXTEEN

JACK STARED AHEAD INTO THE TREES. HIS FIRST INSTINCT was to get in the car, but just before he reached the driver's side door he paused, those keys hanging from his fingers, swaying like a noose. Something pulled at him, like a magnet tugging a metal screw across a table. It was coming from across the road.

Standing next to Arnold's car, he could almost see Charlie and Abigail running into the trees, hand in hand like two best friends. That slow pull assured him that he was right about the two dashing across the street, but it wasn't to go on a lighthearted expedition. Aimee was right: Charlie did take Abigail. But she hadn't taken Abby because she wanted her—she had taken Abby because she wanted Jack.

The keys slipped from his fingers. It was oddly poetic: instead of taking his father-in-law's showboat into the abyss, he'd simply step into the darkness and let it engulf him the way it had always wanted. Like stepping into the gaping mouth of a whale, he'd either be swallowed whole or he'd find a wooden boat.

But Jack knew there wouldn't be a boat; there wouldn't be an "other side." No light at the end of the tunnel. Not the welcoming faces of his mom and dad, smiling, reaching for him, inviting him up to a bright white heaven.

Jack stood on the front lawn of their small Southern home for a few moments longer, remembering the day he and Aimee first spotted this place while they'd been taking a late-afternoon drive. He remembered how hard it had been to get the king-sized mattress through the front door, and how even more impossible it was to maneuver it through that narrow hallway. He saw Aimee painting the walls of what would become Abigail's nursery a pastel yellow that felt like sunshine. He remembered how she had yelled for him to come as fast as he could when Abby trod down the hall in a half-walk, half-stumble that made up her first steps.

Then there was Charlie—beautiful, amazing Charlie, who had mesmerized Jack so fully he had been afraid he'd love her too much. There was her bubbly laughter as a toddler, her dress-up sessions as she got older, the *SpongeBob* theme song that, for a whole year, she'd sing at the top of her lungs at random intervals, making Jack laugh every time she did.

There was Aimee's garden in the backyard, where she planted sunflowers that came back every year, and the way she'd stand in front of the full-length mirror on early summer mornings and look herself over like a surgeon, picking herself apart while Jack wondered how a woman could be so beautiful. It seemed as though his entire life had happened in this run-down house. It began here, and it would end here. Thirteen short years of bliss. It hadn't seemed like bad luck until just then.

Jack sucked in a steadying breath and stepped forward, his back to his home and wife and all the memories that made him who he was. That magnetic tug pulled him forward like a string tied around his heart. He had no idea where he was going, no idea whether he'd find Abby or Charlie or anyone out in those trees. All he knew was that he was through running. It was time to face the shadow with the jagged teeth and hungry smile, time to look himself in the eyes and face the demon he was and the killer he'd always be.

If you lead a man into a fog-covered field and tell him to walk straight, he'll walk in circles instead. The farther Jack walked, the more disoriented he became. He swore he was passing the same landmarks, seeing the same scars on tree trunks. He knew that if he was lost, he'd stay lost whether he kept going forward or tried to go back. And if he wasn't lost, he'd eventually come across the thing he was seeking. His instinct assured him that the second was correct, to disregard the first. And so he did, because there was nothing left to do.

And he did find what he sought. Spotting Charlie in a small clearing, Jack stopped dead. Something about finally setting his eyes on her while knowing what she truly was felt like a miniature death. The part of his heart that Charlie once owned shriveled into a black, brittle husk. She stood with her hands at her sides and her hair hanging limply around her face—but the face wasn't hers. Her smile was jagged, her eyes had lost their spark, and her skin had turned a fetid gray-blue—the color of a bloated, half-buried corpse. Her lips twitched when she saw him stop. Jack couldn't control the emotion that washed over his face. There was his little girl, his angel, a monster.

"Oh, Daddy, I knew you'd find me," she said with a perverse grin. "We've been waiting for you for a *very* long time."

"Where's Abigail?" Jack asked, and for a brief moment he was surprised he remembered his purpose for wandering into the woods at all. Staring into the twisted face of a demonic six-year-old was enough to make any mind go blank, but the thought of Abby pushed through, reminding him that he needed to find her. Both he and Charlie were gone, hopeless, but maybe Abby still had a chance.

Charlie's crooked smile twisted down at the corners, her mouth taking on a grotesque angle of exaggerated disappointment. "Is that all you came for?" she asked, her large eyes now disturbingly huge.

"Let her go," Jack demanded. "You have no right."

The frown disappeared, and for a moment Charlie's expression went frightfully blank before blooming with vicious glee. She exhaled a screeching laugh and clapped her hands together in amusement.

"No *right*?" she hissed, her laughter suddenly gone. "No right? How dare you tell me what right I have, *chief*."

Jack wanted to run. The look on Charlie's face, the warped tone of voice, all of it screamed, *Get the fuck out!* And yet Jack stood frozen, half in fear and half in stupid defiance.

"I want Abigail," he repeated. He tried to sound as imposing as he could—but his tone betrayed him. He knew he was hoping for a miracle. Abby was already lost. She had been lost as soon as she ducked into the trees.

Charlie picked up on that ghost of defeat, and rather than her rushing him and putting him out of his misery, her face settled back into its perfect composition. Her big eyes were bright and doe-like again. Her cheeks were touched with pink. This time the look of disappointment was heartbreaking.

"Oh, Daddy," she said in a voice that made Jack's heart swell. "Aren't I still your favorite?"

Jack looked away. He cringed at the question and clenched his teeth against the answer. "No," he said with a surprising force. "You're not my favorite. Abigail was always my favorite."

That malicious smile returned to her face.

"That's what I was counting on," she hummed in her chest, like a dog growling right before a bark. "Maybe you'll figure out how to get her down."

Jack narrowed his eyes at the statement, then blinked when something wet dripped onto the leaves in front of him. He tipped his chin upward. Above him, a pair of feet swayed in the breeze.

Abby rocked back and forth, the movement making it hard for Jack to see past his panic. After a moment he realized what he was looking at; Abby hung fifteen feet overhead, her small intestines looped around her neck in a makeshift noose.

A sob tore itself out of Jack's heart, punching through his chest.

"So sensitive," Charlie sang with a smirk. "Funny, you weren't that sensitive when you feasted upon the flesh of your own mother and father."

But Jack didn't hear her. She could have said a thousand terrible things, she could have screamed it into the sky; he wouldn't have heard a word over the deafening thud of his own heart. His face felt hot and vertigo kept him low to the ground. Despite his nausea, he scrambled across the earth, scooping up decomposing leaves, trying to steady himself against Abby's killing tree. His nails dug into the bark, his fingertips tearing against the roughness of the wood. He stood, the world hazy behind his tears, trying to claw his way up that tree, trying to save his baby despite his baby being dead.

He didn't see Charlie shift, but he sensed that she was on the move. That gut instinct assured him that he had to pull it together, that he had to gather up the broken pieces of his heart and his mind and glue it all together in some sort of semblance of sanity.

He looked to where Charlie had stood through the blur of tears. She was gone, and he found himself stumbling forward, spinning around like a spooked animal, searching for the predator that was most certainly hiding, waiting for the perfect moment to pounce.

"Charlie," he said, her name cracking with desperation. "Charlie, don't let it take you from me..."

But Charlie was lost; the darkness that had wrapped itself around her soul had squeezed the life out of her long before he or Aimee ever knew she was gone. He dropped to his knees, his hands clasped in front of his chest. "Oh God," he whispered. "Please help me." It was his last hope.

And then he saw her standing next to a tree, her chin tipped upward, her expression as sad as he'd ever seen. Remorse radiated from her eyes. She was looking up at Abigail, her bottom lip trembling as her sister swung overhead. But Jack wasn't convinced. He had been strong-willed as a child as well—sharp as any kid in Rosewood—and the darkness had swallowed him whole. He had murdered his parents and forgotten it ever happened. Seeing Charlie standing like that—her expression grave—he knew that even if she *was* seeing Abby, she'd never remember disemboweling her sister, and she'd never recall how she got Abby's body up into those trees.

Jack pulled the bag he'd brought toward him and reached into it. Groping around until he found what he was looking for, his fingers wrapped around the handle of Aimee's best kitchen knife. He drew it out of his bag like a knight drawing his sword, desperate for it not to come to this, but he saw no other way. It was a cycle: left unchecked, Charlie would be in this very same position in twenty years' time—standing in front of her own child, devastated by the knowledge that her baby was lost. He loved her too much to let that happen. He loved her too much to let her live.

"Daddy?" Charlie was jolted out of her daze by the glint of the blade. She regarded the knife, her face puzzled. Jack held the knife at his side, the long blade pointing straight toward hell. He waited for Charlie's expression to shift again, waited for that monster to show itself once more, but instead of Charlie's face going cold with rage, she stood dumbfounded and scared just the way Jack hoped she wouldn't.

"Daddy, what are you doing with Momma's knife?" she asked.

It isn't her, Jack told himself. *It's a trick, like David fucking Copperfield.* When his eyes snapped open, he half expected Charlie to have disappeared again—but she was exactly where he had left her, spooked and confused. *It's an act. It isn't really her.*

But it *looked* like her. So much like her that it twisted what was left of his heart into a knot.

You have to do it.

Jack pushed on against the throbbing in his chest. He stepped forward even though his ears rushed with blood. Charlie let out a muffled gasp and pressed herself against the base of a tree.

"Please don't hurt me," she whispered, her eyes wide and glittering in the moonlight. "I'm sorry if I messed up," she told him. "I'll make it up, Daddy, I promise I will."

Jack's grip wavered on that blade.

"It isn't me," she whimpered. "It's just like when you were little." Her chest heaved, her breaths shallow. "Do you remember, Daddy?" She began to wheeze. Charlie hadn't had an asthma attack in years, and here was the relapse, appropriately timed as her father held a knife at his side, ready to plunge it into her six-year-old chest.

Nothing could have been any more disarming than watching his little girl struggle to breathe. Her hands pressed over her T-shirt as she tried to gulp air, and all those thoughts of demons and curses and never-ending cycles faded into obscurity. Jack moved forward, catching Charlie by her shoulders, supporting her as she gasped for air. Dropping the knife, he rushed at her, sweeping up his baby girl up in his arms, rubbing her chest, helping her fight for air.

"Daddy?" Charlie panted, her face flushed from the effort it had taken to catch her breath. "Are you mad at me?"

Jack exhaled a breath. He didn't have an answer. He didn't know where to begin. But he shook his head anyway.

"I'm not mad," he told her, crouched on the leaf-covered ground. "I'm just glad you're OK. You're OK, right? Are you OK?" He hoped. Maybe his last-ditch effort in asking God for help was proof: it wasn't too late for salvation.

"I'm OK," she said with a smile, and at first Jack managed a weak smile in return. But her smile kept growing, inching up her face until his heart fluttered to a stop. It was the jagged grin that had haunted him for so long, the smile he saw in the darkness of his bedroom, perched at the edge of his mattress, watching him sleep. Before Jack could react, a burst of air pushed through his lips as though he'd been punched in the gut. He pinched his eyebrows together and his gaze trickled down to his abdomen. Charlie's hand was wrapped around the handle of the butcher's knife, its blade buried in Jack's belly up to the hilt. He hadn't seen her grab it, hadn't even seen her make a move for it, hadn't felt it sliding into him, but he wasn't surprised. Nothing made sense. It was all madness now.

A cold sensation bloomed outward into his arms and legs. He swayed a little, away from Charlie at first, and eventually toward her. Instead of pushing her away, he wrapped his arms around her and held her close. And as the pain began to slither from the blade and into muscles that were beginning to spasm with shock, he let out a cry that made the leaves of the surrounding trees shiver. It wasn't a moan of pain, and it wasn't the cry of a father coming to grips with the loss of his children—one hanging above him, the other sneering into his chest. It was the cry of a child, frightened and tormented, scared by the eyes he saw in the secret graveyard behind his house.

Holding Charlotte close, Jack wept for the things he hadn't allowed himself to weep for until now. Now he understood why he hadn't been allowed to remember the horrors he'd inflicted upon his mother and father. He understood why he had run away from Rosewood despite not knowing what had happened. With pain flaring from the center of his body, hot as the sun, and the soft pitter-patter of blood pooling around his knees, he finally came to terms with why Charlie had been so perfect—why she had seemed like an extension of his soul.

She had been made for him, made for this.

Like a villain putting on a disguise, that wickedness had waited in the shadows, its eye on the finishing move.

It was over.

Jack never had a chance.

When the knife twisted, a gasp escaped his throat. He looked into his baby girl's eyes as she pulled the blade from his belly. The slow drip of blood was replaced by a thin, steady stream. The pain that shot through his head was enough to sway his attention from the cold ache of his stomach.

He felt himself slipping. His knees gave out. He collapsed onto his side in the rotting leaves. Struggling to right himself, all he managed to do was cover his hands in his own blood, leaving his palms slick and warm with the assurance that this was really the end. Pain surged through his brain, blinding him, but not before he spotted the headstones that surrounded him—the rusted wrought-iron fence that caged him in as he died. In a final moment of clarity, Jack looked up to the six-year-old standing above him, that knife held tight in her right hand, and he asked her the first thing that came to mind.

"Why?"

It seemed so stupid, so clichéd, but Jack suddenly understood why all of the dying characters in all the movies asked that very thing. It was the last grasp for an answer, the last chance for understanding. Everyone, it seemed, whether a hardened criminal or a father of two, wanted to find some semblance of peace before exhaling a final breath. Jack was no different. He closed his eyes as Charlotte leaned in to him, her lips brushing the shell of his ear, and heard her whisper, *"Because I love you,"* before that blade plunged into his heart.

But Jack had been mistaken, he realized just before his world went dark. She hadn't whispered, *"Because I love you."*

She had whispered, *"Because I can."*

The next morning, Louisiana State Troopers came across a grisly scene during their second sweep of the area. They gathered around the crumpled body of an adult male, early to midthirties, who had been stabbed eighty to ninety times around the face and chest. The wounds had been caused by a serrated knife, but they came up empty on the murder weapon. It was only after they called the coroner that one of the troopers spotted something in the trees, stumbled backward, and nearly fell ass-first into the victim's minced body. Overhead, they found Abigail Winter. Officer Marvin recognized her from the tiny photograph tucked in the front pocket of his shirt.

Officer Marvin found himself standing on the front porch of that quaint Southern home for a good ten minutes before putting his knuckles to the door. There was no answer. He knocked again but received no reply. After a third attempt he started for his cruiser, but something made him pause. Squinting at the glare cast by the front room window, he cupped his hands around his face and looked inside. Nothing seemed out of place.

"There's nobody home here," he reported through his walkie, trudging back to his patrol car. "I'm swinging by the in-laws' to see if the wife is there."

A few minutes later, the blood that had pooled on the kitchen floor would crawl across the threshold into the hallway. The police would spot it through the window on their second trip back. They'd kick the door in, and with their guns drawn they'd hug the walls of the hallway until they made it to the kitchen. That's where they'd find Aimee Winter facedown on the floor. Except she wouldn't really be facedown, because they'd find her head in the sink, staring blankly, her wide eyes asking what took them so long.

By then, Charlie would be out of Louisiana. Less than half a mile from home, a rusty red pickup would pull up along the side of the road, and a bearded man would push the passenger door open for the scrawny barefoot girl.

"You need a lift?" he'd ask her, and rather than replying, she'd crawl up onto that bench seat and stare forward through a dirty windshield.

"What's your name, kid?" he'd ask, and when he didn't get a reply, he'd exhale a gruff laugh and nod. "That's OK," he'd say. "How about I just call ya chief?"

ACKNOWLEDGMENTS

My endless thanks go to all the people who made this book possible, to those who've helped make this crazy, far-off dream a reality: to my agent David, who has gone above and beyond the call of duty and has dealt with my freak-outs like a champ; to Terry, who saw potential in this crazy story and gave me nothing less than the key to the kingdom; to my editor Tiffany, who respected my vision and helped me elevate this story to levels I never expected; to Dani, who has shared in my hopes and frustrations the way only a best friend could; to Capiz, who has believed in my talent for as long as I've known her; to Lorenzo, for staying interested in my progress despite traveling the world; to Blake, the most genuine friend I could have possibly made in this industry; to my friends and family, who have cheered me on every step of the way; and of course, to my best friend and husband, Will, I love you.

And last but certainly not least, to my earlyreaders and fans—the ones who believed that this book would go far, and I even further—you are all amazing. I can't thank you enough.

Also by Ania Ahlborn:

THE NEIGHBORS

(Preview Chapter)

"It's a beautiful day in this neighborhood,

A beautiful day for a neighbor,

Would you be mine? Could you be mine?"

—Mr. Rogers' Neighborhood

CHAPTER ONE

ANDREW MORRISON SAT AT A RED LIGHT IN HIS FATHER'S beat-up Chevy. Bopping his head to an old Pearl Jam CD, he shrugged off that morning's tension, put the past behind him, cranked up the stereo, and drove. *This is it*, he told himself. *This is freedom.*

Somewhere down the line, he had convinced himself that freedom didn't exist in Creekside, Kansas—that it couldn't. Hell, nothing could survive in that corner of the world except for an endless expanse of wheat and corn. But he had been wrong. As it turned out, liberty *did* exist, and he was mere minutes from his first taste.

Mickey Fitch…Drew could hardly believe it. To think that he'd be rooming with his childhood friend, living with the guy he'd looked up to for so long—a guy who had bailed him out of tight spots as a kid. Mickey was extending his hand to Drew after all these years, and Drew was determined to show his gratitude. He didn't have much cash, but he could spare twenty bucks; buy Mick dinner and make sure his friend knew he was thankful. After all, Mick was doing Drew a solid. He was letting Andrew move in on short notice, and with only a half month's rent. That in itself assured him: despite the time that had passed between them, they were still brothers in arms, and living together was going to be a great experience—the *best* experience.

He'd dreamed of this moment for so long, it felt nearly surreal to be knee-deep in it. Magnolia Lane was still a few intersections away, but Andrew was already there.

The light turned green and Drew stepped on the accelerator, rolling his rickety pickup through the interchange. He turned up his music, sucked in air, and belted out the chorus to "Even Flow" before laughing at himself. Lifting his right hand over his head, he nodded along to the rhythm, mouthing the words, not caring who saw. He had nothing to hide. The sky was bright, the breeze was warm, and the air smelled of honeysuckle and endless promise.

His eyes lit up when he turned onto Magnolia Lane, like Dorothy getting her first glimpse of a Technicolor Oz. Ahead of him: freshly laid tarmac, black and glittering in the sunshine; trees shaped like giant, leafy lollipops, perfectly pruned, not a single leaf out of place. He slowly rolled past a white picket fence— *a white picket fence!* A tiny Pekingese stuck its face through the whitewashed slats and barked, bouncing like a cartoon character with each yappy arf. Across the street, a woman in pink capris watered her flower garden. A few houses from hers, little kids screamed in glee as they jumped through an oscillating water sprinkler. They waved as Drew rolled past them, yelling out a unified *Hi!* when he waved back.

Glancing in the rearview mirror, he hardly recognized himself. He was grinning like an idiot. His chest felt full—like the Grinch, his heart had grown three sizes, threatening to break every one of his ribs.

His gaze snagged on the carefully painted curb numbers, bright white and reflective against the concrete. He pressed the brake a little too hard. The Chevy's tires gave off a half-second shriek—gone in an instant, but enough to momentarily mortify him.

"Shit," he whispered, shooting a look at his side-view mirror. The kids had paused in their antics, staring at the pickup that had come to a dead stop in the middle of their street.

Suddenly he realized just how out of place he was. His Chevy was a relic. It belonged in a junkyard far more than it did on the road. His windows were rolled down, his rock music turned up way too loud.

He jammed the volume knob against the stereo console, the music replaced by the kids' laughter and the occasional bark of that smash-faced dog. Easing his truck along the curb, he stared at the house just outside his window. It was gorgeous, like a gingerbread house pulled straight from a fairy tale. This one had a white picket fence as well, rosebushes bursting with bright red blooms. Matching hydrangeas, heavy with blossoms, dangled from pots that hung beneath the eaves of the porch. A wind chime shivered in the breeze, small rounds of capiz shell sparkling in the sun. A hammock stretched across the right side of the patio.

Andrew exhaled a slow breath and reached for the door handle, stopping short when his attention paused on the house next door. He had been so dazzled by the residence in front of him that he hardly noticed the one directly beside it: a dwelling that, much like his truck, simply didn't belong. It was set back from the street more than the others, ashamed of itself. But it seemed inevitable—every neighborhood had a sore thumb. It was as though all of Magnolia Lane was filmed in brilliant color, but this sad little house existed in dreary monochrome. Its gutters sagged in a frown. The screen door hung at an awkward angle, like a water-logged Band-Aid trying to hang on with all its might. There was no doubt that the next storm would tear it from its hinges, sending it tumbling down the street into someone's award-winning garden.

Drew couldn't help but feel sorry for it. Being an outsider was never easy.

He pushed the driver's door open to the cool early evening air, its metallic whine cutting through the murmur of a tranquil, tree-lined suburbia. This was a world apart from the street he grew up on. Less than five miles away, Cedar Street was desolate and lonely, snatched out of one of the seven circles of hell and thrown onto the flat Kansas landscape. The trees that existed there were sparse, exposing old houses to a relentless prairie wind. The ones that had survived the storms were husks of what they had once been: stripped of their branches, left dead in the ground by tornados that had done their damnedest to wipe that street off the map.

He inhaled the scent of lilacs and honeysuckle before grabbing a box from the bed of his truck, then began his trek toward the white picket gate. Balancing the box on his knee, he fumbled with the latch, blinking when he saw a silhouette move past the front window.

That was when he noticed the house number tacked next to the door.

Drew took a step back, placed the moving box down on the sidewalk, and fished the scrap piece of paper out of his back pocket. 668 didn't look right, and that's what the door of the fairy-tale house declared. He nearly laughed when he realized it, his stomach turning behind the faded cotton of his *Nirvana* t-shirt: this wasn't Mickey Fitch's house.

Mickey's was the sad monstrosity next door.

Disappointment bloomed into blighted hope. He had been stupid to think it would have been so easy. Nobody simply walked into paradise.

Drew narrowed his eyes, plucked his box off the ground, and marched down the sidewalk toward the sulking home next door. He had spent a good portion of his summers fixing up the house on Cedar Street—it, too, was a sad sight. If he could keep that old lean-to upright, he sure as hell could resurrect this place. All it needed was the straightening of gutters and a fresh coat of paint. Magnolia Lane was handing Drew his own private metaphor: His life was a mess, and he was here to fix it.

Reaching the house, he pressed the box between the wall and his chest, balancing it on a raised knee before reaching for the bell. Before his finger hit the button, he reeled back, staring at the fat spider that sat beside the glowing button. It sat there, illuminated from behind, as if giving Andrew a final opportunity to forget the whole thing—to turn around and walk away. Shuddering at the thing, Drew knocked instead.

There was a long, dead silence. Was Mickey even home?

Then the front door swung open, and a death mask emerged from behind a tattered screen.

Mick peered through the screen door with a squint, as though he hadn't seen daylight in years. Dark circles under his eyes implied he hadn't slept for weeks, their shadows contrasting against his white shock of blond hair. He appeared older than Drew remembered, like he was aging at twice the natural speed. Kansas did that to some. It may have been the sun or the wind, the tornado sirens in the dead of night, or the hypnotic sway of wheat fields beneath an endless sky. This place pushed people to the brink of madness, assuring them that the wide-open landscape proved that the world was flat; the horizon held nothing.

This wasn't the bright-eyed kid Andrew had run to when Drew's dad had gone missing, when his mom had drunk herself into a stupor.

Drew had been preparing a wide smile for his old friend, but it wavered as he stared.

"Hey," he said, trying to appear as enthusiastic as he had felt a few minutes before. "Dude, this neighborhood is intense."

No response: Mickey remained motionless, staring out through the frayed screen door. Drew furrowed his eyebrows. The dead look in his old friend's eyes scared him.

Had he made a mistake? He swallowed against the lump in his throat, his pulse drumming in his ears. Mickey looked like he was deciding whether to let Andrew inside or tell him to hit the road.

Drew dared to pose the question, figured it was just a matter of time before it came bursting forth: "Are you okay? You look rough, man."

More silence.

He opened his mouth to speak again, to give Mickey some reason to go through with the deal and invite him in, but Mickey finally roused from his trance.

"Hey, man," he replied in a dry monotone. "Yeah, sorry." He motioned with a swoop of his arm for Andrew to enter, pushing the screen door open to let him inside.

Drew's heart sank. The inside of the house was as unfortunate as its exterior. An obvious path had been worn in the dirty carpet from the kitchen to the couch and then to somewhere down a hall, but beyond that, the house looked unused, albeit coated in a layer of dust. Dingy curtains flanked the windows, one of the rods hanging low, as though someone had caught themselves on the drape to break a fall. Another window was covered by a bed-sheet tacked to the wall by an army of staples, hundreds of them punched into the drywall in a crooked, glittering line. The smell wasn't as bad as it should have been: stale, with an undertone of dust and sweat, but otherwise innocuous.

Drew carefully placed his box down at his feet, allowing himself to fully take in the squalor. This was worse than Cedar Street. At least there, he had kept things under relative control. He spent weekends washing windows, painting the deck with leftover paint he found in the garage; anything to keep his grandparents' pride and joy from disintegrating in the wind. But *this*...this looked like Mickey had moved in and never lifted a finger.

Mickey had made a beeline for the couch as soon as Andrew had stepped inside. He mashed the buttons of a game controller, oblivious to the fact that Andrew was standing just beyond the front door, a box at his feet, waiting to be acknowledged by a guy he used to consider a close friend.

Andrew shoved it aside the pang of apprehension that seized his heart. He could hear his mother slurring her words: *You need me, you know; you can't move out, who will take care of you?* At least here he had some freedom—at least here he could improve himself rather than try to fix someone else.

"Um, should I just put this anywhere, or..." Andrew tapped the box with his sneaker. Rubbing the back of his neck, he continued to watch his new roommate from a distance.

"Mick?"

"Sure," Mickey said. *Put it anywhere.*

Drew closed his eyes, exhaling a muted laugh. This place was a pit. A hole in the ground would have been better. He didn't want to think about what the kitchen was like, let alone the bathroom—but this was the way these things went. First houses and first roommates were supposed to suck. This was the kind of stuff that made stories good for the telling.

He stepped away from the door, marched across the house to the window, and pulled the curtain back. A ray of early evening sun cut through the gloom, dust sparkling like diamonds in the daylight. Mickey paused his game, shielding his eyes as he peered at Drew's silhouette.

"So," Drew said, "you own this place?"

Mickey was unresponsive, despite staring right at Andrew. Drew considered asking him what his problem was, but he decided to wait it out, watching Mickey squint against the sunset as if it was the first one he'd ever seen; a vampire rousing from a thousand-year sleep. After what felt like an hour of tense, contemplative silence, he watched Mick's face lighten. His expression shifted from dejection to something that almost resembled hope. When Mickey actually *smiled*, Drew's heart leapt out of his stomach and back into his chest.

"Yes, sir," Mickey finally replied.

"That's good. So you won't be opposed to some paint."

Mickey raised an eyebrow. "Seriously?"

"Um..." Drew looked around the place. "Seriously?" he echoed.

"Shit," Mickey mumbled, "you're not one of those germaphobes, are you?"

"You're not one of those people who show up on the Discovery Channel, right?"

Mickey shook his head, completely confused. "You mean like a zoologist?"

Drew bit back a laugh and shook his head. "Where's my room?" he asked.

And just like that, Drew had a new house, a new roommate, and a hell of a lot of work to do.

Creekside was but a blip on the map, yet over the years somehow Drew and Mickey had managed to lose touch. The last time they had seen one another as kids turned out to be the last time a nine-year-old Andrew had ridden his bike down the block to play Mickey's new Final Fantasy game after yet another fight with his mom.

Drew could hear screaming from inside the house.

He skidded to a stop just shy of the Fitches' driveway, two ambulances and a handful of cop cars blocking his way, as a pair of EMTs wheeled a sheet-covered gurney down the front steps and onto the walkway. Mick's mother burst out of the house. She ran for them before they could load the stretcher into the back of the ambulance, her face swollen with hysterical tears. Andrew's eyes widened as a police officer dashed across the lawn after her— just like in the movies his own mother didn't know he watched— but Mick's mom was a waif of a thing; she was quick, and the cop was slowed by his roundness, and the pistol that hung heavy at his hip. Drew watched Mrs. Fitch's hands fly out in front of her, her fingers clawing the sheet covering the gurney, screaming at the ambulance workers to *get away from him, get away!* One of the EMTs tried to fend her off, but she recoiled on her own from what was underneath.

As that sheet slid away, something heavy punched Drew straight in the chest, something that toed the line between queasiness and horror: that sensation of seeing something terrible but not being able to look away. What was once a head was now little more than a wad of pulp attached to somebody's neck. It was Mickey's dad—a man Drew had said "hi" to a hundred thousand times.

Mrs. Fitch screamed again, reeling away, her hands pressed to her face. Her torment shot straight through him, forcing an involuntary gasp out of his mouth. With his bike frame between his scrawny legs and his sneakers planted firmly on the ground, he could manage only to turn his head away from the scene, dizzy with dismay. His heart palpitated within the cage of his chest. Mrs. Fitch's cries sent chills tumbling down his spine despite the sun baking the back of his neck.

When he dared to look back, Mickey was in the open door-way of the house. His eyes were fixed on the ambulance, on the men who slammed the back doors shut, taking his dad away for-ever. Drew wanted to call out to him, to run over to him and ask his friend what had happened and whether Mick was going to be okay. Their eyes met from across the yard. Mickey's blanched expression curdled Andrew's blood.

And then Mick turned away and disappeared inside.

There were rumors about Mickey and his family after that. The neighborhood kids whispered about how Mickey's dad had gone crazy. The ladies at the supermarket would gather in the produce department on Sunday afternoons, using words like 'drunk' and 'abusive' and 'no surprise'. Andrew had wanted to get the story firsthand, but Mick wouldn't talk to him. Mickey's dad was dead, and somehow, as if by magic, their friendship had died with him.

He was surprised how much he missed his friend after Mick moved away. He'd ride his bike to the empty house nobody wanted to buy, the 'for sale' sign staked into the Fitches' lawn sun-bleached and weather-worn. Drew would spend summer after-noons sitting on their wilted lawn, pulling yellow blades of grass out of the ground, spinning his bicycle tire, as though each revo-lution was one spin closer to Mickey showing back up.

Occasionally, he'd catch himself staring up at the ceiling when he couldn't sleep, wondering whether Mickey was alive or dead. After each inevitable fight with his mother, he thought back to the day he watched Mick lose his dad, wanting to make contact again. He ignored the impulse, convinced that if Mick wanted to get back in touch, he'd do so himself.

But that didn't stop him from searching for Mickey's name on Facebook, tugging on his bottom lip as he stared at his old friend's profile photo, which was little more than an old Metallica record cover. He had written Mick countless messages, only to hit delete instead of send, always feeling stupid at how sentimental he sounded. He didn't want Mick to get the wrong idea, didn't want him to think that Drew was some whacked-out obsessive weirdo who couldn't let the past be the past. But when Andrew reached the point where he didn't have anywhere else to turn, Mick was always the one he'd reached out to.

And Mick was always the one who had saved him.

Drew spent most of the night unloading boxes from the back of his truck while Mick played video games, struggling with the screen door each time, trudging down a hall dark without a working light. It would have been nice to have had some help, but he didn't want to complain. Mick had offered him a place to crash, and that was more than enough.

His bedroom was small but sufficient. The wallpaper was a hideous floral pattern, damaged by what must have been a water leak, but if all went according to plan, it wouldn't be long before he had those walls painted over, as well as covered in posters and cork boards and whatever else he could find. His favorite part of the room was the big window that overlooked the side yard and the perfect house next door. He could imagine living there while drifting to sleep, a house that would inevitably smell of cleanliness and home cooking.

Once the truck was empty, Drew stood in the center of his room and assessed his army of boxes. He hadn't thought to bring any furniture after the blow-up back home. With no mattress, he settled in for the night atop a pile of his own clothes, thinking about his mother, about how she was sitting in that big house on Cedar Street all alone.

His dad's leaving hadn't been his fault—he knew that—and that was why he resented her that much more. She made him feel guilty with how helpless she'd become, her illness twisting her into something unrecognizable, something far removed from what she used to be. It wasn't his fault—but she wanted Andrew to be responsible.

Pushing a handful of clothes beneath his head to serve as a pillow, he promised himself that he had made the right decision. This was what he had to do to get on with his life, to get out from beneath her control. But even as he drifted to sleep, the guilt hung heavy in the back of his mind, swaying back and forth like a noose without a neck.

The sun made the insides of Andrew's eyelids glow red. When he finally peeled his eyes open, he winced, raising a hand against the glare. As he rolled onto his side, his lower back screamed against the movement.

There was something about waking up to the cheerlessness of an empty room, the bareness of blank walls, that made him feel helpless. He pressed the heels of his hands against his eyes. As soon as he set up his space, he'd feel better about the whole thing. He needed furniture. He needed to settle in. He needed to reestablish his relationship with Mickey. His intention of taking Mick out for a bite to eat had been pushed aside; he'd be appreciative later, after Mickey helped clean the place up.

He hadn't labeled any of the boxes he'd packed. It took him twenty minutes to find his toothbrush and a half-used tube of Colgate. Pushing a pair of earbuds into his ears, he let Bob Marley assure him that every little thing was going to be all right. Singing along beneath his breath, he trudged down the hall toward the bathroom. He'd used it the evening before but had kept his eyes half-closed, partly out of exhaustion, but mostly because he didn't want to see just how bad it was. But now, with the morning's light trickling through the window above the bathtub, the filth was undeniable—so staggering that even Bob couldn't sing his way around it.

Andrew stood in the doorway for a long while, staring at a sink covered in dried toothpaste and stray albino-like hairs. The mirror was unusable, sprayed with what looked to be toothpaste-laced backwash. There was no soap. There were no towels. The linoleum, half-covered by a dirty bath mat, was crusted in hair and grime. He pulled his headphones out of his ears and swallowed against the disgust crawling up his throat. Backing away with his toothbrush pressed to his chest like a cross in the hands of a frightened Catholic, he did an about-face and marched away.

A few minutes past eight in the morning, Harlow Ward watched a beat-up white pickup peel away from the curb next door. She smiled, shifting her weight from one red pump to another. With the truck out of view, she turned her attention to the pristine living room behind her, smoothed the full skirt of her dress, and regarded her husband with a bright smile.

"We have a new neighbor," she announced. "I'll make cookies."

Other than the Wal-Mart across town, there wasn't much in the way of big retail in Creekside, so that was where Andrew went. Staring down a seemingly endless aisle of cleaning products, he knew exactly what he was looking for. He'd been going to the store for his mom since before he could drive. Grocery shopping came naturally, and buying cleaning supplies was even easier. His philosophy: buy the cleaner that had the brightest color, the one that looked like it would instantly kill you if you threw your head back and chugged. He was naturally drawn to the purples and blues, deciding on something called Kaboom not because of anything on the label, but because of its name. He imagined Mickey's bathroom exploding beneath a violet mushroom cloud, giving him just enough time to bolt out of the house and tuck-and-roll onto the patchy front lawn. Or maybe it would cut through soap scum like a knife cuts through butter and leave Drew pleasantly surprised, like the smiling women on TV. *It's so easy!*

After tossing a few more household cleaners into his cart, including some Scrubbing Bubbles—because his inner child couldn't pass up cartoon-endorsed cleaners—he wheeled his way to the grocery section and considered his options. Anything requiring refrigeration meant he'd have to venture into the kitchen, and he was willing to bet that it was as nasty as the bathroom. So instead of getting his usual orange juice, he got a box of Capri Suns instead; and instead of getting cereal that required milk, he settled on some non-refrigerated pudding cups. If he wanted *real* food he'd have to go out for now, which was fine by him. The dining area at Casa de Mickey needed to be excavated from beneath its scrim of dust before it could be used in relative safety.

Dropping fifty-six bucks of his three hundred at the register, he drove back to his new home to scrub the toilet. There was something fundamentally wrong with taking a dump in a can that was dirtier than the inside of your own ass.

He parked along the curb and gathered his blue Wal-Mart bags, dreading the task that awaited him inside. He paused mid-stride and turned his head toward that pristine house with the white picket fence. Drew bet their toilets sparkled the way clean things sparkled in Saturday morning cartoons. He bet the inside of that house smelled like cookies and fresh-cut grass, because those were the best smells in the world. His mom used to bake chocolate-chip cookies every weekend, a whole sheet just for him. That was before his dad disappeared. After Rick left, the only cookies they had came out of a bag. Drew wasn't sure, but he doubted the oven had been used since he was nine years old.

Inside the fairy tale house, something shifted. He only saw it for a fraction of a second, but he was sure it was there. Someone had been watching him from behind the window curtains, staring at him while he stared right back, his arms weighed down by pudding and juice. Something crawled just beneath the surface of his skin, but he turned away. He was the one standing slack-jawed in the middle of the street, probably looking like a lunatic freshly moved out of the psycho ward and into the crappiest house in town.

In the driveway, Mickey's TransAm dripped oil onto the concrete. Drew had tried to give the guy the benefit of the doubt the night before, but after getting an eyeful of the bathroom, he was feeling a lot less chipper and a lot more judgmental. Mickey had always loved video games, so the idea of him being the type of guy to sleep all day and play MMORPGs all night wouldn't have surprised him. But the more time he spent inside that house, the more Andrew pictured Mick screaming into a headset, starting cyber-fights with kids half his age, smashing beer cans against his forehead like a modern-day Cro-Magnon.

These thoughts barraged his brain while he scrubbed grime out of the corners of the tub, scoured so hard that even Joan Crawford would have been impressed. He imagined Mickey stumbling into the bathroom, heady with sleep, his white hair wild like a blizzard, a wire hanger held tight in his grasp. *You think this is clean?* Wearing canary yellow gloves that reached halfway up his arms, Drew exhaled a laugh, inhaled chemical fumes, and was overtaken by a choking fit as he continued to scrub.

ABOUT THE AUTHOR

 Born in Ciechanów, Poland, Ania Ahlborn is also the author of the upcoming thriller *The Neighbors,* and is currently at work on her third novel. She earned a bachelor's degree in English from the University of New Mexico, and enjoys gourmet cooking, baking, drawing, traveling, and watching movies, as well as terrifying readers with her macabre tales. She currently resides in Albuquerque, New Mexico, with her husband and two dogs.

DID YOU ENJOY THIS BOOK?

Visit Ania Alhborn's website at www.aniaahlborn.com to sign up for her e-newsletter and to receive exclusive offers and bonus content such as custom-curated playlists.

Made in the USA
Columbia, SC
16 February 2022

56354867R00150